For my late grandmother, Virginia Roosa, who always believed in me.

1
THE STOLEN VEHICLE

A PIERCING ALARM blared, sending a surge of dopamine straight to the reward center of Marcus Kemp's brain. He squeezed the steering wheel tight with both hands, ears and lips tingling. Flipped on the cruiser's siren and lights and spun the wheel, whipping a U-turn, early morning on Abbott Street in Ocean Beach, San Diego.

His hypnotic, one-handed computer-key clacking had paid off again: entering plate numbers into the county's database in search of stolen vehicles. He had spotted a meter maid ticket on the windshield of a newer model, blue Nissan Altima parked on the west side of the street—thirty yards south of the lifeguard station. Ran the plate number and got an immediate hit. The match set off the unrelenting, high-pitched alarm that would cause the average person to jump through their skin, like when a smoke detector goes off in the dead of night.

Grinning, Marcus swung the cruiser into an open street parking spot, across from Ocean Beach Hotel on the corner. The sidewalk-lining light poles still beamed yellow skirts onto the concrete below.

Recovering stolen cars was not the sole responsibility of his beat, but it could be if he let it. Marcus was the San Diego Police Department's best at recovering stolen vehicles three years running. He'd set a personal best—forty-eight—the previous year. This recovery would bring his current tally to forty, and it was only June. Keeping this pace, he would shatter his own record, but his sights were set on the all-time department record for a year of sixty-seven recoveries.

Bragging rights aside, the year's top three finishers were honored at a lunch reception held at Bali Hai, the Polynesian-themed restaurant in the San Diego Bay Harbor. It was a semi-casual affair with remarks from supervisors, an award presentation by the Chief of Police and a generous buffet spread of pulled pork, creamy coleslaw and purple sweet potatoes. The winners each posed with the chief while accepting their plaques, and the photos and a write-up went out in a department-wide e-mail newsletter.

"Dispatch. Six-fourteen John. I've got a hit on a stolen vehicle in the 1900 block of Abbott Street. Vehicle appears unoccupied. Stand by."

"Shit, man. Another?" asked a voice that wasn't dispatch, but one he recognized immediately.

"That's right, McKenzie." He smiled before dispatch interrupted their exchange.

"Confirm, six-fourteen John. Running the plate number, one-D-Y-P-one-nine-four now."

Marcus licked his lower lip and opened his cruiser door bearing the SDPD seal with *"America's Finest"* above it and *"To Protect and Serve"* below. He stepped out, his boots crunching on sand spilled over asphalt.

Waves crashed on to the beach, the dull roar echoing off the buildings across the street. A dozen or so surfers dotted the water and a couple more were running into the surf. A ponytailed, original hippie swept sand off the boardwalk into the grass with a push broom held together with duct tape. A homeless man sleeping at the base of a palm tree in Veteran's Park began to stir.

Across the street, restaurants with desolate, ocean-facing patios that would be packed at lunchtime. All around, the cardboard paper fronds of Mexican palm trees rustled in the slight breeze.

Besides the police officer's intrusion, everything appeared normal. A few people—lifeguards, three young women in wetsuits with surfboards under their arms and a few shop employees showing up for work—stopped where they were headed to look on. Just in case he was up to something interesting.

While dispatch searched for a report of the theft, Marcus approached the car to make sure it wasn't occupied. Finding the thief in the car would be the cherry on top though, a highlight accomplishment. He'd only ever recovered stolen vehicles after they'd been ditched by the thief or misplaced by the owner. He assumed the latter with this Altima, it being parked in proximity to so many bars and restaurants. The owner probably had a few too many drinks, forgot where they parked their car and took a rental scooter home. This one would be easy one to clear.

Marcus pushed down the hood of his service weapon's holster, releasing the self-locking mechanism. He rested his hand on his sidearm and slithered around the front of the car to the driver's side door. There were a couple of packing boxes on the back seat; the contents spilled out. Noticing the driver's side window was open, he tucked his face to his shoulder.

"Dispatch. Confirming interior is unoccupied. Popping the truck. Stand by."

"Ten-four."

Marcus pulled the trunk release latch on the left side of the steering wheel and sprang to shield his body with the back half of the car. Using the gap between the back windshield and the top of the trunk, he made sure no one had jumped out before exposing himself completely on the side of the trunk.

In the course of more than a hundred stolen vehicle recoveries, Marcus had perfected his moves. The actions were muscle memory by this point. His next task would be to clear the scene with dispatch after finding an empty trunk.

Marcus swung around the back of the car and faced the open trunk with one hand on his gun and the other on his radio. There was someone inside. Marcus startled. He shouted, "POLICE!" and whipped out his gun, aimed it at the form. A shiver shot up his spine. "Don't move!" The person complied. A little too well, remaining face-down, their arms and neck gray. Then a sour, putrid smell smacked Marcus in the face.

A murmur spread through the group of onlookers.

Marcus shook his head and holstered his gun. He pressed two fingers to the thick neck, adhering to protocol. No pulse, as expected. He relayed his discovery to dispatch with a request to notify his lieutenant he had an 11-44 (coroner's case).

Dispatch confirmed.

Warm orange splashed the scene with the sun now peeking over the top of the shops. Marcus shielded his eyes with his hand and hunched over to survey the trunk. The odor of death intensified from the cavity. With no marine layer, it would be a toasty one by June coastal San Diego standards.

"Dispatch. Units needed for scene containment as well."

"Ten-four."

This wasn't the first dead body Marcus had encountered on the job—far from it. His beat was notorious for hit-and-run accidents with pedestrians, bicyclists and tourists on rented scooters, not to mention fairly routine overdoses. Finding a murder victim was more unusual, but he had been a responding officer on one other during his time on the force.

This murder victim was an older, stubby white male. Blood had soaked the carpet of the trunk underneath his nearly bald head, the short gray and brown hair on the sides wet and matted. Blunt force trauma to the back of the head the likely cause of death by the look of it. The ash-colored body was not yet bloated. He wasn't thin, but not obese either. His skin was weathered: wrinkled and scaly in patches around the elbows, knees and shins. His clothes screamed tourist: a pink, short-sleeve casual shirt with repeating palm tree and stingray pattern and a cream pair of cargo shorts, from which varicose-veined legs and bare feet stuck out.

"614 Baker. Dispatch, show me the way," came McKenzie's voice over the radio. "I'm four blocks over, Smooth Chocolate."

Marcus rolled his eyes and looked back at the victim.

His right arm was bent, the palm and forearm pinned awkwardly against his back. Then Marcus did a sharp double-take. His eyes locked onto a birthmark the size of a small nectarine on the victim's forearm. Marcus glared. His heart started to pound. There was no mistaking that birthmark. With every breath, his pulse quickened—he could feel the vein on the side of his neck throbbing. Sweat beaded his forehead and his vision blurred.

He knew that fucking birthmark. Ancient, buried memories swirled up with the force of a tornado, chaos attacking his brain. He could feel the bruises, the violations he'd endured. All of it, fresh. Why was this man—now a corpse—in San Diego to begin with?

Marcus stumbled back a step and then two.

"You okay, man?" asked one of the lifeguards from the small crowd of onlookers.

Marcus squeezed his eyes shut and shook his head as if trying to clear water out of his ears.

"Get back!" he snarled. He flailed out a hand, not noticing in his stupor the group hadn't budged from the opposite side of the street.

He steadied himself with one hand on the stolen car's taillights and then quickly pulled it away, worried about contaminating the crime scene before realizing he was wearing black nitrile gloves. He had put them on out of habit before getting out of the cruiser.

Just then, McKenzie pulled onto Abbott and parked across both lanes on the south side of the street, adjacent to Marcus' cruiser. Jumping out of his cruiser, he waved his arms in a crisscrossing pattern at the onlookers while looking toward Marcus—who was obscured by the trunk— and then back to the crowd.

"Nothing to see here. Go about your business," McKenzie said.

The crowd kept their distance and none of them moved while he popped his trunk and grabbed police line tape.

Marcus gulped, then took a deep breath. Grabbing the short sleeve of his uniform, he sopped up some of the nervous sweat from his forehead. His vision was still narrowed, like looking through the wrong end of a pair of binoculars, but no longer blurry.

Something took over his next actions, but it wasn't his police instincts or training. His response was reactive and motivated by something different entirely. Marcus hovered over the trunk with his shins pressed against the bumper. He crouched down until he could see McKenzie through the opening between the trunk door and the vehicle. He was starting to box-in the scene, wrapping police tape around meters and trunks of palm trees.

Marcus only had a few seconds. His eyes darted back to the birthmark. He cringed. Scanned the area around the body. Nothing but a factory jack in the right corner of the trunk. Avoiding the bloodied carpet, he ran a gloved hand around the torso and legs of the corpse, tucking his fingertips underneath the body and trying not to gag.

"Fuck." Nothing there.

Careful to not to draw any attention, he held his body stiff and continued to search. Onlookers wouldn't have a clue what he was doing. McKenzie would, so Marcus darted his head up every few seconds, watching for his eyes. One more sweep of the body is all he could get away with. Maybe a pocket or two.

Marcus caught a glimpse of McKenzie over his shoulder, police tape in hand. He straightened up and let his colleague pass behind, watching his slender frame move with purpose. Remaining still, Marcus blocked the view from onlookers. McKenzie looped the tape around the parking meter behind the stolen vehicle and then ran it toward the police cruisers.

Surely, he could find some kind of lead on why this man from his past was in San Diego and where he had been during his time in town. His eyes locked on the back, right pocket of the man's shorts. The body was so twisted his right butt cheek was facing nearly straight up. The pocket appeared to be empty; where a wallet might have been was just an impression of a bulge. The killer had likely taken the victim's wallet but Marcus reached into the pocket anyway. To his surprise, his fingertip stubbed against a thin, stiff object. He grabbed it out of the pocket and pressed it against his right thigh to keep it from view.

McKenzie was securing the tape to where he began the containment.

The fact the man's wallet was missing could work in Marcus' favor. He certainly didn't need it. Didn't need the dead man's Texas driver license either to know who he was—the same piece of shit he last saw when he was eleven years old.

Marcus tucked his chin and shot a glace down to his thigh. He turned over the business card, eyed it for a split second. Nothing immediately revelatory. He then stashed it in a cargo pocket of his tactical uniform pants.

"You good, Kemp?" It was McKenzie, startling Marcus.

He nodded. "Yeah… all good."

Another police unit drove up on the south end of Abbott, an SUV.

"Make way," said Officer Cristine Romero from the SDPD K9 unit. She cut through the crowd, ducking under the yellow police tape with her police dog partner at her heel.

McKenzie flicked his chin in Romero's direction.

"She'd make me cum so fast," McKenzie said.

Marcus ignored him.

When Romero made it to the back of the car, she patted him on the shoulder.

"Good job, man," she said.

"Thanks," Marcus said.

The three officers stood at the back of the car. McKenzie and Romero looked at the body and Marcus turned away. Squeezed his hands under his armpits.

A couple minutes later, Western Division's lieutenant pulled up to the scene with McKenzie and Romero still leaned over the trunk.

"Poor fucker," McKenzie said, shaking his head. Romero agreed.

Marcus stiffened with the approach of their lieutenant.

"Homicide should be on scene in a couple minutes," Lt. Berry said. Pointing a finger at Marcus, he added, "Good work, Kemp."

Marcus cleared his throat.

"Thank you, sir."

As predicted, two Homicide detectives pulled up two minutes later and parked on the north end of the scene.

The passenger, Det. Aaron Barnes, a white guy in in his early-forties, got out of the SUV first. His leathery skin showed he'd grown up going to the beach daily. He hobbled down the street toward them with a pained gait.

Next to him was Lt. Jorge Castillo, a more seasoned detective than his partner. In his late-fifties with a full head of jet-black hair, he was also a San Diego native, but grew up in South Bay.

"You three didn't touch anything did you?" Castillo said.

"Hey, Jorge. Check it out… It's the SDPD stolen vehicle champion… OF THE WORLD!" Barnes hollered with his hands cupped around his mouth, performing his best boxing ring announcer impersonation. He walked up to Marcus with a big grin and jabbed his chest with two fingers.

Marcus felt himself sway, partly from the poke, but mostly from the nerves buzzing under his skin.

"Yeah, yeah," Marcus said, straightening up. "Doesn't Homicide have better things to worry about?"

"Apparently so." Barnes motioned to the trunk and laughed.

"McKenzie. Romero," Lt. Berry barked. He pointed across the street. "Start canvassing."

"Yes, sir," they replied in unison.

The crowd gathered outside the police line had doubled by this time, but it was the growing police presence that felt like it was closing in on Marcus. Smothering him. A feeling he'd never before experienced on the job.

With his hands at his sides, he ran the tip of his middle finger along the outside of his pant pocket to ensure the business card hadn't escaped somehow.

"Show us what you found, officer," Castillo said.

"Yes, sir," Marcus said.

2
(HIS) OCEAN BEACH BEAT

HOURS LATER, MARCUS was back on patrol. He'd driven the perimeter of his beat a few times, his mind preoccupied with the information he'd found on the business card. It was for a landscape company located in El Cajon, a city twenty miles east of downtown San Diego. There was phone number on the card, but it went directly to voicemail. And no physical address listed. It was too far away to check out while on the clock anyway. Marcus tamped down the itch to investigate further and cruised Ocean Beach.

The San Diego Police Department considered Ocean Beach a "junior beat" because so much action happened there constantly. The area was ripe for new cops. A beat where they could get their feet wet, fast. Most officers moved on to other beats after two or three years, choosing to work out of a division closer to their homes, or work a less active beat, but not Marcus. He'd stayed on the OB beat for all of his seven years on the force. He told people he stayed put because he enjoyed the constant action. No day as same as the last. Everything from burglaries to disturbing the peace to breaking up fights. The work kept his mind focused.

At the murder scene, Homicide detectives wanted to know the following of Marcus: 1) What he observed before the discovery; 2) How he found the body, step-by-step; 3) Did he touch the body, and; 4) Did he touch or move anything else?

Ensuring an uncontaminated scene is paramount to the success of any murder investigation, they had prefaced, sounding scripted.

"No offense, we just have to ask," Barnes said to Marcus.

He nodded. "It's cool."

Marcus gave Castillo and Barnes thorough answers to their questions, but left out the part where he lifted evidence from the victim's pocket. He also neglected to tell them he knew the victim, intimately.

Dispatch located the owner of the stolen car shortly after Homicide arrived on scene. A police report from three days prior was on file. Marcus overheard the call between Barnes and the car's owner. She had apparently parked it on the street in Little Italy to get drinks with some friends the previous Friday night. The car was gone when she left the bar a few hours later. In the process of moving at the time, she was relieved to hear her boxed-up belongings were still in the back seat, but was soon disappointed when Barnes broke the news that her vehicle and all its contents were being held as evidence in a murder investigation for the foreseeable future.

Marcus drove through a residential section of Ocean Beach. OB, one of San Diego's lively beach communities. The neighborhood the '60s never forgot. OB nestles against the Pacific Ocean, with Point Loma and the San Diego Bay to the south and Mission Bay, SeaWorld and Pacific Beach to the north. Sunset Cliffs Blvd cuts a main artery through OB, a few blocks east of the ocean.

His mind was a blur. So many racing thoughts. The main one: What business did a newspaper editor from Texas have with a landscape company in El Cajon, California?

With several hours remaining on his shift, he turned onto an east-west-running residential street to kill time. This part of the neighborhood was fairly quiet during the day. Most residents were at work and those who were home were retirees, potheads or night shift workers.

Evenings were a different matter. And on busy weekend nights especially, drunks spilled from the bars along the main stretch just two blocks over, and passed out—or worse—on front lawns. Marcus couldn't keep track of how many vomit-covered drunks he'd hauled in over the years.

The look of this street was as diverse as its residents. Not one house or lot the same. Beach bungalows neighboring two-story, Craftsman homes with wood siding, sat next to a five hundred square-foot stucco flat, across from a six-plex rental unit. Looking down from the hill toward the ocean, the houses and apartments alternated in colors and no color went unused.

Normally, Marcus would finish out the rest of a slow shift by running plates, looking for stolen vehicles. Instead, he crept along, his mind wandering. He held his arm out the window. At full peak, the sun's rays punched straight through the canopies of Queen, Canary Island and Mexican Fan palm trees lining the sidewalk. Their majestic crowns blanketed the concrete beneath with dappled shade, while the sun smothered the street and warmed the underside of his outstretched forearm. The intoxicating smell of citrus blooms filled the cruiser's cabin. His radio crackled to life.

"Noise complaint in the 4600 block of Granger Street."

Marcus patted his pant pocket.

"Ten-four, Dispatch. Six-fourteen John responding."

The call came from a couple blocks away. A neighbor reported a young couple for disturbing the peace. It wasn't the first time this particular resident had called police with a noise complaint.

When Marcus arrived at the home, a man in his sixties named Mr. Green pointed across the street. With a scrunched, red face he yelled, "The GIRL, er, woman, was yelling nigg—I mean…" Red exploded on his face. "She was yelling the n-word at her boyfriend or whatever he is."

"Aren't they white?" Marcus asked. He smirked and turned to look at the house.

"Yes! It makes no sense." Mr. Green kept his voice raised. "It's always like that over there."

"Weird." Marcus looked back to find Mr. Green staring a hole into the ground.

"Sorry, I didn't mean to say *that* word," he said.

Marcus touched his elbow. "It's OK, Mr. Green. You're just reporting an incident."

Marcus stepped off the front porch of the bungalow. Flipped down his sunglasses, double-tapped the red button on his body cam, and walked across the street. Loose mortar between the bricks of the duplex's skinny walkway crunched under his steps. Reaching the yellow front door, he called out. Waited a beat and called out again.

A woman came out of the house and left the door open. Before he could introduce himself, Marcus pointed at a crack pipe in the front pocket of her short-sleeved shirt and she blurted out a confession.

"We been smokin' meth."

"For how long?" Marcus reached behind his back for his handcuffs.

The woman shrugged. Her worn-out red eyes blinked erratically.

"All night? What time is it?"

While he was handcuffing the woman, her boyfriend stumbled outside. Marcus held up a hand and told him to stop walking. The man complied. After handcuffing the boyfriend, Marcus instructed both to sit on the concrete step of the front porch.

He was set to take them in, but an officer and her trainee from the department's Psychiatric Emergency Response Team pulled up to the scene and wanted to process the couple for training purposes. Marcus obliged.

Leaving the scene, Marcus worked his way out of the neighborhood, hit Sunset Cliffs Blvd. and drove north. Distracted, he picked at the greasy, torn-up vinyl armrest in the cruiser he took out that morning. He didn't like taking the SUVs out, even given the choice. He preferred the more agile Crown Vics. Sure, most were beaten to hell rust buckets that smelled like it, but their low-to-the-ground profiles made him feel one with his beat, invested. Not riding above it in an SUV like an Old West Sheriff. With each dig of his nail, more of the vinyl tore away, exposing the piss-yellow foam padding, which he then pinched out and flicked to the floorboard.

The winding road provided a picturesque drive Marcus loved. His eyes were always drawn to the sandy cliffs that dropped off and fell dramatically toward the blue ocean below.

Marcus spotted a van parked in a three-space pullout overlooking the Pacific. Ratty beach towels covered the van's windows. He pulled over and informed the two women inside they couldn't have their windows obstructed. It constituted a living domicile, he told them.

"Pull them down and you're good."

The stop didn't take long and the young women thanked him for the heads-up.

Marcus continued on his beat.

His mood began to sour. It was an alien feeling, an anxious one.

Normally, these calls would be cake. Easy work. And keeping residents feeling safe, giving the hippies, beach bums and homeless reason to trust him, the icing. He cut back into the neighborhood and drove slowly.

Ocean Beach suited Marcus perfectly, so much so he made it his home. He grew up in neighboring Pacific Beach from the time he was a preteen until he graduated high school. And while PB and the other San Diego beach towns were great, OB matched his laid-back personality. And it had just enough grime to keep him feeling grounded. The mix of original hippies and hipsters; wealthy and broke; locals and tourists; cheesy tourist restaurants and legit OB originals—he loved it all.

Marcus crossed Niagara Street, looked left toward his place. He rented a one-bedroom apartment at Surfcaster—a small, semi-recently renovated complex at the end of Niagara Street. The units weren't anything special, even though the property owners kept the façade and landscaping fresh. He had minimal furniture and kept the drab, off-white walls bare. He stocked the kitchen with the bare essentials required for a menu of boring dinners: boneless, skinless chicken breast and broccoli, grilled fish or delivery.

His on-again, off-again girlfriend, Megan, didn't object to his bachelor way of living because of the apartment's proximity to the nearby bars, restaurants and shops. Not to mention how close it was to the beach and the Ocean Beach Pier, just a few steps away.

All beach activity in the area seemed to center around the OB Pier. In the summer, surfers staked claim at sunrise and sunset to the waters on the north side of the pier. Even on evenings with flat waves, the water still teemed with surfers who spent the majority of the time waiting for a decent wave by chatting about how one was sure to come in soon.

On low-tide evenings, families explored the tide pools exposed on the south side of the pier. These pockets varied in size; crystal-clear, natural aquariums where fish, anemones, urchins, lobsters and several species of crabs were just some of the creatures they could observe. Sea grass and kelp swept back and forth in the current, and the rocks created islands used to hop from one pool to the next that a high tide would otherwise obscure.

During the week, retired men parked along Niagara in front of Marcus' apartment building before sunrise to cast fishing lines off the pier. On weekends, they ceded their territory to younger, working men.

Perhaps its main appeal to Marcus, was watching the sunset from the OB Pier with Megan. They'd walk to the end, lean against the wooden rail, arm in arm. Turn and marvel at how the sun's warm rays saturated the coastline in gold and amber. Squeeze each other when the sun kissed the water, and then kiss each other. Stay and hold each other well past the point where the horizon swallowed up the last bit of light in the sky.

Marcus took it slow on Sunset Cliffs, passing Ocean Beach Elementary School. Stopped at a red at Santa Monica Avenue. Rubbed the card through his pant pocket and stared at the church across the street. "OB One Church." Megan snort laughed every time they drove past it. Marcus smiled, remembering. She'd had to explain the *Star Wars* pun to him the first time when he didn't get why it was funny.

Megan was a free spirit with a chill Southern California vibe to her. She spent most of her time at the beach, either laying out reading true crime books alongside picnicking tourist families or stealing waves from surfers on her standup paddleboard. The rest of the time she worked at one or more of the many restaurants in OB, Mission Beach and Pacific Beach.

They met when Marcus stopped for some fish tacos while on duty one day. Megan was working behind the counter at a taco shack in OB, and he was third in a line stretching out of the restaurant. The front door was propped open by a broken piece of brick, allowing the salty beach breeze to blow in. Sublime crackled through a couple of cheap speakers and amateur water paintings hung on the walls for sale.

Megan's dirty blonde hair was tied up in a haphazard bunch and bounced when she scooted from the register to the kitchen window putting in customer orders. She looked his way a few times as he inched closer to the front of the line. His size made him stick out in any normal line, but being in uniform surrounded by boardshorts and bikinis really made him hard to miss.

When Marcus stepped up to the register, Megan was at the kitchen window. She stood leaned to one side with her ass popped, repeating the previous customer's order. Marcus looked her up and down as if she was a suspect. He noted a tattoo on the outside of her left leg that ran from knee to ankle: a mermaid holding a sword with a skull on the end, the tip running through one of the hollow eye sockets. He was attracted to her right off the bat, but it was her generous smile that pressed him to make a move after he put in his order.

"Can I get your number? I'm Marcus." Something caught in the back of his throat with the words.

Customers snickered behind him. Guess they had grown tired of the two flirting with each other for the better part of ten minutes.

"For sure." Megan held out her palm.

Marcus unlocked his cell phone with his thumb print and handed it to her in one motion. She took the phone and her thumbs tapped away at the screen. Then, a chime rang from the front of her black half-apron.

"I sent myself a text," she said, and handed him back his phone.

He looked down at the text she sent to herself from his phone and it read, "You're hot." Marcus smiled.

"You better call me," she said.

"I can't text you?"

Megan winked at him.

They hit it off on their first date—a sushi dinner and a walk on the beach. It led to another date a few days later. After brunch on a Sunday, Marcus brought her back to his place at her insistence, and that's when they had sex for the first time. They were inseparable the next three months. They spent time with each other nearly every day, usually in the afternoon after he got off duty and before she had to work the dinner shift.

But catching her by total surprise around the three-and-a-half-month mark, Marcus asked Megan for a break, not knowing completely why himself in the moment. They got back together soon, however, and made it another few months before another break, and back on again.

Megan was perfect for him. No argument to the contrary. The irregular status of their relationship wasn't for a lack of shared feelings. Whenever the two were on a break, it was completely because of Marcus, even if he hadn't been able to fully understand his motivation.

Marcus found himself back on Newport Avenue, at the corner of Abbott Street. Footsteps from the murder scene. He pulled the cruiser up to the red fire lane curb on the side of the Ocean Beach Hotel. After turning the ignition off, he opened messages on his personal cell phone.

Clicking on the contact "Megan R.," he typed, "Can we talk later when I get off work?" He hit send.

He stepped out of the car and stuffed the phone back in his pocket. Faced the ocean. He adjusted his sunglasses, securing them firmly against his eyes. From where he stood, the OB Pier was within view, which put his apartment two blocks away, to his left.

To his right, the scene had been cleared—the Altima towed away—and normal activity had resumed. Marcus walked across Abbott Street to the long, concrete wall running along the beach, sand crunching under his boots.

OB Rob sat on the wall, about thirty feet down to the left. A mountain of clothes, beach finds and haberdashery in a rolling cart accompanied him, as always. Hot pink flip-flops balanced on top of the heap, alongside a bright yellow rubber duck that served as a bubble wand.

Marcus plopped down on the wall, slung both legs over, twisting into position to face the ocean. The breeze carried cool moisture from the two-foot waves to his face. He turned down the volume to his police radio earpiece low enough the noise wouldn't break his concentration, but not so quiet that he would miss a call.

"Hell of a day, man!" OB Rob shouted.

"You can say that again," Marcus said.

An older homeless man, OB Rob was a regular, as his name suggested. He had a wiry gray beard and one eye, having lost the other at some point in his youth and was evasive about the cause. The crusty man was also indignant about wearing his eye patch, and only put it on when the stares and commotion overwhelmed him. Or when cops pleaded with him to stop scaring the kids.

Marcus gave him a half-hearted wave. Watched the breaking waves. In his hands, the business card he got off the body earlier that morning. In a trance, he held the piece of stock paper pinched between his middle finger and thumb. Glided the card from one side of the long end to the other, then rotated the length back up, only to push it down again. Over and over.

Glazing over on the crashing waves, he allowed memories of his childhood to surface. The ones before he worked so hard to keep pushed far from reach.

The California half of his childhood had been rich and fun. Like living a life on vacation. His mother moved them to San Diego from Texas when he was twelve, leaving his father in the middle of the night. She packed their bags, a few meals and took off in the family's only car to give them a fresh start in a place she had always wanted to live: near the ocean.

After making it across the Arizona/California border, she didn't pull over again until their two-day journey dropped them in Ocean Beach. The last "official" bathroom Marcus used was in Yuma when they stopped for gas. Fifty miles later, after whining incessantly about needing to pee again, his mother snapped. Told him to go in an empty water bottle. Marcus sat stunned for a few seconds, but complied.

Several times during their trip, Stacey meekly asked Marcus if he was upset about leaving his father, having explained where they were headed, but not telling him why. He had other pressing concerns on his lips, so he mumbled he was fine and didn't care.

Marcus overheard the frequent arguments between his parents through the paper-thin-walls of the family's two-bedroom apartment. The sharp, unmistakable sound of skin slapping against skin. The last time it happened it was right in front of Marcus. Driving to the store, his father had slapped his mother's face so sharply, her head thudded against the passenger's side window. She'd sobbed the rest of the trip and Marcus pretended he was asleep.

So, it wasn't his mother's decision to leave his father, but something else overwhelming him on that drive to California. With his temple pressed to the window, he struggled to arrange the correct words in his head. His eyes bounced along the jagged boulders of the highway's granite cutouts. He spied dusty white, plump plants anchored in the rock. Each time his confession pushed up in his throat, the words snagged against a lump and stopped at his lips. A skittering stutter escaped instead.

"What was that, honey?" she asked after one such attempt.

Stacey's eyes sparkled when she looked over at him. She turned down the volume on the radio, pausing her singalong with Jewel.

"Nothing, Mom. I forgot what I was going to say." Marcus looked back out at the desert landscape sweeping by. She smiled. Then turned the volume back up, bellowed along with the chorus line to "Who Will Save Your Soul" and patted to the beat on his leg.

Marcus had never seen the ocean before that day in November, 1995. When they left, it was already cold in Plano. Well, cold by Texas standards. Once they made it to San Diego, mother and son stood side-by-side on the beach. The alien salt air danced in his nose and the subtropical sun felt soothing on his skin. He sucked in a deep breath and pushed out his chest for the first time in months. Stacey Kemp let out her own series of healing sighs, staring at the water. Marcus leaned into his mother and she stopped rubbing his back to draw him close and squeeze him. The pressure of having to divulge his horrible truth started to relent. He was out of danger and so was she.

Now a grown man, Marcus sat facing the ocean from nearly the identical spot as he had almost twenty-four years earlier. He looked down at the business card. On the front, two embossed palm trees flanked either side. In between the trees read: All Green Landscape Lighting and Design, and below it a P.O. Box in El Cajon.

Where would a newspaper editor from Texas get a business card for a landscape company in El Cajon? The question had been nagging at him and an idea finally popped to mind. He pulled out his cell phone. Turned on the private browsing option, hoping his search wouldn't be captured in his phone's search history. He typed in "San Diego conventions" and clicked enter.

The first hit was a link to a calendar of events at the San Diego Convention Center. He clicked on it and scrolled down the list, passing listings for seminars and conventions that had already been through town. He got to May, then June. There it was, or at least a likely place to start. "San Diego Home and Garden Show: Hundreds of Exhibitors; shop the latest in home and garden goods and find the newest trends emerging in the industry. Runs Friday, June 14 through Monday, June 17," the preview read.

"Shit, they're still there."

His arms bristled with goose bumps. Overwhelming him, a strong desire to tear off for the convention center. The thought made his skin flush and his throat go dry. Then his mind admonished him for wanting to insert himself into a case of which he had a considerable conflict of interest. Not to mention, he wasn't a detective or part of the official investigation.

Marcus had found his childhood abuser, dead, in the trunk of the stolen car that morning. Everything in him told him the world had set things right. The universe, or whatever, had gifted him retribution, something many victims of evil never come close to sniffing. But there was no closure. It wasn't enough. He knew so in the pit of his stomach. He'd wrestled with that truth for hours.

If Marcus was honest with himself, he would admit he knew the second he found his abuser's corpse that he wanted to help the killer get away with the murder. Who was he? Were they connected to the newspaper man from Texas for the same reason?

Marcus stared at crashing waves, the newspaper man's dead body flashing behind his eyes. His skin—those hands, so gray and lifeless. They were strong and forceful the last time Marcus had seen them.

3
THE PAST FLOODS BACK

Plano, Texas 1995

MARCUS AND HIS three best friends bounded down the concrete front steps of their elementary school. The eleven-year-olds had just finished their last day of the fifth-grade. The curriculum had been movie-watching and throwing a school's-out-for-summer popcorn party courtesy of an old-timey popcorn machine. They'd go to Armstrong Middle School in the fall and each were excited to get out of "baby school," especially Marcus who was eager to try out for the sixth-grade football team. But their shared, immediate concern was on summer, each of them chomping at the bit to make the most of it.

They spent the majority of their time the first week playing basketball, riding bikes a couple blocks up to the 7-Eleven to get soda, candy and chips, and swimming at their apartment complex's pool. The same pool being the scene where they had seen bare breasts for the first time the summer before, with much shared curiosity.

"They look...squishy," Charles said after they spied a teenage girl pulling up her one piece in the restroom, courtesy of a janky lock.

Over the summer, the boys' parents remained hands-off as far as supervision went. The boys came and went as they pleased for the most part. Simpler times. Perhaps it was the insular feel of the walled apartment complex with its one way in and out layout that provided the parents peace of mind.

Two of the friends, Chris and Thomas, had parents who both worked. Neither had to worry about checking in as a result. Charles was the only one who had a single-parent situation, and his mother did require him to call her at her work during lunch or sometime in the afternoon each day. If she didn't hear from him—which was all too common in the hurried excitement to get back to a tied game of "Twenty-One" or some similar pressing vacation concern—she would call Marcus' mother, who was the only stay-at-home parent of the four, to ensure the boys were staying close to home.

Marcus was the undeniable, natural leader of this scrappy group. Taller by a couple inches than each of his three friends, and had been the case ever since they all met in kindergarten. He had been gifted an athletic ease despite his lanky frame. He exuded confidence, but was content to let his friends voice their opinions first when deciding what the group would do for fun on a given day. Because once Marcus showed interest in an idea or provided one of his own, that's the one the group would go with.

They were well-behaved kids most of the time. But one day, on the Monday of the fourth week of their summer vacation, their boredom got the better of them. On that June morning, they were sitting in the shade, leaned against the wall on the other side of Marcus' apartment unit.

"It's so hot already!" Thomas moaned, and tugged at the collar of his shirt to force in air.

"Shit ya," Charles said. He fanned his face with his ballcap. "It's already hot as balls and it's not even 9 a.m."

"My dad says it's the humidity," Thomas said.

Marcus huffed and slammed his back against the white bricked wall.

A short-lived breeze rustled the wispy leaves of the mature pecan tree in front of them but provided no relief. This specific tree had produced a bumper crop of pecans the previous summer, due in large part to the consistent rainfall the North Texas area received that spring. Every day, women of the apartment complex congregated around the stately giant, some dragging child helpers along, to gather up the ripened treasures from the ground.

Stacey Kemp, Marcus' mother, was among the foragers. She collected so much due to the family living right around the corner from the tree and her being able to constantly monitor the day's bounty. Stacey was able to generate a little hide-away money by selling quarter-pound packages of raw, shelled pecans at the library, bundling them in scraps of sewing material tied closed with strips of different colored ribbon.

There would be very few pecans this summer in comparison, since it was the off year for this tree.

Marcus threw a pebble at its trunk while the boys sat thinking. He struck it dead-on in the center, about three feet up from the base, chipping off a small piece of the thick bark.

"Slurpees!" Charles exclaimed. "Perfect, right?"

"No doubt. A Slurpee run is critical," Chris started. "But let's save it till later when we're really dying."

Marcus nodded. "True, true," he said. "We should do something now that we won't want to do when it's scorching," he said to the group.

The boys sat for a moment reflecting on the possibilities.

Charles pulled off the Cubs cap he wore every day and slapped it against his thigh.

"That thing is NASTY!" Chris said, pointing at the ring of brown sweat built up around the bill. "And it stinks to high holy hell!"

Both points were true. But despite their mocking and disgust, Charles wore the cap every day anyway. He was counting down the days until he would rejoin his city league baseball team.

It took only a few moments of contemplation before a sly grin smeared across Chris' face, evidence of a masterful plan on the tip of his tongue.

He sat up straight and spun around to face his three friends, all on his left.

"FIRE!" Chris growled, wiggled his fingers with upturned hands; his eyes flickered with crazy. His grin grew to a gaping smile, exposing the holes where baby teeth had been just a few weeks earlier, completing the madman portrayal.

"What? What the hell are you talking about, Chris?" Thomas asked.

"Let's burn up some shit up. *Our* shit." Chris said.

The boys looked at each other.

"We do have a lot of stuff," Marcus said.

The group took no more time to deliberate. Marcus, Thomas and Charles jumped up from the ground to join Chris.

"Race ya!" Charles shouted, eyeing Marcus, the benchmark of speed in the group.

The boys lined up the way Olympic 100-yard dash sprinters do: each lowering into a crouched position with one knee down and hands formed into a bridge in the grass, set shoulder width apart.

"Readyyy!" Charles sang out.

With the cue, the four boys stuck their butts in the air.

"Set!" Chris said.

They all raised their heads and stared forward.

"GO!" Charles yelled.

The boys jumped from their positions and took off running. Blades of St. Augustine grass flew from their sneakers. Their hand-me-downs and thrift store-bought T-shirts and shorts flapped in the breeze. They sprinted the length of the complex. Their destination: a vacant, bottom-left unit of a four-apartment setup a couple hundred yards away.

Charles hung with Marcus most of the way, but Marcus pulled ahead and beat him by a couple of strides, slapping the side of the brick building with one hard smack, crossing the imaginary finish line. Chris brought up the rear by a good eight to ten paces, grabbing his left hip. He came to a stop next to his three friends who were bent over, hands on knees sucking air.

"I almost beat you that time!" Charles said to Marcus between huffs.

"Ha! Keep dreaming, chief!" said Marcus.

Thomas and Chris snickered at Charles.

Charles snapped. "What do you know about it, Chris? You were so far behind you couldn't see anything!"

Chris, the smallest of the group, waved a hand. "Whatever, man."

The apartment's small, fenced-in patio faced out to a six-foot high cement block wall encircling the complex. The wall was painted white, but multiple layers of old colors showed underneath where the cheap paint had flaked off under the constant beating from the Texan sun. The revealed colors coincided with the numerous facelifts of the apartment complex over the years.

"Coast is clear!" Charles said, dangling with his chest pinned on the top of the dog-eared pickets of patio fence.

Looking in through a glass sliding door at the back of the apartment, Charles saw the inside was empty, ensuring the apartment was still indeed vacant.

The friends jumped the rickety board-on-board wooden fence, landing on the concrete pad on the other side. Even the smell of the patio—a musk, mildew odor—validated it had not been occupied in months.

Chris grunted and grimaced in discomfort, making it over the fence last.

"What's wrong, man? You ok?" Marcus asked, squeezing his shoulder.

Chris stammered. "Nothing, I'm just, I hit my leg on my bed this morning is all."

Thomas slung open the narrow utility door on the patio and retrieved a trash bag full of the junk they had been collecting since sometime in the spring and hid in the space. The oldest of the friends by a mere eighteen days, Thomas turned the bag on its end and dumped the contents onto the patio.

"Okay!" Chris jumped into a stance in front of his friends like a dog guarding its meal. "I get to burn the Dr. Pepper can, promise me!"

Chris had been obsessed with wanting to burn a soda can—specifically a Dr. Pepper can—ever since his older cousin told him how cans turn colors: yellow, then green, and finally blue in a campfire. His cousin did it on his scout trip last summer, he had reminded Charles, Thomas and Marcus multiple times.

"Fine! We know!" Charles said, rolling his eyes and pressing his fingertips to his sweaty temple.

The rest of the junk was literal trash one or the group of them found and thought, "That would be cool to burn." A hairbrush missing rows of bristles, a doll head Charles popped off one of his sister's baby dolly collection being sold at their family's sidewalk sale, cigarette butts, candy wrappers, some string, newspaper, cut-up credit cards they found in a dumpster at the complex during a particularly fruitful dumpster dive one Saturday, and broken pieces of a wicker chair.

"Who's got a lighter?" Chris asked.

Thomas and Charles each pulled cheap translucent lighters from their jean shorts. Chris grabbed the blue one from Charles.

"Ahhh!" Chris smiled delight when the lighter sparked after a few flicks and shakes.

"Light this, Chris," Marcus said, holding out a tightly wrapped cone of newspaper.

"Mine too," Charles said, holding out another rolled up section of newspaper to Chris' lighter.

"Oh, ow! It's hot," Chris hollered. He let the flame die and waved his hand back and forth.

Charles put his newspaper to Marcus' and they used the makeshift torches to light the pieces of the wicker chair on fire. The newspapers burned hot and fast and the ink caused a thick billow of black smoke to build.

"Shit, that's too much smoke. We're gonna get caught," Marcus said, furrowing his eyebrows.

"Ok. Put out the newspapers, guys," Chris said.

They threw down the newspapers and stomped the flames out, which caused charred, black flecks to rise out of the fenced patio, carried on the smoke.

The wicker chair pieces were maintaining a flame by then, as well as the doll head, which was smoldering: the flames mutating the blue-eyed brunette slowly and methodically, turning her chubby cheeks inside out and making her nose run down to her chin like it was made of taffy.

"Now it's time for the can!" Chris held the perfectly undented can above his head like a trophy.

Before he could toss it on the wicker chair, they all ducked at the "bleep" of a walkie-talkie.

"Who's in there?" came a deep voice with a thick East Texas drawl.

"We're deaaaad," Charles whisper-shouted to the others.

Marcus worked to stomp the fire out with his right foot from a squatted position, nearly falling over. Just then, four meaty fingers wrapped down on the top of the fence and a burly man dressed in a dark blue dungaree-style shirt peeked over and stared down at them.

"What'n the hell do you boys think you're doing?"

. . .

STACEY KEMP WAS the first parent to arrive at the manager's office. The maintenance man who caught the friends had marched them there, calling ahead to the manager on his walkie-talkie to inform her of what he found.

"Thank you for coming in so quickly, Mrs. Kemp," the manager said, greeting Stacey in the lobby.

The four boys were lined up like insubordinate students waiting to see the principal, sitting in chairs gathered from empty office desks.

Chris fidgeted. Charles and Thomas were slumped in their chairs and Marcus sat upright and relatively still, hands in pockets. His head dropped when he saw his mom walk in.

"I don't know what you were thinking, Marcus." Her eyes searched for his, but he turned his head to avoid her glare.

"I've already spoken to your father and he will deal with you when he gets home."

She pulled at the sleeve of his shirt and he dragged his feet after her, the soles of his sneakers squeaking on the tile floor. He kept his face hidden from his friends leaving the office.

Once they got home, Stacey sent Marcus to his room, where he spent the rest of the day. His mom did let him leave his room once to join her for lunch.

"What?" he said, noticing she had been staring at him the entire time he was pecking at the ham and cheese sandwich and chips she prepared for them.

"Oh, don't "what" me, mister." Stacey pulled the length of her handmade headband off her head for thematic emphasis.

"Your father isn't going to be happy when he gets home," she said.

"So, what else is new?" Marcus rarely gave his mother lip. Knowing his father mistreated her and yelled at her all of the time, it seemed, he always told himself he wouldn't do the same.

"What did you say?"

"Nothing. Sorry."

"Mmm. Finish up and then back to your room."

After poking at his lunch a little longer, Marcus did return to his room. There he sat on the floor and stared at the large map of the United States of America that hung on the wall to the right of the doorway to his eight-by-ten-foot bedroom.

The map was one you would find for sale at the time in a bookstore or library, perhaps: full color with each state a different shade, the nation's interstate system intersecting through counties and cities and every major city's name at the heart of an intricate spider web of streets fanning outward. Capitals were marked with a gold star. Canada and Mexico did not exist on this map; the U.S. floated on its own and its non-continental states of Alaska and Hawaii licked its western shores.

Marcus was proud of what he had accomplished. Effectively, he had created a piece of assemblage art of sorts, without knowing what that was.

For months, he had gathered every sports magazine he could find: at giveaway piles at the library and in dumpster diving campaigns. He meticulously cut out the helmets representing each of the teams of the National Football League from the 1995 season preview issue of *Sports Illustrated*, guiding the scissors slowly, careful not to cut off any parts.

He did the same for baseball caps of each Major League team he found in a special spring training issue of *The Sporting News*. He had to settle for non-glossy, newspaper cutouts of the National Hockey League teams, the logos set on top of hockey pucks he found in *The Hockey News*. Lastly, he cut out the logos of NBA teams from an issue of *SLAM*.

Staring up at the map, he looked at the cluttered Northeast where he had quickly run out of room for all the teams homebased in New York and New Jersey. He was forced to put the New York Islanders, New Jersey Nets and New York Jets logos in the Atlantic Ocean and draw lines from each to the team's respective home.

The Midwest was practically barren, by contrast. The Kansas City Royals and Kansas City Chiefs stood out predominately with plenty of elbow room from a lack of teams in the states to the west. It looked as if a pebble had been skipped from Chicago, with the Bulls, White Sox, Cubs, Bears and Blackhawks, bounced at St. Louis with the Cardinals and Rams, then Kansas City, and then not again until Denver before splashing and rippling out on the west coast with pro teams spread across California, Oregon and Washington.

His friends gushed over his creation and the pro team map's detail even drew praise from his father, which surprised Marcus.

"Looks like you worked pretty hard on this," Terry Kemp told Marcus after the map caught his eye one night when he walked past his son's room. Marcus' chest rose in response to the compliment and his eyes welled.

Marcus wondered how his friends Charles, Chris and Thomas faired in their punishments. He worried about what Thomas would get. Marcus had been at his house on one occasion when his friend got into trouble. Though Marcus' father hit his mother, Terry had never touched Marcus, but the opposite was true for Thomas' homelife. His father had a quick temper and took out his frustrations on his only son physically.

At around 5:30 p.m., according to the red numbers glowing from the hand-me-down AM/FM radio on his dresser, the front door opened. After Marcus heard his parents bicker briefly, the door slammed shut and he heard his father's heavy footsteps stomping down the hall.

He sat up straight on the edge of his bed and held his breath. His father's presence in the hallway smothered the sliver of light filling the gap and Marcus gulped. A gurgle squealed almost simultaneously from his stomach.

Terry walked into the room, still dressed in his work uniform: brown shorts and an untucked brown short-sleeved shirt, with an embossed "UPS" patch on the left breast, above a pocket. He walked to stand over Marcus and got right to the point.

"Your mother told me what you did. You lucky they didn't call the police on you dumbasses," he said. His deep, gravelly voice punctuated the "yous."

Marcus hung his head and picked at some dried skin he found on his left palm.

"You hearing me, boy?"

"Yes, sir." Marcus kept his eyes fixated on his flakey skin.

Terry had no idea the punishment he was about to give Marcus would serve his son up to a monster.

4
THE PUNISHMENT

TERRY STOOD OVER the child he had been indifferent on having and still hadn't warmed to eleven years later.

Waiting for his punishment to be handed down, Marcus looked up at his father, then choked, catching the suffocating stench of his father's heavy smoking habit in the back of his throat. His work uniform always reeked.

Terry smoked two-and-a-half packs a day, even under Stacey's pressure for him to give up the "nasty habit." The monthly budget was a constant source of friction between the two and the rising cost of his addiction due to increasing taxes didn't help matters. His smoking habit was one of several regular topics the two argued about. Most of their arguments centered around money, or more precisely, the lack of it. Compounding their financial situation: Terry's refusal to allow his wife of thirteen years to get a job, despite her regular appeals.

"You wanted to have a family, so how you gonna be a mom and work, too?" was his usual argument-ending go-to on the matter.

Further straining the family's finances, Terry wouldn't allow Stacey to apply for government assistance either. Food stamps and WIC were "for poor people. I got a job," he would tell her.

It was true, he did have a good job. Stacey just saw no correlation between the late hours Terry worked as a delivery driver and their floundering budget. An affair wasn't out of the question and she entertained the possibility as a reason for his late nights. After all, Terry looked every good-looking woman up and down in public, his family in tow or not.

Turned out, most nights he sat parked at one of a dozen fast-food restaurants between work and home eating dinner off a dollar menu instead of spending time with his family.

Stacey was powerless to say anything about it. She lived a damned if she did, damned if she didn't existence. The family would have been much better off if she was allowed to work. She could buy Marcus new clothes and she could plan more nutritious dinners for the family, ensuring not every meal consisted of a cheap pasta dish, something battered or coming from a box. She dreamed of exposing Marcus to fresh fruits, exotic fruits even; quality meats of cuts more varied than ground beef in a roll or pork chops on manager's special. Mostly, she wanted to simply feed his growing body with real food.

Stacey had attempted to put her vision into practice one random week, only to run out of grocery money after just a few days of meals. Feeling defeated, she fell back on handouts of boxed pasta, canned foods and powdered milk from the food pantry to augment the week's menu so she wouldn't risk angering Terry by asking for more money.

For most of their marriage, Stacey covered for Terry's faults. Ignored the mounting control and violence. Didn't consider leaving him. The way they met had been fate, she told friends, and that as much as anything kept her overly optimistic about their relationship for longer than she should have.

Stacey caught Terry's attention when the two bumped into each other at the DMV. After wildly swinging open the heavy, aluminum-framed glass door to the government office into Terry's back, the two spent the next hour-and-a-half learning all about each other and left the DMV with valid driver's licenses and a plan to go to dinner.

He was attracted to her bright personality and organic beauty, and she his brash confidence. When the pair eloped four months later, Stacey's grandparents were reluctant to approve of the nuptials after the fact. When they voiced concerns about Terry's ability to support her and about him being raised in a single-parent home, Stacey bristled.

"Terry is no different than me, Granddaddy," she said. "At least he has a mom and she raised him right."

Terry's mother was overjoyed for her youngest, telling him she was glad he finally made something of his life. She kicked him out of her house at seventeen when he was expelled from high school during his senior year, after being caught stealing from the cafeteria. He had been on his own for three years prior to meeting Stacey. First couch-surfing at friends' houses, then splitting a two-bedroom apartment five ways.

The young couple moved to Plano after they were married. Terry got a referral for a job at UPS at its hub in Garland, northeast of Dallas. The job paid more than his sporting goods store job and had prospects to advance.

Stacey, by comparison, had very little job experience at the time. She had been taking some community college courses here and there without any real direction since graduating high school. Living with her grandparents afforded her the ability to coast. But now that the couple wanted to be adults, she needed to get a job, too.

They looked at apartments around Terry's work but didn't like the Garland neighborhoods. They found a place in the neighboring city of Plano, on the east side, instead. The rent there was affordable and the neighborhood they chose was diverse: Mexican, white and black families all occupied the complex where they signed a one-year lease for a one-bedroom unit.

The first few months of their marriage were good, but it didn't take long for things to change.

The first time Stacey felt threatened by Terry was three months before their first anniversary. By then, she was working as a cashier at Albertsons, a grocery store two blocks east of their apartment complex. She walked to work and back each day to allow Terry to use the couple's only car—a Honda Civic Stacey's grandparents gave her for graduating high school—to commute to his job.

That night, they settled in to watch some TV after dinner. Stacey brought out a bowl of tortilla chips and salsa. Terry had been quiet through their store-bought lasagna dinner.

Before she knew what she had said to set him off, he flipped the bowl from her lap. Chips flew in the air and landed all over both of them, the tan couch, and the floor. The plastic bowl careened off her leg before falling to the carpet, where it bounced a of couple times and settled like a wobbly top.

Stacey sat stunned and could only manage to say, "What? I, I…" with her mouth wide open and her hands turned to the ceiling.

Terry stormed off to the bedroom and slammed the door behind him, the force shaking the thin, textured walls of the small apartment and making Stacey jump.

What started as testy spats early in their marriage grew from then on. Terry yelled at her constantly. Maybe he hated his job. Maybe he resented where they chose to live or how they were more behind on bills than ever. It likely was any and all of these things, but their fights never exposed a root cause in her mind. And she was confused why every little thing became an excuse for him to yell and frighten her. Her questions and pleading for answers only enraged him all the more.

His outbursts would have made more sense if he was a drunk, she told her friends. A couple of whom encouraged her to "take a break" from Terry, but Stacey would hear nothing of it at first. He loved her, that much she knew. He always made up for their fights by showing affection and even apologizing on most occasions, she rationalized to her friends.

When she found out she was pregnant, she was overjoyed and thought Terry would be happy as well. But the yelling continued and their arguments escalated, leading Stacey to put her foot down one evening when she was seven months pregnant. The two had calmed down after a heated disagreement over whose check they should pay the cable bill with. She demanded a condition be followed from then on. Period. End of story.

"Terry, my love," she started. She stroked her round stomach and held out her right hand to take his hand. He reciprocated and offered his hand.

"I don't want us to fight in front of our baby. I don't want our child seeing their mom and dad like that," Stacey said.

Terry nodded and seemed to concede to her request. Her good intention had a devastating unintended consequence for her, however.

A year after Marcus was born, their arguments intensified. Emboldened by the privacy their bedroom afforded him to technically adhere to Stacey's condition, Terry became physical. It started with little finger pokes, then shoving and progressed to slaps with his open hand. If he wasn't winning a fight, or felt belittled or frustrated, he ended the argument with a hand to Stacey.

Over the years, Stacey convinced herself she was the problem. She told herself she questioned her husband or acted better than he, after all. She knew where the line was and she simply wouldn't cross it.

Marriage is about compromises, she convinced herself.

So, it wasn't a surprise when Terry came home with a punishment for Marcus after the fire incident that Stacey easily gave up her protests when Terry threatened her.

"You'd best not tell me how to handle him, woman," Terry said, pressing his index finger between her eyes and then slamming the front door.

It took less than a minute for her to back down, partly because the discipline he intended for their son could have been worse in her mind. And partly because she knew she had no chance of changing Terry's mind anyway. But mostly because she had woken up to the fact by this point in time that she needed to leave Terry. Her friends—now long-gone from her life—had been right. She had to bide her time. Focus her energy on how and when she would break free from the mold Terry had cast her in.

TERRY STARED DOWN at Marcus.

"Your mother called my work. They had to call my truck." He rubbed his trimmed goatee with his left thumb, index and middle fingers. "What ya need to learn is some responsibility, boy."

Marcus felt his eyebrows arch, listening to his father's words. His eyes blinked rapidly, out of his control.

"That's why your gonna spend less time horsing around with your friends. I got you a job," Terry said.

A job?! The words made something jump in his chest. Excitement. Marcus realized he was going to get to go to work with his dad. They would deliver packages and load his big, brown truck and sweep up... his mind raced with all the possibilities and he couldn't remember a time when he had been more excited about anything.

"With...you?" Marcus asked, sitting up as straight as he could on the edge of his bed without standing up.

"No, dummy," Terry snapped. "I was delivering a package at the newspaper and got you a job helping out there."

Marcus stared up from his bed and looked into Terry's dark-as-blacktop eyes, the skin between them wrinkled. Marcus exhaled and slumped over on the edge of his bed, his body deflating; his hopes of spending time with his father dashed.

His mind wandered to what working at the newspaper would involve. Then a flare of panic shot down his chest and into his stomach. Of course. Working a job meant no more 7-Eleven runs. No more riding bikes for hours, swimming at the pool every day or playing basketball. He probably wouldn't see his friends again until school started and by then they would probably have replaced him.

In reality, Marcus would still have four days a week to hang out with his friends, but in the moment, his social world was crumbling.

"Let's get some dinner," Terry said, catching Marcus off guard and snapping his concentration.

"Oh-okay," he said.

That's strange. Marcus looked over at his AM/FM radio and saw the time read 5:59 p.m. His father was home early *and* would eat dinner with them.

One corner of his mouth raised and a smirk popped up on his face.

"I mean, ok!" Marcus exclaimed, changing his tone to elation.

He jumped off his bed and followed his father out of his room.

"I'm tellin' ya, boy. I like that," Terry said, tapping Marcus' pro team map twice with his middle finger on their way out.

The smirk on his son's face turned to a gushing grin.

The family enjoyed a rare, pleasant dinner together that night, but none of the Kemps knew the next day would be the start of the longest, worst summer of Marcus' life.

5

THE CAR THAT SMELLED LIKE NEWSPAPER PRINT

MARCUS SAT AT a wooden table, waiting for instructions. The table served as a catch-all desk of sorts for everything in the newsroom; from the editorial team's space to lay out the broadsheets for final review before sending the edition to the printer, to a station for pot-luck casseroles.

Marcus rubbed the worn finish of the table with the heel of his palm and then crossed his arms again, each hand cupping his opposite elbow.

He let out a sigh, and found himself taken with how the tone of his skin had to be the exact fifty-fifty combination of his mom's and father's skin.

"Wow," he mused aloud.

It bugged Marcus how his friends thought his father was cool simply because he was black, but he never argued with them because it was easier than breaking the truth to them. That Terry was more of a bully than anything. He wondered what his friends were doing without him, but then remembered Charles, Thomas and definitely Chris were all probably grounded.

Leaning back in the rolling chair, the springs in the old fabric-covered back gave out, sending Marcus flying backward. He giggled like a much younger child might with the sensation of a cheap rollercoaster. He righted himself. His lanky frame allowed his feet to touch the floor, but the desk table was too high for him, causing his shoulders to hunch when he propped his arms back on its surface.

Methodic taps of a typewriter echoed in the otherwise quiet newsroom of *The Plano Register*.

Marcus looked around.

Jennifer was the older teenage receptionist with caked-on foundation who had let him in the front door when Terry dropped him off at roughly 6:30 a.m.

"Oh. Bill doesn't get here till eight or so, but he can come in anyway," she said, holding the metal-framed glass door open.

The clacking of the typewriter keys continued, like a chicken pecking sporadically at the dirt without rhythm.

Marcus scanned the far side of the room and saw computer monitors on top of every desk and a corresponding CPU underneath each. Holding the side of the table with both hands so he could lean to one side dramatically, he craned and saw an older woman—who he guessed was "probably a hundred" to himself and snickered—pecking at a typewriter on her desk. In her mid-fifties in reality, she was indeed hammering away on her assignments.

Seeing someone using a typewriter reminded Marcus of his great-grandparents, his mom's grandparents, who both passed away within weeks of each other when he was nine. His great-grandmother used a typewriter to do her "correspondence," as she once told him. He still hadn't figured out what that meant. He would watch her type away at a fevered pace in comparison to the writer in the newsroom.

Marcus started to make his way over to the older woman. His gaze fixed on her large, baby powder-white arms, exposed just below the shoulder. The full, fleshy underbelly of each arm jiggled and swung with each hammered keystroke. *Click. Swoosh. Clack. Swoosh.* And then the typing stopped.

"Yeeeeees? Can I help you, little mister?" the writer asked, looking up from her work and over her glasses at a curious Marcus standing next to her desk.

"I'm…Marcus," he said, and looked up at her soft face. "What are you doing?"

"I'm typing up Mr. Dale Howard's obituary."

"What's that?" His right eyebrow arched with the question.

"Well, when someone passes—"

"You mean, dies?" Marcus asked.

"Yes. When someone passes away, their family requests an announcement to go in the paper to tell everyone about their life."

Marcus blinked and stood quiet.

"My name is Opal. Bill told me you're going to be helping us out around here?"

Marcus shrugged his shoulders, pouted his lips.

"I guess," he said. "I got in trouble."

"Ohhhh, I see," she said, smiling. She hesitated a minute and Marcus caught her eyes darting around the newsroom.

"Let me show you something that might make you feel better about your punishment. I know it cheers me up when I'm having a rough go of it."

Opal pushed off one armrest, attempting to stand, wobbling for a moment before throwing out her other arm to Marcus. He caught her hand with both of his, feeling instantly helpless and absurd. He grunted and winced. She managed to right herself without losing her balance and didn't need his assistance after all.

Marcus felt relief and blew out a hard breath.

He followed her back across the newsroom, past the wooden table to the far wall. Pushed against it—in the middle between the door to a restroom on the left and a big copy machine on the right—was a short, brown piece of furniture. It reminded Marcus of the nightstand his great-grandmother had used to display Precious Moments figurines and other trinkets.

This one in the newsroom was just wide enough to hold a black microwave on top. From on top of the microwave, Opal wrapped her hands around an eight-sided, glass container filled with various individually-wrapped pieces of candy. She lowered the jar right in front of Marcus and lifted the glass lid, of which the rim of the inside was insulated with blue painter's tape.

"Go ahead, take one. It's here for everyone," she said in a soft, kind voice. She winked as she held the lid and pushed the container closer to Marcus. Her gold-chain necklace swung and the cross pendant hanging from it clinked against the glass.

Marcus surveyed his choices. The jar was alive with color: shimmering gold and yellow foil, blue and brown wrappers trimmed in silver; and the brilliant red of Kit-Kat bars. He reached his hand in the jar and grabbed out one mini-Snickers bar.

"Why's there tape on it?" Marcus asked, pointing to the lid with his free hand.

Opal dropped the lid back onto the jar and her eyes widened in a "watch this" moment of theatrics.

"No clink!" she said. "We fool ourselves and say the tape is so we don't disrupt others while they work, but I think it's really so we can sneak a piece or two of candy and no one will catch us."

She winked at Marcus and set the jar back on the microwave.

Marcus unwrapped the candy bar and took a bite. The gooey texture elicited an immediate smile and slow blinking eyes.

"I guess I should have made sure you ate breakfast first," Opal said.

"I did!" Marcus said with a smack, exposing a mouth of sticky caramel and chocolate.

At that moment, the front door swung open and Bill, the editor, trudged in. Marcus only caught a quick glimpse of him, as Bill turned the corner into his office, flipped the light on and shut the door behind him.

"I suppose we better get back to work, Marcus," Opal said.

She waved her arm and escorted him toward the table in the middle of the room. He plopped back down in the chair and Opal walked to her desk and began pecking away at Mr. Howard's obit again.

After only a short time, Bill emerged from his office and started toward the open newsroom. Marcus sat up a little straighter and watched him move into his line of sight. He didn't look in Marcus' direction, but rather shuffled over to Opal's desk.

Marcus snorted suddenly and quickly covered his mouth with both hands.

"He looks like Penguin," Marcus muttered under his breath and snickered. He wished Chris was there to laugh at his spot-on comparison. The two had watched "Batman Returns" on videotape one morning just a week earlier at Chris' house while they waited on Charles and Thomas to arrive.

Bill was a squatty, round man who wore glasses. Marcus couldn't tell if it was his stomach or the short-sleeved shirt tucked into his pants creating the roll below his waistline.

Only visiting with Opal for a minute, Bill now walked toward Marcus. His sneakers squeaked on the linoleum floor. Marcus sat up as straight as he could and tried to swallow recurrent giggling from his Penguin joke, pursing his lips and scrunching his face.

"Hi there, Marcus," Bill said. His voice boomed, deeper than Marcus had anticipated it would be.

Feeling fooled and bad, Marcus said, "Hi," in a soft voice.

"We're glad your dad let us borrow you for the summer. We have a lot you can help us with."

Marcus' ears perked up. He'd rarely received words of encouragement from a male before. His mom was his lone reassuring voice. A sensation numbed the back of his neck. It never occurred to him in the twelve-ish hours since receiving his punishment that he might be needed. His father never once asked him for help or sought to include him in anything.

Marcus gave Bill his full attention. His eyes lit up and stared at the man, eagerly awaiting his assignment.

"We've needed to organize our archived issues for a while now," Bill said. "Actually, Jennifer has been working on it for some time." He shot a glance over his shoulder toward the receptionist and back to Marcus.

As if on cue, Jennifer dropped two dusty Bankers Boxes full of old newspapers onto the table.

"Jennifer will get you started. Glad to have you here, Marcus!" Bill patted Marcus on the shoulder, sending another chill up the young boy's neck.

Jennifer spread out the old copies of *The Plano Register* and explained her process of organizing the back issues, thumbing a few of the copies. She detailed exactly how she wanted Marcus to go about it, but Marcus' attention was elsewhere.

He'd noticed how good the older girl smelled. Something about the way she wore the oversized black T-shirt—hung just an inch above the hem of her faded jean shorts—captured his attention. He looked back at the table and he couldn't see any exposed wood, there were so many newspapers laid out. Jennifer patted him on the back and left him in charge of organizing the issues from 1986.

Most of the hundreds of copies had acidified yellow from age years ago. Marcus picked up the March 1 issue with the headline, "Council hears comments on Plano Parkway expansion," printed on the top of the page in large print and brought the paper close, curious if the musky odor filling his nose all of the sudden was coming from the newspapers.

He drew in a big whiff of the paper and memories popped to mind of summer afternoons at the library with his mom when he was younger. The two attended a summer reading circle every Tuesday when he was eight, and Stacey would let him check out nature books about animals afterward. The library was close enough they would walk there, but even with the short walk, the air conditioning inside felt so good.

Over the next couple of hours, the hum of the newsroom grew with the arrival of the sales team, reporters and photographers. The volume rose as the sales reps started "smiling and dialing," as Bill referred to it later.

While reporters came and went throughout the day, Opal only left her desk for restroom breaks, grabbing a piece of candy on her way back each time. Marcus followed her lead and grabbed a piece for himself whenever she did. A few times he stuffed a second piece in the right pocket of his jean shorts as well.

The eleven-year-old drew looks, nearly all of which turned into smiles aimed his way, especially from the women in the newsroom. A man, he guessed a reporter, and one of the male photographers walked past him without so much as a glance.

Marcus was finding the work enjoyable with each passing minute, regardless.

"You're doing a great job," Opal said to him on the way back from one of her bathroom trips.

The encouragement revved him more than any 7-Eleven sugar high ever had. And when he thought he couldn't ride any higher, Bill poked his head out of his office, moved to where Marcus could see him, winked and gave him a thumbs-up raised above his head.

Marcus sucked and held a breath. His eyes widened and his chest swelled. He returned the thumbs up enthusiastically, not realizing until later that Bill's intent was to ask if everything was going well, and not saying, "You're doing a great job, Marcus!"

The afternoon flew by and Marcus finished organizing 1986 and most of 1987.

The clock hanging on the wall above the microwave behind him read 4:30 p.m. and it was then that Bill walked over to the table. He gave Marcus another pat on the back, this time keeping his hand on his shoulder for a few seconds before dropping it to his side.

"Ready to go home?" he asked. His deep voice reverberated inside of Marcus.

"Sure," Marcus said. "Is my dad here?"

"Oh, no. He didn't tell you?" Bill placed his hand back on Marcus' shoulder again and rested it there.

Marcus felt his insides cringe. He heard his mother's voice berating people in the grocery store for touching her son's head. But Bill's wasn't a wrinkly old hand rubbing all over his hair, combing through it and examining it like a child does an underwater sea creature in a petting zoo.

Bill leaned in, smiled and said, "I'm taking you home after work."

Marcus hesitated to answer but had no reason to question his boss of one day.

"Ok," he said.

Marcus grabbed his lunch bag from under the table. It was heavier than he expected, and he realized then he had forgotten to eat his lunch because of all the candy he had eaten.

"Can I go to the bathroom first?" Marcus asked. He looked at Bill, their eyes practically at the same level.

"Sure thing. Don't forget to wash the ink off your hands," Bill said, pointing at Marcus' hands.

Once inside the bathroom, Marcus unzipped his lunch bag and looked at the ham and cheese sandwich wrapped in plastic wrap Stacey had made him. She also packed him a bag of Doritos, his favorite. His stomach gurgled. Marcus stood over the trash can, conflicted, but decided to save his mom's feelings. He ditched the lunch and ran to meet Bill in the parking lot.

The air conditioning was on full blast when Marcus jumped in the passenger's seat of Bill's Honda Civic. The inside still felt like an oven, thanks to the ninety-eight-degree heat outside.

"Ready? Buckle up," Bill said, but simultaneously reached over Marcus and pulled the seat belt across his body before he could respond, and fastened him in.

The air blew so hard the force created a whistle. Little bits of black foam insulation flew out of the vents and landed on his shirt.

"Sorry about that," Bill said. He picked a particularly large chunk off Marcus and dropped it to the floorboard. "She's holding together as best she can."

The car reminded Marcus of his own family's vehicle, just messier.

The dashboard, the top of the steering wheel, the radio knobs, the handle and area around in of the glove box—really every vinyl surface in Bill's car—was mucked up with black smudges.

Bill finally gunned it on to Plano Parkway, after the two sat for what seemed like an hour waiting for traffic to ease up. The air began to cool. It had already dried out Marcus' eyes and so he looked out the window.

"So," Bill started.

Marcus swung his head back at him.

"You're kind of a quiet guy, huh?"

Marcus shrugged. "Guess so."

"That's alright," Bill said, letting him off the hook easy enough.

Marcus sat silent.

"I know one thing," he continued. "You're a good worker and we're lucky to have you."

Marcus smiled.

"I mean it," Bill said. He looked at Marcus and dropped his chin to look at the boy over his gold-rimmed glasses. "It's too bad you can't help me every day."

"I wish I could!" Marcus blurted out. He flushed and looked away. "I mean…"

"Oh, I know. You probably don't want to spend every minute of your summer working. Just saying, you're a good kid, Marcus."

Marcus bounced back in his seat. His smile pulled his cheeks tight.

Bill turned on to his apartment's street. Marcus kicked his right foot, swung it.

Then, he identified the smell in the car. Maybe he wasn't able to before because the air conditioning had masked it. But once Bill turned the air conditioning down, Marcus realized Bill's car smelled like a thicker version of the archived newspapers he had organized all day. It was a little sweet, but stale at the same time. Marcus sniffed.

"It's newspaper print," Bill said. "That's what you're smelling. Good, huh?"

Marcus nodded, but wasn't sure he agreed it smelled good.

"I roll and deliver papers when I'm down a man, so the smell lingers."

Bill stopped the car in the front of the entrance to the apartment complex, pulling over to the curb.

"Here we are."

Marcus looked up and it took a second for him to know where they were.

"I like the smell," Marcus fibbed.

Bill smiled.

"See you Thursday, little man."

"Thanks for the ride!"

"My pleasure," Bill said.

Marcus hopped out of the car and shut the door with two hands. He ran home with his lunch bag swinging at his side. Inside, his mother greeted him.

"Hi, baby!" She threw out her arms.

Before he could answer, he saw confusion overtake her wide smile. She looked over the top of Marcus and asked, "Where is your father?"

Marcus shrugged. "Bill said Dad said he should take me home."

"Wait. Who brought you home?"

"Bill. The newspaper man."

Stacey's eyebrows went from scrunched to arched. She then rolled her eyes.

"Figures," she whispered at the ground.

Marcus tensed.

"Not you, baby," she added, rubbing him on the shoulder. "Your father. Never mind...Tell me about your day!"

Stacey led him into the kitchen and took his lunch bag from him. He began to share, and she opened the pantry and pulled out a package of fruit snacks for him.

"It was fun!" Marcus said. "Bill is really nice and thinks I'm a good worker, and—"

"Well, of course you are, sweetie!" She handed him the snack and a cup of watered-down red Kool-Aid and waved her hand for him to continue.

"And there was this old lady that was nice, too.

"*Who* was nice," Stacey corrected.

"Who was nice," he repeated, and then continued. "I got to help put these newspapers in order. They have a candy jar and you can have as much as want and it's cold inside and—"

"Well, it certainly seems like you enjoyed your punishment more than I expected," she said, smirking.

Marcus looked up at his mom's bright face and his cheeks flushed.

He went to bed full that night. Not from dinner—though he did eat every bit of the Stouffer's chicken and vegetable lasagna his mom served with two hunks of garlic French bread on the side. If he had a tank in his chest, he pictured his feelings building up and sloshing and spilling over the top.

Laying on his back in bed, he couldn't contain himself. Grinning from ear to ear, Marcus squeezed his fists in front of himself and shook his entire body.

Fighting his runaway smile from prying open his mouth, he squealed in the back of his throat, keeping the noise muffled like screaming into a pillow. Marcus stared at the ceiling and exhaled a long breath. He had never experienced the rush associated with pleasing a father figure until that day.

Marcus spent the entire next day thinking about how he couldn't wait to go back to work at the newspaper, which would be that Thursday and Friday, two days in a row. He learned about his schedule from Bill. For the next eight weeks, Terry would drop him off at *The Plano Register* on Tuesdays, Thursdays and Fridays.

Wednesday dragged. Chris, Thomas and Charles were all grounded until the following week, so basically, Marcus was as well. The moms all agreed the boys needed some "separation time."

Marcus was actually free to go outside and play, ride his bike or whatever, but the anticipation of returning to the paper kept him distracted and he stayed inside the entire day as a result. Every time he thought about Bill, he experienced the same rush of feelings he had the night before. He was sure Bill would greet him with a big smile on his second day and give him another pat on the back for doing a great job.

Marcus was correct. Bill greeted him warmly on Thursday, heaped praise on him during the day and on the car ride home. Marcus warmed up to his boss quickly as a result. He pelted him with questions on Friday, when Bill drove Marcus around town to collect fees from the newspaper's week-to-week subscribers.

"Where are the papers printed?"

"Who is your best worker?"

"How do you pick the stories?"

"Ha! Ha!" Bill laughed heartily at the precocious preteen. "You're the best worker, of course!"

Bill rubbed Marcus' head and continued. "I love your curiosity, Marcus. That's the best quality a reporter can have, if you ask me."

Marcus looked at Bill's face and saw his smile was warm, the same as his mom's when he would catch her looking at him for no reason. With his hand still on Marcus' head, Bill pushed his glasses up with his other, gliding them along his nose until they fit snug against his eyes. He blinked. Just as Marcus felt a twinge start through his stomach, the newspaper man removed his hand and held it up for a "high-5."

Marcus hesitated. One of his eyebrows rose. He looked at the hand for a second and then gave Bill five up top but just missed when offered "down low."

"Too slow!" Bill hollered, pulling back his hand. But then placed it on Marcus' bare left thigh, his palm resting just above Marcus' knee.

Marcus flinched like when being shocked by static electricity. Bill patted Marcus on the leg with two beats and pulled back his hand, playing off the interaction.

"Well, anyway. I bet you will make a good reporter one day," Bill said.

Marcus was flushed, but Bill was not. The newspaper man was calm and his lips slightly pursed. The car had come to a stop. Marcus stared at Bill for a second longer and then shook his head, blinked and looked at the small ranch-style brick home on his right that had brown wood shutters and a front yard full of overgrown weeds.

"Uh, how much…does, um, this house owe?" Marcus asked. He hoped the change in subject would help him ignore the funny feeling in his stomach.

Bill whipped out a clipboard from the pocket of the driver's door. He bit down on a pencil, skimming the paperwork. After raking the pencil in his teeth some more, he gave the figure to Marcus.

It took a few more stops, and driving in mostly silence, for Marcus to shake off the uneasy feeling. Bill tried to break the tension a few times by asking Marcus questions such as, did he like baseball and what kind of candy was his favorite.

By the end of the afternoon, the two were back to normal. Walking along a broken concrete pathway from Bill's car to the front door of another subscriber's house, Marcus convinced himself the behavior was no different than when old ladies in stores liked to touch his hair.

No biggie.

Later in the afternoon, Bill dropped Marcus off in the front of his apartment complex and wished him a fun weekend.

"I'll see you next Tuesday, partner."

Marcus nodded, stepped out of the car and waved at his boss, before closing the door.

It took him longer than usual to fall asleep that night. His stomach gurgled. Dinner hadn't sat well, and he was excited to spend the weekend with his friends, all of whom would no longer be grounded by then.

By the time the weekend was over, Marcus had put the memory of Bill holding his leg completely to the back of his mind. By Monday night, he was looking forward to being dropped off at *The Plano Register* for the start of his second week on the job.

6
FIRST ASSAULT

DRIP.

Drip.

Marcus blinked his eyes open and came to. Small drops of wetness splashed on his leg. It was a blazing hot Friday, but his skin was frigid to the touch. The car's air conditioning blew furiously. Little bits of foam insulation expelled from the vents and landed on his lap after bouncing off his chest. His right arm was stretched precariously and forcibly across his body. The rest of him was tense, pulled in the opposite direction.

Drip.

Drip.

Marcus looked down and watched a few of the drops land on the bare skin of his left leg. He crooked his head slightly, confused and groggy. He blinked his eyes and tried to tell himself to focus on figuring out where the drops were coming from.

The moisture picked up pace.

Drip.

Drip.

Drip.

He raised his head a couple of inches, bringing his eyes in line with the arm crossing his body. A hand not his own held a tight grip around his right wrist.

Another drop splashed on his thigh.

Drip.

Marcus was determined to track the next drop. He blinked, stared intently at his arm, stretching his eyes wide to make sure he wouldn't miss it. The light brown tone of his skin was glistening more than normal. Marcus wondered why his forearm looked different than he had remembered. It was grooved and veins were popping out. A ripple like a valley ran its way from the bend of his arm all the way to his elbow. Then, he spotted it.

Drip.

Marcus watched sweat puddle on his upper arm and forearm and flow along the channel created by his tensed muscles. It met and pooled on his right elbow, forming a perfectly tear-dropped, transparent bead that throbbed until gravity could no longer support its mass.

The sweat fell and splashed on his leg.

Drip.

Having found the origin, confusion evaporated and clarity took hold. The droplets of sweat were forming, falling and splashing from many points of his body, not just off his arm. One flowed from his forehead, down his nose and splashed on his blue basketball shorts. Another ran down the length of his ear and dangled on his ear lobe for what felt like a torturous eternity before falling on to his shoulder. A field of sweat droplets beaded on his legs and knees and if he was permitted to stand up, a couple of dozen drops would have showered the ground.

Every muscle, nerve and emotion in Marcus was constricted, twisting and shaping his body parts into multiple, angular points for the sweat to funnel to and cascade off.

Then Marcus remembered what preceded the mystery of the drops of perspiration...

Bill had grabbed him suddenly by the wrist and pulled his hand to him. Marcus squealed, cringed and squeezed his eyes shut.

He felt his hand being guided. He screamed as loud as he could but no sound came out. When Marcus peeked, he saw Bill's striped knit shirt lying untucked over the top of his unbuttoned khaki pants and Bill's hand wrapped around his. He was holding on to Bill but wasn't trying to. His eyes locked on to a strangely-shaped spot on Bill's right forearm. It was an oblong swell with a deep crimson color and thick like chewed bubblegum.

A lump lodged sharply in Marcus' throat. He tried to swallow but his mouth was too dry. His stomach lurched and sank at the same time. Marcus whipped his head away, shut his eyes again and pulled his body toward the passenger's door with all of his strength. But it was like being tethered to a tree by a thick rope or chain; his body hit an invisible wall when Bill tightened his grasp.

He was trapped, unable to break the newspaper man's hold.

Marcus squeezed his eyes tighter and tighter to the point where stars pulsated and flashed under his eyelids, accompanied by streaks of light flying past his peripheral vision in warp speed. Then, his mind became overwhelmed by penetrating black and went blank.

The darkness lasted for about ten seconds, but it might as well have been hours. When he awoke, Marcus unconsciously tensed his body again with all of his strength. It was then he became distracted by the mysterious drops of wetness.

Now Marcus told himself to focus on something else like he had with the sweat, anything else to distract himself.

Don't look at what is happening.

Not until it stops.

Bill moaned and the sound shrieked through Marcus, making him buck violently. He shut his eyes again, but opened them just as fast, not wanting to pass out again. A newspaper on the floorboard between his sneakered feet caught his eye. Marcus could make out the print clearly. His mother was always quick to remind him of the fact he had excellent vision when he couldn't find his backpack for school or when she asked him to get a condiment out of the refrigerator for dinner.

The newspaper was turned over, lying face down so only the stories below the fold showed. There was a color photo of an elderly black man in the middle of the page wearing a military hat of some sort with metal pins adorning it. He had a wrinkly face and soft eyes. The caption read: "Marvin Johnson celebrated his 80th birthday with his family at his home in Plano last week."

Marcus read every word detailing the account of the hometown hero who felt blessed to celebrate another birthday when so many of his brothers came home from the big one in caskets. He was just getting to the part where Marvin's oldest daughter was quoted and the story cut off and continued on A24.

Marcus moved his eyes on to a story running down the left side of the page alongside Marvin's feature and was only about five to six words wide. The skinny piece reported on a bond initiative the City Manager had presented to the City Council the night before.

Marcus wondered if "last night" was his last night and scanned the bottom of the paper to find a date, and, yes, this was a copy of today's issue, which meant his birthday was exactly one week away. He had overheard his mom telling his father a few days ago of plans to celebrate his birthday at his grandmother's house in South Dallas. Marcus loved his grandmother but wasn't as close to Terry's mother as he had been with Stacey's grandparents. This would be the fourth birthday since they had passed away. Their old East Dallas ranch-style house felt more like home then his did. It smelled like baby powder and laundry detergent. He spent the majority of the time during his visits playing in the sizeable, unfenced back yard that backed up to a creek. He learned to skip a rock in the creek and sloshed through it to look for frogs, turtles and crayfish.

Bill moaned again and the low resonance vibrated in Marcus' head like sound waves escaping crashing cymbals in music class. His body recoiled at hearing his forced will bringing the bald newspaper man pleasure.

Bill had grabbed Marcus after the last collection of the afternoon. Marcus thought he was being driven home like every time before, but this time Bill took a detour.

Collecting on subscriptions was fairly straightforward. Bill showed Marcus the ropes on his first day collecting. Going door-to-door together, Marcus listened intently on how to speak clearly and directly to the subscribers and tell them upfront that he was there to collect for *The Plano Register*.

Encouraging Marcus he could do it on his own after a few stops, Bill dropped Marcus off at each house and waited in the car. With a chewed-up stubby yellow pencil tucked behind his right ear, Bill would read off the amounts owed to Marcus from a list pinned on a clipboard he kept in the driver's side door pocket. When he returned to the car, Bill sat waiting, turning the chewed-up pencil around in his fingers, ready to notate the collected amount or lack thereof. Marcus stared at the dents cast from Bill's molars against the ferrule while he told the newspaper man how an older woman answered and said she didn't know about the charge and asked them to come back another time to talk with her husband.

After scribbling the result down and tucking the clipboard in the door, Bill called it a day. Instead of driving Marcus home, however, he pulled over into a field underneath an under-construction overpass.

"What's here?" Marcus had asked, innocently.

"Don't you want to see the new highway they're building with President Bush's name on it?" Bill said, pulling the pencil out from behind his ear and dropping it into the driver's side door with the clipboard.

Marcus didn't answer. He was only vaguely aware of who that was. He looked at Bill's face and into his eyes. They were bright and sparkled behind the round lenses of the gold, metal-framed glasses he wore.

Why was Bill now forcing him to do this?

Marcus continued to stare at the newspaper, but now with blurry eyes. He felt them begin to burn and sting with the same sensation as they had with the sweat. The eleven-year-old began to whimper. Tears dripped from his eyes on to his legs. He blinked and several at a time fell. His skin felt clammy and sweaty but he was cold.

A wave rolled through his stomach and up into his chest. It wasn't the same feeling as the gurgling, which persisted. This feeling was similar to the day when he jumped his bike off the top of a large utility box behind the grocery store his mom worked at before he was born. He was the first of his friends to attempt the trick and when he finally worked up the nerve to jump, the feeling shot through him.

He landed on two wheels and rolled away with Charles, Thomas and Chris pumping their fists and cheering at the top of their lungs from their bikes. The commotion drew the attention of the store manager who was around the corner by a dumpster taking a smoke break. He ran off the friends before the other three were able to try to duplicate Marcus' feat.

The feeling he had now was similar, but not mixed with the exhilaration he felt on his bike in mid-air. No, this was pure, concentrated fear.

His T-shirt stuck to him in several spots. His stomach continued to churn. Surely it was bubbling green, toxic liquid and was devouring the sandwich and chips he'd consumed for lunch a few hours earlier. Next, it would do its destructive thing to the lining of his guts; foaming, churning, sloshing and dissolving his insides with unrelenting fury.

A waft of the sour newspaper print ran through his nostrils, and Marcus gagged at the rotten character the smell took on.

His right arm was tingling now and he shook it in an attempt to loosen the tight grip around his wrist. But Bill maintained his control and Marcus felt his arm numb and fall asleep.

Somehow, his tears had dried up and stopped. Something in his head told him he needed to keep his mind busy if he was going to survive this.

He scanned his side of the car after sneaking a peek at Bill. His head was thrown back against the headrest, eyes closed. Marcus turned his head away sharply in disgust.

Airbag, he read in his head off the dashboard in front of him. He looked around for anything else to read, and there was nothing, just a mucked-up gray vinyl dashboard.

Why was this happening to him? What had he done to anger Bill? He was a good worker. Bill had told him so repeatedly.

Tears welled again in Marcus' eyes. They stung as much as they had the last time.

Marcus sniffed back a trickle of snot threatening to run down his nose and Bill barked, "Stop!" Marcus jumped at the correction and then whipped his head to the right. Bill continued. The soon-to-be twelve-year-old glazed over, looking out the window, wishing someone would walk up to the car and save him.

Excavated soil was piled up a few dozen yards away from the car and the growing concrete skeleton of the highway overpass stood just beyond it. Marcus stared at the T-shaped supports: thick beams of rebar ran up through the massive columns and poked out the top of the poured concrete. An outline of the state of Texas and its flag underneath were pressed into the top portion and flared out on each of the three visible supports. Wild rebar hung from various parts of the construction, especially along the overpass that was being connected to the support columns on site.

A crane loomed over the construction site, frozen in time like a brontosaurus stuck in a tar pit.

The crews were long gone for the day, but evidence of their work was everywhere. Earth-moving equipment was parked awkwardly where the users had been driving when the quitting time bell rang. Rakes, shovels and the like were leaned up against a chain-link temporary equipment pen.

Marcus looked at the pile of dirt again. It had to be over ten feet tall. He pictured it next to an NBA regulation goal and thought the top of the soil would have been even with the rim.

He really wanted a basketball goal for his birthday. He didn't need an official setup: a square plexiglass backboard embossed with an official NBA logo atop a fixed pole. One of the goals on wheels that you fill the base with sand or water would do. The goal adjusted in height: perfect so he and his friends could practice and play on a regulation ten-foot rim but also be able to lower it a few feet so they could dunk on it.

He would roll it in front of his apartment, right up to the patio fence on the edge of the sidewalk, where there would be room for them to shoot on the hoop from the black asphalt parking lot.

To make sure no one parked in the spot after his father left for work, he would have to get up early and put something in the space, but it would be worth it.

He and his friends played on one of the basketball goals at their apartment complex. Even if they weren't taken by older kids, the cheap nine-foot goals sucked. Most times the two goals were missing nets and on the rare occasion when management replaced them, the nets were promptly ripped to shreds in a couple of weeks from teenagers hanging from them.

Marcus and his friends were thrilled when they showed up at the courts the first day of that summer vacation and both goals had fresh new, white, nylon nets hanging from the orange metal rims. They played full court two-on-two and Marcus got a jolt every time his shot swished through with a "whooooshhhh-POP" of the net. They ended the day with Marcus and Chris up four games to three on Charles and Thomas with plans to finish the best of eleven contest the following day. The next day, they ran on to the court, which was next to the apartment pool with a grassy area dividing the court from the pool, and the nets were gone, stolen by god knows who overnight.

The scene was all too familiar in their crummy neighborhood, but the four slump-shouldered boys attempted to continue their tournament without nets anyway. They didn't play long, however. When the ball persisted on making a getaway, flying though the bare cylinder after each made basket, the friends tired of taking turns to chase it down. They called a forfeit and abandoned the activity in favor of a run to 7-Eleven.

Yes, a basketball hoop of his own would be awesome.

The numbness in Marcus' arm was subsiding and caught his attention. He looked to his left and Bill's grip on his wrist was loosened but the newspaper man still kept his grasp. Grunts, heavy breaths and deep snorts fogged the glasses that had slid down the bridge of his nose onto its bulbous end. After one punctuating growl and deep breaths, Bill said, "Hold still while I wipe up." He frothed in between huffs.

Complete feeling returned to Marcus' hand and arm when finally released, allowing him to wiggle his fingers. Bill raked his knuckles with a baby wipe. Marcus' eyes fell to the red birthmark on the newspaper man's arm again, entranced by its size and odd color. Finished with himself, Bill began tugging each digit of Marcus' right hand with the baby wipe. Marcus remained frozen. When he was done, Bill plopped Marcus' arm on to the boy's leg and then let out a series of deep, satisfying breaths. He buttoned up his pants and stuffed his shirt into the waistband.

Marcus stared at his feet, trying not to let any part of Bill enter his peripheral vision. He rubbed his still moist hand on his shorts; first his palm in a swipe and then the back of his hand in the reverse direction.

Bill buckled his own seat belt and put the car in reverse. They were not far from the newspaper office and would be at Marcus' apartment complex in ten minutes. They drove the first eight in complete silence.

Marcus didn't move and kept his gaze on his white sneakers, now more brownish and scuffed with grass stains after only four months of use.

Bill turned the wheel, guiding his car on to the road that intersected with the street Marcus lived on.

"I want you to know that I care about you, Marcus," he said.

Marcus furrowed his brows and didn't look up.

"I mean it," Bill said, not looking at the boy.

Marcus was already confused and now his head started to spin. He wanted out of the car. He thought about unbuckling, opening the car door and jumping for it, but a wave of panic shot up his back, like standing on an overpass and imagining what would happen if you leaped off.

You'll never make it! his inner voice yelled. You'll hit the pavement and your head will be crushed!

The car came to a stop in front of the complex. Marcus sat up and grabbed feverishly for his seat belt only to have Bill's two hands smother his own on top of the buckle.

Bill leaned his face close to Marcus' head, putting his lips next to the boy's left ear. Marcus shut his eyes and a soft whimper escaped his lips.

"Have a fun weekend, Marcus. See you Tuesday. Oh, and don't speak a word of this to anyone."

The thought of seeing Bill again made Marcus' stomach churn violently. Maybe it hadn't stopped.

Bill released his hold on Marcus and the eleven-year-old unbuckled the seat belt, darted out of the car and tore off. Instead of taking his normal route home through the middle of the complex, Marcus ducked to the left behind the concrete block wall that ran around the perimeter, hoping to throw off his predator, fearing he might follow him.

Flinging himself at the wall and slamming his back up against it, Marcus tucked his knees to his chest and buried his head in his folded arms. His white Dallas Cowboys T-shirt was soaked in sweat. He just wanted to get home, but he couldn't move.

Tears poured from his eyes and he buried his head deeper in his arms.

He didn't give himself long to cry. He sniffed the tears back and cleared his throat. Terry wouldn't want him to cry. "Winners don't cry. Babies do."

Marcus balled up his right hand into a fist and punched the outside of his right thigh.

"Stupid!" He growled under his breath at himself. Landed one blow after another. "Stupid!"

Marcus then punched the soft St. Augustine sod beside him, stood up and put his hand against the wall. His fingers found a section of cracked, white paint and he picked away at it with his middle finger. Paint chips fell to the grass. Marcus tried to collect himself.

He started to stagger along the wall, which would eventually turn to the right and lead to his apartment three-hundred yards away. The wide, interconnecting canopies of mulberry and pecan trees growing along this stretch provided Marcus shade from the unrelenting afternoon sun. He shuffled his feet and noticed his stomach was still churning. He could taste the acidity building in his mouth. He tried to get his mind off what had just happened.

Bill's moans and echoes of his unremorseful glee whispered in Marcus' ears. Bile rose up into his chest. He stopped. His body convulsed and Marcus belched; his mouth filling with the taste of aluminum. He took a step and his stomach lurched again. He doubled over this time. His head spun. His face was so hot he could feel his ears and nose burning.

Unable to control his body, it wretched and jerked until vomit streamed out of his mouth and forced its way out of both nostrils in one simultaneous burst. He gagged and wailed out with a roar; the chunky bile burning and stinging his throat and nose as it streamed out.

When the wave finally stopped, Marcus stayed doubled over with his hands on his knees and spat. His insides were fried.

With teary eyes, he stood up and stared at his shaking hands. He turned them over to watch his palms quiver as well. His insides covered a bush planted along someone's back wood-fenced patio. Little chunks of Doritos mixed in with the foamy, stinking vomit.

Marcus spat the remnants from his mouth and shook his head in disgust at the bitter aftertaste clinging to the back of his tongue and in his nose. He started to walk again, and hocked up saliva to expel the remaining vomit.

Marcus stumbled to his apartment in a daze. When he arrived, his mom let him inside when he couldn't unlock the door; his hands still shaking too much.

He went to his room and stayed there that entire evening. Stacey checked on him at one point and he refused to come out for dinner, saying he was sick. She sat on the edge of his bed and rubbed his back in soft, slow circles with him laid on his stomach, his face looking at the wall.

She drew on her boy in a spiral pattern with the ends of her first and middle fingers, growing the path out until her fingertips reached the top of his shoulders and his lower back. She then reversed the pattern until her fingers drew a small circle the size of a silver dollar on the middle of his back and then spread out again, and back and forth.

She hummed a tune he couldn't identify. She hummed it soft enough that parts of the melody dropped off and she went silent, her sound drifting in and out like an intermittent breeze.

Marcus eventually passed out, calmed by his mom's affection. He woke again briefly a few hours later to Stacey putting him under the sheets. It was dark but Marcus saw the red glowing numbers of his AM/FM radio read 9:34 p.m.

When he drifted off again, he had no way of knowing he would be subjected to the same abuse each of the next six Fridays. This day had been the first abuse, but it wouldn't be the last.

When Bill reached to grab at Marcus the next Friday parked at the same location as the first time, Marcus yelled and cried for help. He grabbed for the door handle to free himself. He had set a plan in place in his mind during the previous week. He wasn't strong enough to fight off Bill, but he could run. He was fast. Faster than all of his friends, and surely the doughy, sloppy newspaper man wouldn't be able to keep up or catch him.

He would dart out of the car, or maybe he would yell for help and someone would be right there and they would see what was happening and catch Bill in the act.

Bill quickly engaged the electric locks, however, trapping Marcus.

"You're not going anywhere, Marcus, and let me tell you why." Bill's voice was cool and collected.

"Why?!" Marcus turned to Bill and shouted in his face. "Why are you doing this? What did I do?!"

"Stop it. Don't be a baby," Bill said.

Marcus recoiled at the taunt and withdrew.

Bill's glasses slid down to the end of his nose when he grabbed Marcus' face in a quick, snake-like strike. With his right hand, he squeezed the boy's chin between his thumb and fingers to force him to look in his eyes.

"You will do what I say and you won't fight me or tell anyone about this." Bill lingered on the last word, emphasizing the sound of the last consonant.

Bill released his face.

"If you tell anyone about this, I'll tell your parents you're stealing the petty cash from the newsroom."

Marcus wrinkled his face at the unbelievable scenario and let out a smart-assed, "Hmph!" that instantly enraged Bill. The newspaper man's face turned purple and his irises burned black, refracted behind the lenses of his glasses like crazed ebony marbles with flecks of red-hot embers.

Marcus ducked, having never seen Bill mad like this.

In a deep, evil voice, Bill roared, "I will tell all your friends that you kiss boys! Is that what you want? You want to be a fag?"

The threat sprayed all over Marcus' face. Bill seethed, pointed his finger at Marcus and then pressing it hard against his nose hard enough to make the boy's eyes water.

Shocked, Marcus felt his hands shaking. The threat landed. The very lack of logic of it was lost on him, obscured by the fear of being rejected by his friends.

Marcus slumped his shoulders and he let out a whimpering sigh. Surrender.

"Please. Don't." Marcus whined softly. His eyes teared up again.

"Trust me, I don't want to," Bill said. His voice was silky-smooth with an almost musical quality to it.

Bill moved in and abused Marcus for a second time. But this time, emboldened, Bill molested Marcus also, fondling his privates and moaning. "Feels good, right?"

After this abuse, shock turned to a multitude of other feelings no child should have to feel. Bill's manipulation overwhelmed Marcus, took root and festered. His control grew into a monumental obstacle in Marcus' mind, obstructing any rational thought he could conceive of how to free himself from the weekly molestations.

Only the beginning of the school year and the end of his unpaid employment would free Marcus from his hell.

7

THE CONVENTION CENTER

MARCUS BROKE HIS gaze from the waves rolling and breaking on to Ocean Beach, his mind back on the present. Ready to move.

"What'd you say, boss?" OB Rob shouted. His voice sounded like a shovel scraping broken asphalt.

Marcus stood up, pushed off the wall and waved him off with one hand.

"Nothing, OB. Just talkin' through some shit."

OB Rob wagged his tongue out on the side of his cracked lips and threw up both middle fingers.

Marcus caught the antics in his periphery and grinned. "See ya, OB. Be good." He walked away from the wall, swept away a tear from the corner of his eye that had managed to escape while he had been watching the ocean.

Until finding Bill's corpse, Marcus hadn't thought about his childhood in Texas in years. Moving to California had created a definitive line of demarcation in his mind.

As was the case for his mother, Marcus felt he was always meant to live in San Diego. The city's natural wonders fed his maturing soul. Made him feel at home like he couldn't imagine any other place could.

The rest of his childhood, everything that came before— even the good memories—evaporated. For the first few years when they moved to San Diego, he did wonder what his trio of friends in Plano was up to, but their memories faded eventually as well as he fell in with his new group of friends.

It had been years since Marcus recoiled at the smell of newspaper print, visualized the inside of Bill's car or put his mind through the paces of the trauma he had endured. The adventures of his adolescence and constant activity overtook those memories, allowing them to fade in his maturing brain.

Marcus further buried the memories as a young adult by taking up and keeping to a routine. It was a strategy he stumbled upon when he walked-on as a tight end at San Diego State University.

After graduating from high school, he made the college team his freshman year and fell into a daily routine: Up early to work out/classes/football practice/homework/bed. The only time his schedule differed was on game day and the night before a game when he would be required to study the playbook.

He organized his days to leave little spare time for things such as dating or hanging out with anyone but his teammates and select friends. What free time he did have, he used to go surfing or hiking—mostly alone—but sometimes with high school friends. He and his mom kept up their Sunday morning beach walk tradition, but still, it was part of his routine.

He didn't need to actively keep his mind off the abuse he endured because routine kept his mind and body busy. It's not to say he never thought of Bill, but the memories became more blurred and distant when he wasn't forced to acknowledge them.

Departing from his routine or even the suggestion to skip one or more parts of it caused great anxiety in Marcus. As a result, he became rigid about sticking to his daily routine, leading to an avoidance of social interaction more and more, a consequence that compounded over his adult years.

After graduating college, Marcus organized a new routine, requiring the stability it provided. Having earned a degree in criminal justice, Marcus joined the El Centro Police Department—a two-hour drive east of San Diego. He had the ultimate goal to join the San Diego PD but was content to put his time in at a smaller department first.

Before he could earn his badge, however, he was required to attend twenty-five weeks of training at the regional police academy, and routine is what helped him excel in the all-encompassing program. A five-day-a-week endeavor, academy combined classroom work with a tactical training and physical conditioning program. The latter required recruits to hit the weights, run long distances and ride stationary bikes, clearing mandated scores for each. The physical training prepared Marcus and his fellow recruits to pass an exit exam where each had to complete a timed obstacle course and distance run that involved climbing numerous 8-foot walls using ropes and rescuing dummy drowning victims.

The twenty-five-week training was grueling, despite his physical endurance still being at its peak from playing football since the eighth grade. Being a gym rat definitely gave him an edge. His muscular body was a dead giveaway that he put time in on the weights.

In high school, he had messed around in the gym, lifting regularly but with little direction and no progressive plan in place. In college, the team's strength coach put him on a high-protein, high-calorie diet and high-volume lifting regimen. Marcus took to the structured, five to six-day-a-week workout program, finding fully engaging his body, moving each rep with intensity and fatiguing his muscles focused and calmed his mind to an unprecedented level. It was one more tactic he would unconsciously use to keep his trauma buried for years. Whenever he became the least bit restless or anxious, a hard session in the gym was all the therapy he needed and he carried that bit of strategy with himself through the years.

Marcus would credit his success in life to making a plan for a given goal, setting a routine and following it until he achieved what he wanted.

Romantic relationships had proven different with an opposite outcome. Taken with the excitement of a new connection, Marcus made attempts early in relationships to amend his routine in the hope of maintaining a steady partner. But as with Megan, dating disrupted his routine just the same, and he found it easier to just be alone.

Crossing the street back to his police cruiser, Marcus joked with himself under his breath. "Routine can't do shit when you find your pedophile abuser dead in the trunk of a car."

He got in the cruiser, turned up the police radio and sat, plotting his next steps. He looked at the time. His shift ended in a couple of hours. But his skin itched with anxiousness. He wanted to get down to the convention center and poke around before they packed up the show.

He put the car in reverse, backed on to Newport Avenue and headed out of Ocean Beach.

"Can you cover me, man?" he texted to McKenzie.

Dots blinked on the screen, then a reply.

"How long?"

Marcus punched the gas. It was the confirmation he anticipated. He turned on to Sunset Cliffs, flipped on the emergency lights and flew through the traffic light. The cruiser's siren blared. He drove on to the shoulder, whipped around the right side of a car at the traffic light and sped on to the 8 on-ramp.

"Maybe thirty or an hour thanks exclamation point," Marcus said, holding the phone to his mouth.

Marcus never used this common, unspoken courtesy for himself: beat cops covering for each other. Most who used coverage did it so they could do something family-related, such as pick a kid up from school or take a partner to a doctor's appointment while on duty. This innocent use is why the practice had been allowed to persist as long as it had. But there were cops who took advantage, of course, to do things like hook up with each other and worse. Supervisors across the department were cracking down after a cop at a northern division got busted buying drugs from an undercover DEA agent while on his shift. The cop who covered for him was suspended for a month without pay when he lied about covering.

McKenzie certainly owed Marcus. The gangly, freckled cop had asked Marcus to cover for him so often Marcus couldn't keep track. McKenzie would race home, hell bent on catching his cheating wife in the act. Mind you, he'd never actually caught her being unfaithful on any of the attempts, so he played off his impromptu home visits as though he was simply missing her.

"What happens if you do find some dude in bed with your wife?" Marcus asked him one afternoon while they ate Hodad's burgers off the hood of McKenzie's cruiser.

"Shit, I don't know, man," he said, hanging his head in defeat like the scenario had just occurred.

"You kill a dude and I covered for you? I don't think so," Marcus said, smiling. He gave McKenzie a little poke to the side, then threw a piece of bun to a group of squawking seagulls.

"I wouldn't do that! I wouldn't rat you out. Besides," he said, slapping Marcus on the back, "I leave my gun in the car!"

"Shit," Marcus said, drawing out the word and covering his mouth with his fist. He pulled away from McKenzie and shook his head. "That's fucked up, man. You don't trust what you would do so much that you keep your gun in the car?"

Both cops stared at each other for a second, not wanting to let the other off the hook, and then both broke and doubled over laughing.

Speeding down the 8, Marcus ran the list of his infractions to that point. He'd already violated personal conduct policies 9.8 (Department Reports), 9.29 (Truthfulness) and 9.32 (Conflict of Interest) of the San Diego Police Department's Policies and Procedures Manual. Now tack on 9.18 (Neglect of Duty) and the tally was mounting fast.

Pushing aside his insubordination was the nagging question of why he didn't report Bill all those years ago.

How could he have been so selfish? Whoever the newspaper man's killer was must have surely endured the same horrors as Marcus. Until that day, he hadn't connected how his silence may have allowed Bill to continue his sick perversion with another young boy or boys. Marcus had left them to be devoured by a wolf. It had been within his power to stop Bill's evil, and he fled with his mother and didn't look back. And worse yet, he had buried the truth deep inside himself.

Marcus wiped his face with his hand and groaned.

Maybe the killer was a boy Bill had convinced to assist him with subscription collections the summer after Marcus moved— literally someone who took his place. What if that boy wasn't able to get out of the weekly abuse after one summer as Marcus had? Or worst yet, what if Bill's appetite expanded to preying on his helpers more than once a week and in more penetrating ways than Marcus had endured? Who was he kidding? For this person to murder the pedophile newspaper man, the abuse had to have been much, much worse. Right?

Marcus moaned. Stomach tied in knots, his mind was running away with itself.

He realized he was picking away at the cruiser's vinyl armrest again. He wrapped the offending hand on the steering wheel to stop himself. Up ahead, the city's skyline loomed over the 5. A Southwest Airlines-branded 737 flew over the highway on its final descent into Lindbergh Field. Just beyond the tarmac, the San Diego Bay shimmered in the midday sun.

Marcus passed Little Italy, and took the exit for downtown and the convention center.

He stomped the brakes to take the winding exit and the cruiser jerked. The road looped around ninety degrees and brought him to a three-way stop.

He flipped on his lights and siren for a moment and rolled through the sign, cutting off a car to turn right.

How could he have repressed so much for so many years, he wondered? Was it as simple to explain as he had been plucked from the situation, pulled away from the flames so they no longer licked at his face and burned his soul? Perhaps. Or was he just alibiing for himself?

A call came over the radio and he slammed the brakes, jerking himself and the car to a stop in the middle of the lane.

"Report of a vehicle break-in at Newport Pizza and Ale House."

McKenzie answered. "Ten-four. Six-fourteen Baker responding."

Marcus breathed a sigh of relief, whispering a thank you to McKenzie for covering the call, and punched the gas again. He made every green light to get to Harbor Drive, took left, and whipped into a meter on 1st Avenue. Back across Harbor stood the metal and glass San Diego Convention Center.

Marcus turned off the car and dropped the keys on the seat between his legs and let out an anguished sigh. Holding his face with his hands, he rubbed the sides of his forehead a few times and moaned. He drew in a couple of deep breaths, trying to calm himself and slow his racing heartbeat.

"See what you can find," he instructed himself. He punched the side of his thigh with a fist twice, preparing to get out of the car. Opening the door, Marcus jumped backward to avoid a collision with a flurry of construction workers zooming past on rental scooters, one after another.

"Sorry, man!" one offered, seeing Marcus was visibly startled.

Marcus shut the door and watched the spectacle continue. Their florescent orange vests flapped in the breeze and the sun bounced off the reflective trim, sending little specs of light off the men in every direction. Some of the workers had backpacks on, others balanced their lunch cooler hung from one handle and their water bottle from the other.

Then, as if choreographed, each construction worker played out the same thing. Reaching their street-parked vehicles, each guy popped their trunk or hatchback, threw the scooter in, jumped in and tore off to end the workday. Guys with trucks tossed the scooters in the bed and their protective gear in the cab.

Marcus reacted with an, "Hmph," unwilling to deviate from his purpose to stop them.

A text vibrated in his pocket.

"You owe me :P This bitch tourist left an iPad on her back seat and WE have a sketch neighborhood cause it got stolen?" He'd finished it with an eyeroll emoji.

"LOL Fuck that noise," Marcus typed back, not actually laughing out loud.

McKenzie sent back a fist bump emoji.

Marcus pocketed the phone and started for the convention center. He wanted to find a lead, but the risk of being found out was already eating at his conscience.

Wiping a bead of sweat from his hairline, he jogged across Harbor Drive, his boots echoing off the pavement. Marcus slowed to a walk as he approached Exhibit Hall A, and the entrance of metal-framed doors which ran the length of the front of the building. Once inside, air-conditioning enveloped him. He peered to the left, looking down the long, empty hall.

The police radio crackled in his ear and he responded by turning it off. McKenzie had his back and would text if anything required his attention.

Marcus spotted activity past the escalators: figures moving about 200 yards away from him. He started toward them.

Marcus understood Bill's victimology intimately, that is, the propensities, vulnerabilities and motivations that led the newspaper man to become a victim. And though Marcus was not a detective, he was confident he could figure out what happened to him.

From a college course on victimology, Marcus knew environmental theory suggested the location and context of the crime is what brought Bill and his eventual killer together. The convention center may have been the location, but what was the context that brought them together?

Bill may well have attended the garden show as a part of some work assignment or background for a story or even to network with potential advertisers for *The Plano Register*. Perhaps his motivations made him vulnerable to violence.

Maybe the killer didn't know him and was simply a father who saw Bill inappropriately touch his son at the show, became enraged and attacked Bill. The father would have had to lure Bill away from or wait until he was away from witnesses to make his move. He then would have whacked Bill over the back of the head in his anger and got rid of the evidence in the trunk of a stolen car.

What if Bill made a pass at a younger-looking male who was just older than he looked and took offense? A stretch, perhaps, but plausible.

Marcus came back to his initial hunch: One of Bill's victims grew up, perhaps stalked him over the years, waited for an opening and when a work trip—if that's what it was—to San Diego presented a prime opportunity to murder the pedophile in a different state, he struck. Theoretically, suspicion wouldn't be aroused and the crime wouldn't trace as easily back to the perpetrator in that scenario. Similar to the theory that one can get away with murder more easily if they kill a stranger.

Marcus believed the killer was counting on the police chalking Bill's murder in San Diego up to a robbery gone wrong or something similar, with no other apparent motive present. One reason was the cause of death—blunt force trauma to the head. Plainly obvious when Marcus looked over his abuser in the trunk of the car.

Normally, his instincts would have told him a victim of Bill would have strangled, stabbed or beaten him about the face. The three were hallmarks of a murder with a personal motive like revenge or hatred. But when Marcus put himself in the killer's place, he thought he would have done it the same way to avoid detection.

"Can I help you, officer? You responding to a call?" a voice behind him asked.

Marcus spun around to find an overweight, young black man adjusting a blue cap with "SECURITY" in yellow lettering on his head. His light blue knit shirt was sloppily tucked into dark blue pants, his stomach flopped over the place where a belt would be.

"Oh. No, man," Marcus said. "Just stepped in for the A/C."

"I hear that," the convention center security guard said.

Marcus didn't respond and the two shared an awkward couple seconds of silence, each waited for the other to say something.

The guard caved first. "K, let me know if you need anything. Take it easy."

"Same. Thanks," Marcus said, and then turned away.

Walking down to where he had seen the activity on the other end of the convention center, Marcus wondered if Homicide had found anything yet and if they would show up here too. All they would have to do was ID Bill, find out where he worked and then call *The Plano Register* to ask what he was doing in San Diego to lead them to the garden show.

He quickened his pace.

Of course, they might not get anything with Bill's wallet missing. But then Marcus wondered about IDing him by his fingerprints. If his prints were in the system, Homicide would be on the same track just as quick.

He began sprinting.

8
TRACKING BILL

THE SAN DIEGO Convention Center and Marcus weren't exactly strangers. In fact, he knew the building well. Shortly after he joined the SDPD, San Diego Comic-Con required additional security, as it did every year.

Though he had been on the force just a few months and the plum overtime assignment was offered to those with seniority first, Marcus still managed to be chosen to staff the multi-day entertainment convention. Even more of a stroke of luck, he was assigned to man one of the halls hosting a rotation of panels, which meant air conditioning and the straight-forward task of ensuring the celebrities spanning multiple genres of television and movies, cartoons and pop culture were kept safe and separated from their adoring fans.

The assignment bored him a bit, he would admit to another officer from his division while they staffed the event the following year. Not only was the crowd attending the panels well behaved for the most part, which relegated Marcus to standing in place for the majority of his shift, but the "nerd culture" was lost on him.

From the first day, seeing people dressed in cosplay really confused him. The concept of someone dressing as their favorite superhero, villain, television or movie character did not compute. Unless the person was dressed like someone as universally identifiable as Superman, he just didn't get it.

And though he grew up in the same city as Comic-Con, which drew hordes of fans from all over the country, it had never caused so much as a blip on his radar. He was too busy surfing, hiking or doing something else outside.

Working Comic-Con that year was the first time he had stepped foot inside the convention center. Overall, he'd enjoyed the experience and the easy money and, by the end, the event had grown on him. It might have been the moment when he saw one of his heroes on the last day of his first year working Comic-Con that made him "get it," and want to work security again the next year.

Manning his post—against the wall about halfway between the large conference room's entrance and the stage—with a full room of geeked-out nerds in front of him, a personal security detail was escorting actor Lou Ferrigno down the outer aisle and they were headed right toward Marcus.

His eyes widened when he saw Lou's tan face bob into his line of sight.

"Wow. Lou fucking Ferrigno," Marcus whispered to himself in doting adulation.

Rather than his countless television and big-screen credits, Marcus revered Lou for his Mr. America and two Mr. Universe titles.

When his college football head coach put on "Pumping Iron" for the team to watch one day, Marcus found himself rooting for big Lou while the rest of his teammates rooted for Arnold Schwarzenegger in the legendary 1977 film that documented the two rivals vying for the title of Mr. Olympia. Marcus wanted to see the underdog unseat Arnold—the reigning king and primary focus of the documentary.

As Lou drew closer, Marcus lost himself in a rush of excitement, for a second forgetting he was working, and stepped forward to do what, he wasn't sure. But just as quickly as he made the rash decision to leave his post to reach for or get Lou's attention in some way, he caught himself and stepped back, narrowly avoiding a collision with one of the security guards right in front of Lou.

The San Diego Garden Show's footprint at the convention center and its attendance—even though a biannual event—paled in comparison to San Diego Comic-Con. With it taking up only one of the four halls, it left three-fourths of the convention center cavernously empty.

Ramping down his sprint, Marcus jogged to a stop in front of the entrance to the hall. The open double doors to the hall were unmanned and Marcus walked right in.

Marcus refocused his mind on Bill's victimology and told himself what he should be looking for: young, good-looking males who would have unconsciously lured Bill to their table or booth. He recoiled. Thank god he was in uniform.

The show's floor layout was divided by one central, wide aisle. Marcus scanned the rows of back-to-back booths situated on either side of the middle aisle. The arrangement created four rows of booths to investigate.

He pulled out the business card for All Green Landscape from his pocket and walked up to the first booth on his left. It was some sort of niche fertilizer maker he guessed by the line of products in recycled, brown paper bags with colorful prints displayed on a shelf beside a woman sitting in a blue, folding-style camping chair.

"Do you know where I can find this company," he asked the older woman, holding out the card to her.

She slowly put down a book she was reading in pain-staking effort, her disapproval for being interrupted punctuated with little grunts. Looking over her glasses at Marcus she said, "I am not information."

"I know, ma'am. I'm just not familiar with the setup here."

She snatched the business card from him and looked it over. When she handed it back, she barked, "Around the backside and all the way down on the end."

"Appreciate it," he said, and reached for the card.

She returned it with a huff. Marcus hurried away and around her booth to make his way down the row of exhibits behind her.

More people were working the show than attending it by this point. A couple of crews rushed past him with large flat dollies and hand trucks, likely on their way to break down the impressive pond feature in the middle aisle.

He passed the first couple of booths where three bearded, middle-aged vendors were gathered together, bullshitting with each other. They seemed all but done working and were just killing the clock.

Definitely not Bill's type, Marcus thought to himself.

The next booth caught his eye, but not for purposes of his investigation. The entire space was bordered in bright pink panels with a prominently-placed sign in the middle reading, "Oinker Grills," in large pink lettering on a white background. In italics, the company's slogan, "The Swinest Smokers™" appeared underneath.

Arranged in a triangle in the middle of the booth were three identical-looking pink smokers in the shape of cartoon pigs. Each pig's body was constructed using a 55-gallon steel drum and supported by four steel pig legs, complete with notched, hooved feet.

On the front end of the smoker, a large pig head was painted with oversized eyes, a protruding steel snout and a big smiling mouth propped open by way of a metal apple between its comically goofy, large front teeth. The mouth doubled as an extra place to smoke smaller items. From the back of the smoker extended a curly tail and the end of the 55-gallon drum was embossed with a branding on the side reading, "#porkbutt."

Noticing the display had caught Marcus' attention, the vendor hollered, "Dude! You need to be our spokesperson!"

Marcus snorted and said, "Cause I'm a pig, right?"

"Just messin' with ya, man!" the hipster said, giving Marcus two thumbs up with a shit-eaten grin.

"Yeah, real funny." Marcus shook his head and kept walking.

The show may have only taken up the one hall, but it was a sizeable event still the same; he guessed after doing some simple math there were at least sixty to seventy vendors present.

Next, he walked past an exhibit filled with an elaborate display of live, miniature terrariums, each hanging from a bit of string or displayed on a piece of salvaged wood. Marcus didn't make eye contact with the young, earthy girl staffing the booth, dismissing her as not material to his search. She didn't look up from what she was doing to look at him, either, likely because he didn't fit her target market.

His pace quickened by then and he felt panic rush over him again when he thought about how much time he had been away from his beat already. He grabbed his phone to check the time and saw he had no reception in the hall.

"Shit."

The heels of his boots sent out a "knock-knock-knock" echo off of the linoleum with each faster, longer, more deliberate step. He dodged a few wandering show attendees, apologized for his rudeness. Holding up his hands, he shimmied between the booths and a group of women who looked to be in their late fifties, just wandering and taking their time doing it.

His steps slowed to a final couple of clops when he eyed the booth second from the end to which the grumpy woman had sent him. It was a simple exhibit arranged with three, 8-foot folding tables set up in the space with one of them set against the back of the 10'x10' area with one table butted up along each of its ends.

White, linen table cloths covered each table. On the left table was a selection of different styles of landscape lights, including low-voltage and LED spotlights, pathway lights and security lights. Displayed on the right table were transformation photos of residential and commercial landscapes standing in plexiglass frames.

On the table to his right, Marcus spotted a stack of business cards matching the one he'd swiped from Bill's back pocket.

The back table was empty, save for an empty Coke bottle lying on its side and a half-empty bag of sunflower seeds. Behind the table was the company's pop-up, rectangular vinyl sign with simple green san-serif lettering that read, "All Green Landscape."

Marcus pointed at the sign and asked, "Are you the owner?"

A man standing in the space said, "Yeah, that's me. Jeff."

Marcus took a step forward, held out his hand and Jeff shook it firmly.

"Marcus Kemp."

"Am I parked illegally or something, officer? I don't think I have any unpaid parking tickets." Jeff's eyebrows furrowed.

"Oh, no. Nothing like that," Marcus said. "I'm working a case involving a man who we think attended the garden show and I'm just asking around. Seeing if anyone saw him."

Jeff's shoulders fell and the well-built man let out a small sigh.

Marcus looked him over and felt a second of uncertainty, wondering if Jeff could help with his search at all. The landscape owner looked to be a decade older than Marcus, evidenced by the scattering of gray in his beard stubble and the wrinkles in the corners of his eyes.

But Bill had stopped by this booth, there was no doubt about that. And Marcus wondered why considering Jeff was way out of the newspaper man's preferred age demographic.

"Happy to help if I can, officer." Jeff pushed the black snapback hat up off his forehead to expose the paleness of a receding hairline.

Marcus spread his feet shoulder-width apart, hands gripping the front of his utility belt. Typical cop stance. He watched Jeff adjust his hat again, stared for a second at the bear on the front of it holding a yellow surfboard.

"I'm trying to find out if a man came by your booth yesterday—stocky, short, older guy?" Marcus asked.

"Hmm," Jeff said. He kept messing with his hat, readjusting it on his head. "I mean, I met a lot of older guys the last few days. They're the ones with the duckets."

"This one was nearly bald, had glasses. Maybe mentioned he worked for a newspaper?"

Jeff's eyes rolled back and he cupped his chin.

"We think he has information that could help us with a case." Marcus said. "Heard he may have visited here, so I'm trying to track him down."

"I'd like to help, but nothing is coming to mind," Jeff said.

Two facilities workers walked behind Marcus with flat dollies and set them against the wall. Walking up from behind them was a boy who immediately caught Marcus' attention. Marcus pegged him at fourteen, tops.

"Oh, hey!" Jeff said. "Maybe my son saw your guy."

"What guy?" the boy asked.

His pulse jumping a bit, Marcus asked, "This is your son?" and Jeff nodded.

"Am I in trouble?" the boy asked, looking up at Marcus with no real concern in his eyes.

Jeff said, "No, no. He wants to know if some short, fat guy came to our booth."

"Not fat," Marcus corrected. "What's your name?"

"Brett," the boy said, handing his dad two bottles of Coke.

"How old are you?" Marcus noted Brett's unkempt, brown hair peeking out from a brown Padres hat.

"Thirteen, but I'll be fourteen in a few weeks," Brett said.

"Happy birthday," Marcus said.

"Yeah, if he's good, we're going to take him to see a Padres game and then up to LA to a Dodgers and an Angels game," Jeff said.

"They're all at home on the same weekend!" Brett exclaimed while waving his arms.

"That's cool, man. I like baseball, too," Marcus said.

Marcus paused before asking his next question, making sure he had Brett's attention.

"Let me ask you, Brett. Did you see a stocky, short, older man with glasses? Anyone like that talk to you the last couple of days?"

Brett's face fell in the short time it took Marcus to ask him the question. He looked at his dad and mouthed something. But when Jeff couldn't understand what he meant, Brett scrunched his face, as if in pain.

"Remember?" he asked. "The weird guy I told you about?"

"No, who?" Jeff asked.

Growing more frustrated, Brett's face turned red. His cheeks began to splotch and he clenched his teeth.

"The guy who looked like Frank from Always Sunny?"

"Danny DeVito?" Marcus said, cutting in. He jumped from his stance. "The old guy looked like Danny DeVito?

"Oh, right. I didn't see him," Jeff said. "I guess I was answering some questions at the time, but yesterday. Yeah, about midday, he says some guy who looked like Frank from 'It's Always Sunny in Philadelphia' was asking him creepy questions."

"No, he *was* a creep, I said."

Marcus turned to look at Brett again.

"Can you tell me what he said to you?"

Brett looked at his feet and stammered.

"Uh, he just talked to me... like, like we were friends or, he, uh, knew me. It was creepy."

"Did he touch you or try to touch you?"

"No!" Brett cried.

"It's not your fault if he did," Marcus said.

Marcus dropped to one knee, got to Brett's eye level.

"He didn't touch me like *that*," Brett said.

Marcus saw Jeff staring intently at his son with long eyes.

"He just, he shook my hand—"

"Seems normal," Jeff said nervously, interrupting his son.

"But he put his other hand on top," Brett said. "It was weird. Then he got a text or something and put his hand on my shoulder when he was looking at it."

Marcus widened his eyes at him. Brett hesitated but continued.

"I kind of squirmed away and he said Uber was here for him and maybe we would meet again. I was like, in your dreams, perv."

"Brett! You said that to him?" Jeff asked.

"No, I just thought it."

"You've been really helpful." Marcus looked Brett in the eyes. "You had the correct instincts. But explain one thing for me."

"What?"

"Are you sure he got a text? I don't have a signal in here," Marcus said.

"Oh, yeah. I've been fighting it all weekend," Jeff said. "But you can get a couple of bars right where you're standing, but not three steps this way."

Marcus pulled his phone out of his shirt and hit the home button, and as if responding on cue, two bars blinked to life and notifications for two texts appeared: one from McKenzie and the other from Megan.

"Look at that," Marcus said.

"Is that all you needed?" Jeff asked.

"Yeah, it is. Thank you both."

Marcus turned away from the father and son, but looked back and said to Brett, "Have fun at those games and get a Dodger Dog."

"Thanks!" Brett said. He put up a fist to Marcus, who turned around and bumped it.

Eyes back on his phone, he turned away from the two and headed back for the front of the hall in a fast-walk. He previewed Megan's text, which read, "Busy" and then opened McKenzie's.

"LT asking where you are. I said you were taking a huge dump lol"

The dumb text would have made Marcus snort laugh if he had seen it any other day. He interpreted the text now as a casual warning, but he knew he couldn't spend much more time at the convention center.

He rushed out of the hall, whipping his head side-to-side. The conversation with Jeff and Brett had given him an inclination of what had likely happened to Bill and he knew just the person—even if he hadn't caught his name—who could help him.

Back on the other end of the convention center was the security guard he had been startled by earlier. Marcus jumped to a fast jog toward the guard, his utility belt bouncing, each item jostling with every stride.

"Hey!" Marcus hollered out, holding two fingers in the air. The guard wasn't looking in his direction and Marcus was still a couple of hundred yards away, although he was closing the distance quickly. He turned the jog into a sprint.

"Hey! I need your help!" This time Marcus caught the guard's attention.

Before he could answer, Marcus stomped to a stop in front of him and blurted out, "I need access to your video surveillance."

"Sure, man. Yeah," the guard said. "Follow me."

Marcus knew where they were going, but fast-walked behind the guard who jogged down the hall. He badged them in through a locked door marked "Security" in white lettering. Marcus had been in the room before when he worked Comic-Con.

He squeezed in front of the security guard and flung himself into a rolling office chair in front of a bank of monitors. The guard sat down in a chair to his left.

"Do you guys still have cameras on the rideshare pickup area?" Marcus asked.

"Uh, yeah, it's there," the guard said. He pointed at one of the monitors halfway up a block of monitors on the left.

It showed a long driveway, but the only activity on the screen wasn't human. Just a few seabirds loitering and pecking on the south side of the building.

"Can you bring up the footage for around noon yesterday?"

"Yeah, here," the guard said. He stuck his tongue out of the corner of his mouth while he logged into the system to retrieve the saved footage.

"I'm Marcus, by the way. Appreciate the help."

"It's cool, bro. Always happy to help PD," he said. "D'andre." He held up a fist without breaking his focus on the monitors. Marcus half-heartedly bumped the guard's fist.

D'andre looked at a monitor directly in front of the two and the footage Marcus wanted appeared.

"Ok, here it is. You just have to use this button to rewind and this one to fast forward," he said, pointing to the wireless keyboard before handing it to Marcus.

"Thanks."

Marcus took the footage back until it read 11:00 on the screen and then fast-forwarded on the slowest speed from there. He was sure he would find something in a three-hour gap of time, going off what Jeff had said about Bill and Brett's interaction being around midday. Sure enough, once the footage got to a section where the timestamp on-screen read 13:06, Marcus saw something familiar that made the hair on his neck bristle. He let the tape play.

A dark Nissan Altima swung into the pickup driveway and came to a stop. There were three other cars parked in the driveway in the frame. Marcus hoped the driver would get out of the car to expose his identity, but he remained in the vehicle. The angle of the camera didn't capture a good shot of the inside of the car either, as it was set on a bird's eye view.

Suddenly, a couple of seconds later, a short, squat man waddled into the frame from the bottom of the screen. Marcus leaned forward in the rolling chair. His heartbeat jumped. *Bill.*

Bill walked up to the passenger's side of the vehicle and stuck his head into the open window.

Marcus' mouth fell open while he watched and his stomach let out a low, bellowing groan.

"Whoa, you got a gator in there?" D'andre said, covering his mouth to hide his snickering.

"Yeah. Haven't eaten all day," Marcus said. He kept his eyes locked on the screen. Saying the words, he realized he was indeed hungry, but that wasn't the reason his stomach made noise. Seeing Bill alive, walking, moving... breathing on tape, even though he knew Bill was now dead—it infuriated him.

Marcus paused the tape, raging. Scum. Filth. This goddamn, piece of shit, fucking disgusting, lying, festering open-wound-excuse-for-a-person was not worthy to breathe the same clean California air. Not worthy to see the glistening bay or walk his streets. How dare he come to his city.

Marcus' left hand was clenched into a fist tight enough to make him begin to lose feeling in his fingers. They were red and also white. Blood rushed back into his hand when he unclenched his hold, and his mind relaxed slightly. His fingers tingled to life and he took a deep, deliberate breath, drawing it in slowly and quietly to not draw D'andre's attention. He blinked his eyes and shook his head as if to tell his brain he was ready to refocus on his plan and purpose.

He hit play on the footage and after a couple of seconds passed, then another couple, the pedophile was still discussing something with the driver.

After a bit, Bill walked out of the frame the way he had come, but reemerged just as quickly. This time he carried a small suitcase or duffle bag—it was hard to make out on the video.

At the same time, the driver had gotten out of the car and walked to the back of the car where he stood at the open trunk.

Marcus didn't imagine this would be the time the driver would club Bill over the head and dump him in the trunk, and he was right.

The driver waited and then Bill stumbled or must have. He was on one knee. How did Marcus miss what caused him to be on one knee? He took the tape back a few seconds, and the answer: Bill tripped over the pavement, his own feet or something else and fell to one knee. He stayed down until the driver spotted him and walked over. Bill called out in a weak, whimpering voice to the driver for help, no doubt.

The driver was now in full sight. He was wearing a dark, long-sleeved shirt, jeans or dark pants and a dark ballcap with no visible logo or insignia. He looked to be a good foot or foot-and-a-half taller than Bill.

The driver tried to help Bill to his feet but Bill stumbled again and the driver flinched violently to catch him, like when you drop your phone and all but dive to the ground to keep the screen from shattering. But the stumble was just that and Bill righted himself with the support of the driver. The driver took Bill's bag and threw it in the trunk. At the same time, Bill got into the back seat.

"This what yer lookin' for?" D'andre asked, piping in.

"Yes," Marcus said curtly.

Unblinking, he watched the driver close the trunk and walk to the driver's door, open it and get in. But before closing the door or completely sitting into the seat, he stood up and touched the right side of his head. He retraced his steps back to where he had helped Bill to stand up. The driver's head swung around a few times, looking at the ground. He bent over, put his hands on his thighs and looked under the car.

Marcus sat up straight and leaned in, intrigued. It looked like he had lost something.

Marcus rewound the footage to when the driver walked from the trunk to Bill. He couldn't see anything on the driver's head or face because of the video's lack of clarity. Then he had a thought. AirPods. What if the driver had lost a wireless earbud?

Marcus fast-forwarded the footage and the driver tore his hat from his head and swiped it against his leg a couple of times and in what could best confirm Marcus' AirPods theory, he grabbed at the left side of his head and stuffed his left hand into his pant pocket.

The car drove away shortly after he got back in and seabirds commandeered the area for their pecking and squawking.

"Can you delete this?" Marcus asked without looking at D'andre.

"I mean, yeah. But it auto deletes after a while anyway."

Marcus didn't respond and sprang out of the rolling chair. He patted the guard on the back of his shoulder and bounded out of the room. He jogged down the long hallway until he reached the glass doors leading to the rideshare pick-up area.

He burst through the door and scared some seagulls into taking flight, squawking and screeching.

"It's got to be here somewhere," he muttered.

A "ding" and a buzz in his shirt pocket told him he had received another text message, but he kept his focus on scanning the ground, mimicking what the driver did on the footage. Hunched over, he reached into a pocket on the side of his left thigh and pulled out two black nitrile gloves and snapped them on.

The driveway was clean, as if street sweepers had come through overnight.

"Fuck." Marcus feared he was right. He continued to whip his head around. He stood up and looked back toward the convention center and then to his right. Looked down the long driveway.

Not seeing anything and feeling his will plummet, Marcus walked to the border of the driveway and plopped down on the curb and put his face in his gloved hands.

On one hand, the convention center's surveillance footage had the confirmed Bill's potentially last moments seen alive and didn't expose the ID of his likely killer. Even if Homicide detectives eventually figured out who Bill was, why he was in San Diego and went to the convention center to retrace his steps as Marcus had, they would run into the same dead-end sooner than he had since the footage would be deleted. They would be no closer to discovering who the murderer was.

But that felt like winning by forfeit. His mission fizzled out quicker than it had begun. The disappointment stung hard and the swings of all the day's emotions began to catch up with him. Emptiness and mental exhaustion settled in.

Tears held in his eyes. He lifted his head and stared blankly ahead at a square utility box similar to the one he and his Texas friends had played around on so many years ago. Except this one was painted with a colorful mural depicting the different soil types in San Diego County.

Each of the four sides represented a different region of the county. On one side, "Coastal" was painted across the top in white cursive lettering and below it a three-dimensional cross-section of varying layers of soil types: multi-colored cobblestone under a top layer of white sand. The other three sides depicted "Central," "East," and "South" San Diego soils, each showcasing similar mixtures, but in a different unique layering of topsoil with varied depictions of flora and fauna.

A couple of seagulls were pecking around on the side of the utility box and their commotion snapped Marcus out of his glazed-over state. He jumped up and ran at the birds, waving his hands yelling, "Hey! Hey! Hey!"

There, in the gap between the bottom of the box and its concrete base, was a white AirPod.

"Ahhhhh!" Marcus screamed. From his knees, he pumped both his fists.

He delicately plucked up the earbud from the bulbous end with his still gloved hand and dropped it carefully into a pant pocket.

A sly smile spread across his face, recalling the driver wasn't wearing gloves in the surveillance video. If there was a latent print on the earbud and the driver was in the system, Marcus would discover the identity of his redeemer.

"Shit!" He remembered he had a text waiting.

It read, "narwhal" with no capitalization or punctuation.

His face tensed, knowing code word meant, "Get his ass back on beat."

9

THE AIRPOD

"CAN YOU GIVE me fifteen or twenty minutes more question mark" Marcus sent the voice-to-text message to McKenzie. He pounded pavement to get back his police cruiser, parked way at the other end of the convention center, and then a couple of blocks across Harbor Drive.

The heavy soles of his black, tactical boots thudded with each stride against the street.

A Southwest 737 roared on its final descent in the distance.

His sunglasses slid from their perch on his forehead on to his face when he took off running and now bounced on the bridge of his nose. With his phone in one hand, he secured the pant pocket containing the AirPod with his other.

Marcus reached his cruiser, skidding to a stop with loose bits of tar and aggregate from the street work kicking up. He pushed his sunglasses back on to his forehead with his right wrist. Stole a look at his phone, still waiting for McKenzie to reply.

...

...

A message in the works.

"Come on!" Marcus jumped into the driver's seat. He dropped the phone to the seat between his legs and started the car.

Marcus had sights set on running to SDPD headquarters to drop off the Airpod for fingerprint analysis before going back to OB, if time would allow. It was a quick two-mile drive from where he was and he could make it there in minutes. But he needed an answer, or else he should jump on the 5 and rush back to his beat to avoid being found out.

He was way out of line already by investigating a murder and shirking his patrol. Shit, if he was caught, he would have to come clean with his motive, or at least why exactly he cared enough about some old, dead white guy found in the back of a trunk to steal evidence, run around town asking questions and look at and destroy surveillance video.

Having a conflict of interest was putting it mildly. No way he would let anyone find out the truth, if he could help it. That the bloodied and beaten-to-death tourist made a weekly habit one summer of pleasuring himself using Marcus.

Fuck no. Marcus punched the steering wheel, like hammering a truth to a tree or a wall.

Marcus could smell the musky odor Bill excreted on those Friday afternoons and gagged remembering how pungent he truly was. Remembering it as an adult, the stink and memory seemed stronger than the time he spent in that car. The stench of newspaper print and the stale mildew from the air conditioning had seared into his brain. But even worse, Bill's cologne—or body odor or pheromones—he only realized right then.

Marcus remembered Bill's soft eyes and round face. How he looked at his younger self longingly, confidently. Ready to spring the trap he had baited by showering Marcus with affirmation and appreciation.

"Arrrr!" He hammered the steering wheel with his fist a second time.

His jaw was clenched tight, tears pooled in his eyes. Marcus pushed his sunglasses up with his hands to wipe the tears away, also sweeping away a layer of sweat beaded under his eyes.

Bill would not get the satisfaction of controlling him again, least of which not as a corpse.

Marcus put the car in drive and punched the gas, making up his mind to get back to OB and run the AirPod up to headquarters after his shift. It would take a few hours, at least, for the fingerprint analyst to find a match, so it would have been more efficient to drop it off right then. Get the clock started while he finished his shift, but Marcus wasn't prepared to lose everything over a couple of hours.

While he executed a U-turn on Harbor, his phone started to vibrate between his legs.

"Hello?" Marcus said, picking up the phone and putting it to his ear without checking who was calling.

"Dude. It's Brad!"

"McKenzie, hey man. I'm so sorry, I'm headed—"

"Man, I was just messin' with you. I got you! It's deadsville over here anyway."

"Wait, what?" Marcus asked.

"Do what you need to do and then tell me all about it when you get back—if you know what I'm sayin'," McKenzie said.

"Serious? What the fuck, man?"

McKenzie laughed hard enough he started wheezing. When he could catch his breath he said, "Sorry! Just bored and having some fun with you!"

Marcus growled. Pressed the phone to his shoulder so he could whip the steering wheel to head to downtown.

"Lieutenant did ask for you but said it wasn't urgent. You're probably getting another commendation. Fucker." McKenzie said.

Marcus groaned. "Just tell anyone who asks that I'm running up to HR for something."

"I got you, bro."

Marcus thanked his cover and hung up.

Thanks to hitting green lights and running one red, he made it to police headquarters in four minutes, shaving five off the projected in-transit time.

He parked his cruiser on the side of the building on E Street, and surveyed the scene across the road. The majority of cars parked on E were non-police vehicles and the same went for the parking lot in the rear of the seven-story, glass, white and blue structure. There were four SDPD SUVs hugging the building in the lot bordering E and 14th streets.

From his car, Marcus waited for a uniformed officer to stroll out of a second-story sliding-glass door and down a set of stairs leading to the parking lot. Once he made it to his car, Marcus scooted across the street. He took a short flight of concrete steps to the lower level, and patted the pocket containing the AirPod.

Unlike most cops who worked at headquarters or had business at headquarters and used side entrances, Marcus instead entered through prisoner processing. The entrance didn't require him to badge in and had significantly less foot traffic than the main entrance on Broadway.

Marcus had been to headquarters, even before being on the force. Besides the numerous visits for work-related matters, Marcus first toured the building with one of his college classes. The first floor was reception, Internal Affairs and the Missing Persons Unit. Administration took up the majority of the second floor, save for a sad, windowless room in the middle of the floor, probably no bigger than ten by ten feet. The room where news media room waited for a major police or crime-related story to break.

On the third floor were the Homicide and Narcotics units and Burglary and Theft units on the fourth. The sixth floor housed miscellaneous desk space for detectives, but Marcus was headed to the fifth floor, to the department's latent fingerprint lab.

The elevator opened on five, right in front of the glass-doored entrance to the lab. Marcus stepped forward and paused for a second, then placed the heel of his palm on the metal door handle. "Latent Fingerprint Laboratory" was etched in a semi-circle on the glass, with the SDPD crest nestled inside.

He pushed the door open and walked into a space, which exuded every attribute you'd expect from a lab. The left side of the square room was lined with benches: white, long tables, bolted to the wall with glassware and instruments taking up the majority of the workspace. A large fuming chamber, the size of an industrial air conditioning unit, took up the middle of the room. It was here Marcus and his Civil Justice classmates had watched with fascination as the technician demonstrated how to uncover prints from a Smith & Wesson 357 Magnum revolver with a 6-inch barrel using a squirt of superglue and some humidity.

On the right side of the room were offices for the trained print analysts in charge of comparing the prints lifted from items used in a crime to those a computer matched using federal and state fingerprint databases.

"Can I help you, officer?" said a small woman, who moved to stand in front of him.

She was a good foot-and-a-half shorter than Marcus, but her presence towered over him. She looked down her long nose at him, seeing every insecurity with her serious eyes, nestled beneath a wrinkled brow.

"I, I have an earbud I need analyzed," Marcus said.

Though well-dressed, the woman wasn't wearing a lab coat and didn't appear to be a technician or scientist by any other respect. Her eyes stared intently at him and he fought the urge to look away. The back of his neck tingled. Where was the technician he knew?

The woman flipped over her civilian SDPD work badge hanging by a metal clasp from her blazer pocket and it read, "Mariana Esposito, Lab Manager."

"You are certainly in the right place," she finally said without breaking a smile.

After his shoulders fell, Marcus patted the pant pocket containing his piece of evidence. Held out a hand.

"Can I borrow a pair of gloves, please?"

"You mean you have the evidence on you and not bagged?" Her tone matched her earlier strict posture.

The back of Marcus' neck tingled again and he felt his face get hot. He dropped his head and said, "Yes." Looking back up at her, he added, "But I collected it quickly in pursuit of a suspect."

"You didn't pick it up with your bare hands, did you?" she asked. Condescension stuck to every word.

The words flared his nose and his face burned hot—this time heated with defiance. But just as quickly as the anger rose in him, it dissipated.

"No, ma'am. I keep a pair of gloves on me at all times for instances like this. But I used my last pair to collect this earbud and took them off before I realized it."

Marcus hoped he hadn't rambled too much.

But her sideways, judgmental glare softened and it appeared to be the explanation she needed.

A lab technician was watching the two of them by this time. She had walked into Marcus' view from the office area over to the fuming chamber where she'd been pretending to work. She'd adjusted some dials on the side of the chamber and taken down a small, aluminum saucer from a shelf and put it back, all the while keeping her head cocked toward Marcus and Mariana.

"No problem then," Mariana said. She spun around and walked to the fuming chamber, placed a hand on the shoulder of the technician, who flinched. Reaching over her, Mariana strained to grab a flat, tissue paper-sized box from off the shelf the aluminum saucer was on.

She whipped back to Marcus and held the box of nitrile gloves up to him.

Marcus thanked her and pulled one glove out of the top.

After gloving up, he crept his hand into his pocket and retrieved the AirPod. He then held it out to the technician who waited with a white envelope. She pinched it by the ends to create a pocket and swung around after Marcus dropped the earbud in.

"Kay will start processing the item for exposure of latent prints," Mariana said. "If you could help with some information…" She tapped her index finger on a clipboard she was now holding with just one page pinned to it.

"Sure," he said, and followed her to the office area. On the way, he looked back at Kay, who was already securing the AirPod to a metal clasp.

He noticed another person when he looked back, a man with goggles and a sloppy head of stiff, black hair wearing a lab coat, at the far end of the lab. He was playing on his phone sitting at the lab bench.

"Name?" Mariana said.

Marcus snapped his head back to look at her, startled.

"Uh, Marcus. Kemp. K, as in 'king,' E-M-P."

"Is this item evidence in a crime?"

She knew it was. He said so just minutes earlier. Sure, the story was bogus, but she didn't know that. Right?

Marcus crouched and leaned in to glimpse at the clipboard. He crossed his arms, tucking his right hand under his left arm and felt his sopping wet armpits.

"Mm-hmm," he said. Great. Add another "filing a false report" charge to the list of infractions for the day.

She looked at Marcus out of the corner of her eye. "I assume you want us to run any prints we may find?"

"Yes, please."

She checked a box on the form reading, "FBI Integrated Automatic Fingerprint Identification System." The gold standard for cross-referencing fingerprints, the database is the largest repository of fingerprints in the United States, gathered from criminal, civil and military records.

Mariana also checked the "CA State Database" box, which holds only California criminal and civil fingerprint records.

Marcus was sure his guy would be from Texas, but it didn't hurt to check both and it might look suspicious if he declined to enter the prints into the California system.

"Contact information where we can email you the results if we successfully pull and match the print?"

She held the clipboard and a cheap, black Bic ballpoint pen out to Marcus, who took them from her. She pointed at the line for him to fill out. Marcus held the tip of the pen hovered over the contact line, not sure whether to write down his personal or department email address. He wasn't used to covering his tracks and this moment drove home the reality of what he was doing. He held the pen still for another long couple of seconds.

The lab would have a record of his request either way. If he stayed one step ahead of detectives, none of it would matter anyway. His email, phone—whatever else—would only come into the picture as evidence if he got caught. Which reminded him, he needed to avoid the third floor and Homicide.

Marcus printed his work email on the form and handed the clipboard back to Mariana.

"Thank you," she said. "That's all I need. We will send you an email with our results. If we are able to pull a print, it could take hours to run it through the databases and analyze any hits we receive."

"Appreciate it," Marcus said.

Hours. He knew it could take a while, but it was all he could do to keep himself from rolling his eyes.

He turned away from her, distracted by a sudden poof he saw out of the corner of his eye and a resulting plume in the foaming chamber. He drifted back toward the center of the lab and watched the vapor engulf the glass chamber, filling it with a whitish, thick cloud.

"It's always a trip watching that," Marcus said.

He lingered a second or two, expecting a response from the technician, but she had her back turned to him, focused on her work.

From behind him, Mariana cleared her throat. "If there isn't anything else, Officer Kemp?"

"Right. No. Thank you."

He practically sprinted out of the lab, charged with the urgency to get back to OB and on patrol. Marcus pushed the glass door open and caught the single elevator door before it closed. With a ding, the circular 2 button lit, and the doors closed.

Minutes later, Marcus swung his creaky Crown Vic into the parking lot at the OB Pier and pulled up next to McKenzie's cruiser, which was parked in the middle of the lot facing the entrance/exit.

Their driver's side windows aligned, the two cars facing opposite directions. Marcus took several deep breaths, not looking McKenzie's way until he was ready to literally face him. He drew air in through his nose and blew out with a prolonged, two-three second huff through pursed lips.

After collecting himself, he rolled down his window. His colleague's face was splotchy and he was looking straight ahead.

"What's wrong, fool?"

"O-B fuck-ing ROB," McKenzie said.

"What happened?" Marcus asked. He took off his sunglasses, hoping his friend would mirror his action so he could see his eyes. McKenzie ripped his pair off his face.

The younger cop snorted and turned his head to Marcus.

"I don't know, man. It was dumb. I was telling them all they needed to keep the wall clear of their shit," he said. He was waving his hand, pointing to the direction of the sea wall where the homeless in the area hung out during the day.

"Some dude I've never seen before started yelling at me and got right in my face saying, 'It's OB's stuff, man! He's a good dude...' blah, blah blah." McKenzie changed his voice to imitate his combatant, giving him a whiny, nose-talking pitch with a thick, fake surfer's accent before trailing off and mimicking someone talking too much by opening and closing his hand over and over.

Marcus rubbed his forehead. "So, what happened?"

"I don't know. I just stood there pissed off. I'm not even sure what I said. Probably just told them to clean up Rob's shit or I would."

"So, what's the problem? Why are you still pissed?" Marcus found it hard to stay focused on what McKenzie said next. He was too lost in his own racing mind. So, McKenzie blathered on and Marcus nodded along. What a day. Pssshhh. That didn't even cut it, given all the shit he'd gone through so far.

Marcus looked at his friend gesturing, his face still splotchy and ruddy, while he worked through the frustration that had built up in the time from when Marcus last talked to him before going to the fingerprint lab. That was the thing about the job: You could be fine one minute, then you get one bad call or have one conflict and it could totally undo a solid day's work in your mind.

Words backed up in Marcus' throat. He suddenly thought about spilling his guts to McKenzie. Why now? Why McKenzie? He winced at his friend's shocked reaction, picturing telling him about Bill, about how seeing his corpse made his stomach turn.

But how it had also given him a charge, made him hungry. How the trauma of his youth had surged to the surface of his life that day, like a shark that had lurked for years under the churning glass of a black ocean, waiting for the perfect time to strike and finish off its wounded victim. That same victim who had bobbed along his whole life, like he didn't remember the fatal chunks taken out of his side all those years ago.

Maybe confessing all this would absolve him of his culpability. Or maybe the pull to confess was as simple to explain as needing McKenzie to tell him he wasn't crazy for doing what he'd done.

Whatever it was, the thought passed quickly, and with it the acute attack of panic.

He never had been a good sharer. That went back to his childhood as well. Whenever he should have shared his pain, or just told someone he trusted what he was thinking, he couldn't. But that's exactly the reason he was in this spot now, wasn't it? He should have been able to open up with his mother when his abuse started, but he never wanted to burden her with more problems.

His mother! He hadn't checked in to see how she was doing all day. She had returned home, back to her assisted living facility a week earlier after spending a couple of weeks in the hospital recuperating from a surgery to remove tumors. It had been a long, tough road to this point, but they hoped things were looking up.

Marcus made it a point to call her every morning to see how she was doing, and also went to see her after he got off work at least every other day. He had done neither so far today.

He mm-hmm'd McKenzie, whose venting had started ramping down. Marcus felt his still-soaked underarms, more so now than when he'd first noticed in the lab. With his nerves shot—or maybe he was just running on fumes—it wasn't surprising a shaky feeling had taken hold as well. But when he checked his hands, they weren't shaking. Flipping them to check his palms, it was the same. No shaking. Letting loose all of a sudden, however, his stomach gurgled out a low bellow that rose and crescendoed into a high-pitch squeal.

"Whoa!" McKenzie yelled. The sound snapped him out of his bitchy fit for good. His commemorative coin-sized eyes stared at Marcus. The two froze looking at each other for a long second, and then McKenzie burst into a hacking laugh, punctuated with hard HAs, one after another, until he couldn't catch his breath.

Marcus laughed along, but in a sheepish kind of way.

"I guess I'm hungry," he said.

"I would say so, bro!" McKenzie wiped his teary eyes. His once splotchy face was now beet red like a ripened tomato. When he finally caught his breath, he asked Marcus if he wanted to grab a beer after work.

Marcus looked at his instrument panel for the time. They had an hour left in their shifts and his inbox was waiting for him, hopefully with a print match from the lab.

"Ah, man. I would but—"

"Oh, I get it." McKenzie winked. "Going back for seconds, huh?"

Marcus hadn't told him about breaking up with Megan this last time. McKenzie had just rotated back on to the early morning shift, so the friends hadn't hung out in a while.

"Whatever," Marcus said. "I told you I went to HR"

"Sure, man. Well, let's grab some lunch at least," McKenzie said. "You'll need fuel for round two!"

10
HOMICIDE'S JOHN DOE

BACK AT SDPD headquarters, Homicide detectives Lt. Jorge Castillo and Aaron Barnes were getting nowhere on their murder case. After spending the better part of the day combing over the scene for clues, they still had no leads, including an identity for their John Doe. The scene—apart from the victim's beaten and bloodied body—contained nothing of consequence in the way of physical evidence.

The forensic specialists from the department's Field Services Unit dusted every inch of the Altima for prints and found none on key areas including the steering wheel, driver's side door and the trunk. However, the passenger's front and back door handles were mucked up with prints, as were the interior panels.

They scoured the driver's seat for hairs, skin or any other bodily remnants that could lead to the identification of a suspect, but there had been nothing. The detectives were confident the killer vacuumed the area. He might have used a lint roller. Point was, the driver's seat and the surrounding areas were immaculate.

Forensics did find numerous medium-length brown and long black hairs on the back seat behind the passenger's seat. But, as with the fingerprints found in the same areas, Barnes dismissed the physical markers, figuring they belonged to the many different passengers the car's owner had picked up and dropped off as a part-time rideshare driver.

Attempts to ID their victim failed soon after they started. Detectives took note of the stretched-out bulge in the back pocket of the victim's shorts where a wallet would have likely been, but it wasn't on the body or in the car. The victim's prints, expedited with the latent fingerprint lab, came back negative for any kind of match in state and federal fingerprint databases.

"What about surveillance video from one of the restaurants or the hotel?" Castillo asked his partner, stroking his salt-and-pepper goatee while the two detectives sat at their desks.

Their workspaces butted up to each other on the third floor of SDPD headquarters and they had been going over the case there on what little information they had for the better part of three hours, after returning from the scene.

Barnes squeezed a purple stress ball in one hand and rested his chin on his other fist, arm propped on his desk.

"Hotel didn't have an angle. Too far down on the corner," Barnes said, staring at Castillo with an indignant glare, squeezing the foam ball. "Still waiting for a call back from the manager at OB Surf Lodge."

"And none of the light poles had our cameras? Castillo asked.

"Nope."

The dead ends were mounting up and, with each loss, the partners grew more cantankerous with each other, and after they began their day on such a high, too.

They'd arrived on the OB murder scene that morning coming off a huge success. The morning before, they officially cleared three cold case murders dating back thirty-seven years, long before either of them had been cops.

The arrest earned them a night of celebratory craft beers with colleagues at a bar in Little Italy. They had also been featured prominently in a story that chronicled their dogged, leather-to-pavement police work, printed in *The San Diego Union-Tribune* with the headline, "Online ancestry, detectives' work snares serial killer."

"I was quoted three times," Barnes said, holding up the print issue, taunting his partner as they drove to the OB murder scene.

"Yeah, yeah," Castillo said, keeping his eyes on the road.

Working with an online ancestry company for two months—ancestry DNA tracing being the new craze—the detectives got a hit in the database. They had found a relative whose DNA was enough of a match for the original samples of semen and skin collected from the slayings of three separate women in the early eighties. From that relative's DNA, they were eventually able to narrow their focus to a single suspect, who they put under surveillance, trailed and collected a fork he used at a restaurant as their source of comparative DNA.

The strategy had been put to use up and down the state by law enforcement after it had been successfully employed by a Contra Costa County investigator to catch the "Golden State Killer," Joseph DeAngelo, suspected of killing thirteen people and raping more than fifty women in cities ranging from the Bay Area to Orange County between 1974 and 1986.

SDPD's Homicide unit supervisor gave Castillo and Barnes the green light to try the same tactic with their cold cases.

When they dug into the old case files, they found the original detectives suspected the three cases were linked, that a single person killed all of the victims. Examining the killer's behavior, they were inclined to believe their hunch was correct.

The killer severely beat each of the unidentified women with an object thought to be a hammer or some other kind of heavy hand tool. After bludgeoning each woman, he stripped her clothes off and threw her into a canyon in the county. In each case, hikers stumbled across the bodies within days of the murder. The suspect was unoriginally dubbed "The Canyon Killer."

The original detectives on the cases noted the most disturbing part of each murder was discovering that the killer had hiked down to each body and raped the corpses post-mortem. As if throwing a person down the side of a canyon to tumble over cactus, dried scrub, rocks and boulders wasn't sickening enough. Learning that he had then raped their mangled and broken bodies added a level of sinister heinousness the detectives of the time weren't used to seeing in the small-big city of San Diego.

After defiling the bodies, detectives believed the killer moved his victims closer to well-trekked trails for easier discovery.

No family or friends filed missing persons reports consistent with the descriptions of the victims, and even the physical evidence didn't amount to much, given the state of forensic science and technology at the time. Few to no leads were generated. There were no eyewitnesses, and the cases had gone cold.

Thirty-seven years later, when the DNA test connected the saliva on the fork to the samples from the three crime scenes with a 99.9 percent certitude, the original detectives were proven correct in their hunch of a serial killer working in San Diego.

The suspect was John Alan Webber, a sixty-seven-year-old, white recluse who lived in Lakeside, California, in East County San Diego.

The SDPD SWAT team led the arresting party, charging into his shack of a home that smelled like stale sweat and rancid cooking oil. Barnes slapped handcuffs on the man, who inquired, matter-of-factly, "What took you so long?"

So, surely a dead guy tossed into the trunk of a car that the killer abandoned in a busy part of town would be an open and shut case. Right?

Not so much.

"Do you think that cop was acting strange?" Castillo asked Barnes.

"The responding officer? Kemp?" Barnes asked.

Castillo sat up in his chair.

"Yeah. Seemed jittery, like—"

"Like he opened a trunk and found a dead guy?"

Castillo paused a couple of seconds in reflection.

"Yeah, I get that. But he looks like a tough guy. I mean, he's huge."

"What are you even saying?" Barnes said, scoffed.

"I don't know." Castillo's voice trailed off and he leaned back in his chair to reflect some more.

Barnes stopped squeezing the purple stress ball and leaned back in his chair, too. He tossed the ball up in the air with a flick of his wrist, like perfecting his free throw form. He caught it and threw it above himself again and again.

With each toss in the air, he spoke a word and paused before the next word to catch the ball.

"Seems. To. Me. We. Should…"

"Spit it out!" Castillo propelled upright in his chair and lunged over the desk to swat at the stress ball.

Barnes snatched the ball on its descent, stood up, held it out in Castillo's face and said, "Ha! Not with those T-Rex arms!"

"Fuck you," Castillo mumbled under his dejected breath.

Barnes tossed the ball underhand to the lieutenant, who caught it despite wincing and blinking from the surprising delivery. Both sat back down and went silent.

A couple of minutes later, Barnes said, "Let's move on to something else, is what I was going to say. If we get video, then fine, we can go back to it. But this case is a dud right now."

"I don't know," Castillo responded.

"What's not to know?" Barnes asked in a higher-than-normal pitch. He ran his hand through his hair, making it stand up in sections, splayed out.

"Let's go over everything we have again, starting with what Kemp told us," Castillo said.

"Man, I'm tellin' you, bro. We're wasting our time."

"There's a killer out there," Castillo said.

"Oh, for real?" Barnes said, mocking his partner. "No one is even looking for this John Doe. This should be low priority."

Castillo drew in a deep breath through his nose and stared at his partner, who wasn't returning his eye-contact. After blinking a number of times as if to an internal rhythm, he gave his partner instruction in a low, metered response.

"You should go take a walk."

Barnes jumped out of his chair and threw it into his desk, making Castillo jump in his seat.

"Might I suggest the stairs while you're at it?" Castillo shouted.

"Whatever," Barnes stomped across the office and stiff-armed open one of the two swinging glass doors to the Homicide unit.

Castillo didn't react to the childish behavior. Barnes was a good detective and his reasoning might have struck Castillo with merit if their previous cold case closure hadn't pumped him full of so much confidence. Besides, he had years of experience on Barnes and like any seasoned detective, he knew sometimes another hour or a fresh look could break things open in an investigation.

Castillo looked down at the papers strewn across his desk and on his partner's. He turned his attention to his computer and double-clicked on an email from the San Diego County Medical Examiner's office.

He clicked and opened two attachments—an examination report and a death certificate for John Doe—to print. The ME sent both on a rush an hour earlier and Castillo and Barnes had reviewed them at Castillo's desk. None of the information shed much light on their victim, however. The ME's email also informed the detectives, as with roughly seventy-five percent of deaths, that the ME's office was legally obligated to perform an autopsy on their John Doe. Be that as it may, they weren't hopeful an autopsy would help them ID their victim or his killer.

Castillo listened for the printer across the office to beep and spurt to life, letting it finish up before he got up and trudged over to retrieve the County reports.

A senior by both stature and age, Castillo's colleagues playfully called him Chicano Antiguo when they caught him doing things like printing emails, looking something up in a book or not embracing technology in other ways.

A man of size, Castillo hunched when sitting or standing, carrying his frame as if embarrassed by it. When he walked, his feet splayed severely to the sides with each step, though his legs didn't protrude sideways like someone who walked bowlegged.

On his way back to his desk, Castillo looked over the sparsely populated work stations in the unit and then peered out the windows on the south side of the office at nothing in particular. He plopped back in his chair, letting out a labored sigh and dropping the papers to his desk. Then, he organized the papers by report type.

The death certificate was straight forward and provided information either of the detectives could have guesstimated. The time of death of their victim was somewhere between six and eleven p.m. the previous night, as determined by the state of decomposition of the body. "John Doe" was listed on the top of the report and the bottom was signed by "Ruben Sacks, MD."

Castillo pinched the form up with his fingers and slapped it down on a pile of papers on the right edge of his desk. Next, he looked at the examination report and stroked his goatee while thinking.

Under cause of death, it read: Blunt force trauma to the head; trauma to the rear and back of the skull. That much the two detectives had already observed just looking into the trunk. Blood had soaked the ring of hair on the victim's head and had run down on to his neck where it had then dried. Though his hair had still been damp.

The Medical Examiner didn't find pieces of foreign object or paint or anything else that could have chipped off the murder weapon and lodged into the victim's skull during the attack. On the "Murder Weapon" line it simply read: "N/A—Not found."

"He's a robbery victim," Barnes had exclaimed when they read the report the first time. "His wallet is missing and he was dressed like a tourist."

"But why would he kill him that way if it was a robbery?" Castillo wondered aloud.

"Here's what I'm thinking," Barnes started. He held out his hands, palms up. "We know the car was stolen, right?"

"Right," Castillo said.

"Our killer steals the car, uses it to pick up a mark—we keep hearing about people getting in the wrong Uber or Lyft and getting robbed or worse—"

"I'm with you so far," Castillo said, encouraging him to go on.

Barnes pumped his hands and continued.

"Picks up our guy, from… wherever. Drops him off at a secluded place."

Castillo's nose squished and one eyebrow dropped. Barnes noticed, causing him to rattle off the last part of his hypothesis in two-time speed to get it out before his partner could make another disparaging face.

"And whacks him over the back of the head, dumps him in the trunk, steals his wallet and anything else he might have and ditches the car in OB."

The lieutenant straightened up in his chair. Didn't react and stared through Barnes.

"Well?" Barnes said.

"It's a decent theory. It's basically the facts as we know them, so you probably have a lot of it right."

"But?"

"Nothing, it's just—" Castillo hesitated. "I'm still stuck on how he was killed. And why even kill him? The report says the killer hit him multiple times. One hit would have disabled that old man long enough for the killer to rob him and make a getaway."

Barnes stared at the floor, then lifted his head.

"What if it's as simple as he didn't mean to hit him over the head and panicked? Then he felt like he needed to get rid of the witness? People kill people for the stupidest reasons. I mean, we know that."

"Sure," Castillo said. "But if he didn't mean to hit him, why the back of the head? That tells me he snuck up on him. That he meant to assault him."

Barnes looked at the floor again and hummed.

"I just wonder if he wants us to think it was a robbery," Castillo said.

"I'll ask him when I find him," Barnes said. He winked and shot Castillo with a finger gun.

Barnes had been on his walk for about twenty minutes now. Castillo continued to scan the ME's examination report he had printed off. Tapped his foot.

He looked out over the empty bullpen, then re-focused on his computer monitor.

"Where is everyone?" he muttered. He kept tapping his foot, but he also fanned his linen shirt, forcing fresh air into it. He hit his SDPD Headquarters ID badge and it swung violently from the lanyard hanging from his neck.

He stopped and palmed the report up and slapped it on the pile with the death certificate and other papers. Sighs grew into huffs. He shuffled loose papers: the actions of busy work or delaying the inevitable. Papers flew, his lanyard and badge swung and bobbed about and his draws of air grew deeper. Just about the time Castillo's visible frustration was reaching its apex and the look on his face telegraphed surrender, his phone rang.

"Lieutenant Castillo speaking."

One of his eyebrows rose as the caller spoke, and he shrugged his shoulder to secure the phone receiver between his neck and ear. He scrambled for a pen and notepad.

"Thanks for calling," he said, prompting more information while writing "OB Surf Lodge manager" on his notepad. As the caller spoke, his eyes widened and he circled the words several times.

"You do?" Castillo asked. "Could you email the footage to me?"

Keeping the receiver pinned to his ear, he clicked on Outlook.

"Great, yes. Are you ready?"

After giving the caller his email address, Castillo hung up the phone and pumped his fist and let out a "Yeah!" under his breath.

He impatiently clicked between "Inbox" and "Sent Items" a few times in an effort to refresh his inbox. A few minutes later, the email arrived with the compressed surveillance video file attached. Once opened, Castillo fast-forwarded in fifteen-second intervals repeatedly, looking for the time when the blue Altima pulled into the metered spot to hopefully give him the first glimpse at their suspect.

About ten minutes later, the double glass doors to the unit flew open and Barnes skipped in.

"Ho-oh-oh-oh-leeeeee SHIT!" he bellowed, raising his arms above his head as if celebrating a touchdown in a sports bar.

Castillo's head shot up to look at his partner, who stood there with wide blue eyes and his mouth open so big, if he spread it any wider, he might have dislocated his jaw.

"What?" Castillo said.

Barnes clapped his hands several times, the echo of his sing-songy cadence bouncing off the walls.

"George, wait until I tell you this shit. You'll never believe what—who—I just saw."

A few other detectives had made it back to the office by this time, and they poked their heads up at their desks to see what the commotion was about.

"I've got news, too," Castillo offered.

Barnes dropped his arms and furrowed his brow at his partner's attempt to steal his thunder. "For real?" The younger detective walked over to their desks and stood over Castillo, who was still sitting down.

"I saw our man," Barnes said with a shit-eating grin.

"What? Our suspect?"

"No, no," Barnes cut him off. "Kemp! The responding cop!"

"What? Where?" Castillo's eyes got big.

"Get this. Leaving the fingerprint lab!"

Barnes splayed both hands as if he had just dropped a heavy weight—the figurative representation of his apparent truth bomb.

"Ohhh-kay," Castillo said. "Wait. Back up. How exactly did you see this?"

"Right. Right," Barnes said. "So, I went for my walk. I took the stairs like you said, and walked around the building a few times. Foot was feeling sore, so I sat down for a minute. I took a few deep breaths and then went back inside. But I wasn't ready to come back to the office. I took the stairs again and got off on each floor, walked the floor to the other staircase and up to the next floor, zig-zagging my way up to five."

"Ok," Castillo offered.

"That's when I saw him leaving the lab and getting on the elevator when I got to the third floor."

"Did he see you?"

"No. It was a split second, but it was definitely him."

"Ok," Castillo said.

"Turns out, he dropped off an item for analysis," Barnes continued. "Mariana told me Kemp said it was off a guy he chased, but got away." Barnes held his fingers in front of himself and used air quotes when he said, "off a guy he chased, but got away."

"He's a beat cop. Sounds normal to me," Castillo said, looking confused.

"Maybe normal some other day, But *tuh-day*? The day he was acting definitely not chill at the scene of a murder? A scene where we didn't find shit?"

Castillo rolled his right hand at the wrist, telling his partner to go on.

Barnes did just that, saying bluntly, "I think he knew our victim. I got to thinking, that's how I would act. You know? Distracted. If I knew the person that I had just found dead, but didn't want anyone to know I knew him."

"He *was* pretty distracted when we talked to him," Castillo said. "Didn't I say he was acting strange?"

"You were right!" Barnes said, holding his palms out.

"What if he's looking for the suspect *and* knows where the victim had been?" Castillo riffed, now in synch with his partner.

"Yes!" Barnes bit his lower lip and jabbed Castillo on the shoulder.

"And we might be able to answer if that's what he's up to, with what I just found," Castillo said, almost triumphant.

Barnes leaned back. "That's what I'm talking about!" Then checked himself and added, "Wait. How?"

"The restaurant called and sent over video, and it has our killer on it," Castillo said.

"Sick!" Barnes shouted at the ceiling like howling at the moon. "So, all we have to do is see if our guy could fit any of the matches Kemp's prints bring back. Tell me he's unique looking!"

"Well," Castillo began. "Not really. White guy, tall, and his face was covered."

"Ah, shit. Ok," Barnes rubbed his chin in thought.

"Let's bring this to Kemp's lieutenant," Castillo said.

"No way!" Barnes shot back. "If he's busy investigating this, let's let him do the job. Don't you want to find out what his angle is?"

His partner thought for a few seconds, stroking his goatee.

"Maybe you're right," Castillo said at last. "We aren't Internal Affairs."

"Damn straight," Barnes said. "If it's nothing, we still have video of the killer to work with. But, what if his prints are sitting two floors down?"

Castillo lifted his face and the cautious look melted; his eyebrows arched and a sly smile of intrigue took hold.

"Tell me you asked for the print analysis," he said, clenching his teeth and fists.

In a smooth, lounge singer's delivery, Barnes said, "Well, let me tell you, mi Chicano Antiguo... Mariana's going to blind copy me on the email she sends to Kemp."

11
SETBACKS

MARCUS CRUMPLED THE yellow wrapper from the footlong sub he'd just devoured and tossed it across the deli.

The ball cleared the mouth of the trashcan, landing inside with a whack against the back of the container. "Score!" McKenzie yelled with his hands raised above his head.

The cops each waved at the kid working behind the counter on their way out, set to part ways for the final ticks of their shifts. Each had started the day at 5 a.m. and Marcus, for one, was anxious to end his 10-hour shift.

"I'm gonna cruise Sunset Cliffs," McKenzie said to Marcus, smacking his lips. His tongue glided back and forth along the top row of his straight teeth, searching for any trapped meat and cheese.

"Cool, man," Marcus said. He flipped his sunglasses down. "Think I'll hit the beach."

"Make some fools pour out their forties? McKenzie had a wide smile plastered across his face, sitting in his cruiser with the door open. Not giving Marcus time to respond he added, "Always keepin' it one hundred. Catch ya later, Smooth Chocolate."

"You got to stop it with that," Marcus said. He glared at McKenzie with a straight look and serious eyes as stern as his words.

The goofy smile on McKenzie's face drooped and he fumbled for a response. He struggled to form words as if a bear trap had just snatched his tongue.

"Uh, I…uh…yeah. Sorry, bro."

The awkwardness didn't last long, thanks to an aversion for confrontation Marcus had exhibited his entire life. It was a character flaw he'd identified recently and had a growing distaste for, having reminisced on his childhood all day.

"I'm just messin' with ya." Marcus said. He knew his friend didn't mean anything by it, but the passive racial jabs were getting old nonetheless.

McKenzie barked out a "ha-ha" without laughing, and kept his eyes on Marcus for further cues if he was truly in the clear. Marcus sensed this and reluctantly cracked a smile. In response, McKenzie let out a series of nervous chuckles and started his car.

They waved to each other and then Marcus turned to walk the few blocks to the beach as McKenzie drove off.

Shuffling down the sidewalk, Marcus noticed his legs felt fresh. He had figuratively and literally run all over the city that day, and was surprised he wasn't feeling any ill-effects. Quite the contrary, he felt invigorated. Lunch had definitely helped—the calories had soaked up the anxiety churning in his stomach from violating numerous department policies, but hadn't touched the deeper trauma of finding his former abuser's corpse.

The afternoon sun now beamed intensely in a naked sky. The radiation warmed his arms. He looked up, closed his eyes, and stretched his neck toward it in response, as a basking lizard might. He pulled back his shoulders, pushed his chest out and closed his eyes briefly before continuing down the sidewalk.

It was creeping on 3:30 p.m., and a slight breeze had picked up, licking up the cool moisture from the ocean on its tail. Most evenings in San Diego were that way: it cooled off quicker than you would expect. But it was a little unusual to feel it begin so early, especially given the clear, warm day it had been. Then again, what about this day had been normal?

Trying to temper his excitement about seeing the fingerprint results, Marcus hung a left on Bacon Street, pointing him toward OB's main drag on Newport Avenue. He passed a new bar and grill under construction on his left, a floral shop and a deserted CrossFit gym. Some sort of electronica-influenced music caught his attention, blaring out of the empty brick building. The multiple garage-style doors were open. No one hung from the Olympic rings or pressed, squatted or deadlifted any of the rows racked barbells. If it had been any regular day, the scene would have Marcus thinking about his workout the next day. But he kept walking, his mind strangely quiet. Not focused at all on his usual routine. He didn't know what the next day would bring, but the uncertainty excited him, and that surprised him.

Before he reached the corner Starbucks, he stopped. There in his path on the sidewalk, a large utility box, like the one he found the AirPod under at the convention center earlier, except this one was wrapped in an image of a massive, tsunami-sized wave in full crest, barreling toward the beach on all four sides. Riding the wave was not a surfer or even a whimsical stand-in like an English bulldog or something, but the Target stores logo. Marcus wasn't focused on the anti-corporate imagery but stared at the box all the same. This was the spot where he responded to the only murdered person he had encountered while on the San Diego Police Department, until today.

Tammy had been a regular panhandler who lived on the streets of Ocean Beach. Marcus knew her well. The day he'd responded to this spot, she had been stabbed in the stomach over a drug dispute. Specifically, Tammy had some and her attacker wanted them. At a scrawny eighty-five pounds after a full meal, she didn't survive long after the attack and was dead by the time Marcus arrived just minutes after getting the call.

They caught her killer the same night—several sitting around the utility box with Tammy had witnessed the attack.

Marcus hadn't stopped to look at the spot since it happened, even though he had driven past the box hundreds of times on patrol. He looked away when he realized this, and continued his walk.

He crossed the street and saw the ocean about a block away. Close enough that sand spilled over the sidewalk, tracked there by foot traffic and the wind. Marcus exhaled after breathing deep. Normally the unmistakable smell of beach instantly relaxed him. But he couldn't keep his mind off his case. All he saw when he closed his eyes was himself sitting at a computer back at Western Division, scouring the fingerprint analysis report. The more he gave into the daydream, the more his mind filled in details of what he hoped to discover about Bill's killer and where it would lead him.

Age? Probably a little younger than him. Race? He went back and forth between black and white.

He had reached the beach and stood facing the water when a guttural condemnation from a curvy Latina snapped him out of his state of mind. The young woman was lying on a towel on the beach, tanning. She was on her back with her feet closest to the water and her head pitched back toward the street so she was able to see Marcus staring at her with a dumb look on his face.

Holding on to her unsecured seafoam green bikini top, she rolled over on one elbow and propped herself up, hyperextending her back. Her leg kicked sand in the air as she made the move. She glared back at Marcus, scrunched her face and huffed. When he didn't respond and kept staring, she huffed again, this time loudly and with a growl in her throat.

Startled, Marcus said, "Sorry. Sorry, I didn't mean…" He trailed off, looking away quickly. His face warmed and he covered his mouth, realizing he was smiling. He turned away and walked toward the pier.

Underneath the pier, he saw a few regulars sitting in the shade. A waxed box of old soggy bagels and donuts sat untouched at the base of the stairs to the pier. Likely dropped off by some well-meaning restaurant owner or someone from one of the many churches in the area.

The beach was already getting crowded and the 9-to-5ers hadn't even made it home yet. The breeze was a little stronger right on the water than where he been walking blocks away, but the air felt good. It cooled his body. The black police uniform was exceptionally proficient at absorbing and trapping heat on a sunny day, so he appreciated the combination of the breeze and shade under the pier.

The beach bums started to scatter. Most of the half-dozen or so walked back down the beach, headed north to the boardwalk.

Though they knew Marcus, it wasn't like they preferred hanging out with a cop. It might have bugged him any other day, given that he prided himself on maintaining relationships with everyone on his beat. But not today. Even so, he felt like the weirdo no one wants to sit next to at lunch in junior high

With the area to himself, he hopped up and sat on the concrete base to the pier that backed into the cliff. The waves were starting to build. A few surfers sat on boards on the north side of the pier, waiting for a good set to come in.

Marcus looked up at the pier, and Megan came to mind. He felt a strong desire to tell her everything. It pulled at him. The last time they had talked in person had been their most recent breakup.

"Why are you so closed off?" Megan had said. "You're being such a stereotype right now."

"What does that even mean?" Marcus asked, without looking at her.

"You can't stay with me for more than a few months without getting scared off," Megan shouted, holding out her arms, palms face-up. Exhaustion written all over her face, she bobbed her head at him, attempted to make eye contact.

"That's not it," he said. His shoulders slumped and he dropped his head. "Lots of cops have relationships. Families."

Megan blew out a long sigh of exasperation. "So, what? Good for them. I'm not asking you for a family. We have fun together, don't we?"

"Yeah." He plopped down on his couch.

"I'm not asking you to marry me."

"I know that," Marcus said.

"So, why can't you stay with me if you care about me so much?" she asked. He didn't have an answer.

Marcus' pocket vibrated. A text from Megan. A chill ran up the back of his neck from the coincidental timing. He sat up straight and cupped his hand over the phone's screen.

It read: "Sorry. I've been swamped at work…"

She was working on another text. He jumped to his feet and his boots sank into the soft sand.

"TBH I don't think we have much to talk about right now."

Marcus stared at the screen and all he could spit out was an exasperated, drawn-out, "What?!" His face burned hot.

Marcus had forgotten he was waiting on a follow-up to her earlier "Busy" text. He stared at the phone. No dots blinked.

He growled and squeezed the phone. Shook his fists.

Tapping out a lengthy response, his anger influenced multiple mistypes leading to an autocorrected incoherent message.

"Arrrrggg!" Once he corrected the message, he hesitated to send it. His thumb hovered over the send arrow for several seconds until he tapped the x over and over.

He typed in, "I understand," but again backed out of sending the message.

"What. Ever," was the message he sent at last.

Marcus stared at the screen and waited until 'Delivered' appeared under the text bubble. He stared at the screen, hoping the jab would land, but also had to know she wouldn't respond either way.

"Fuck this." He pocketed the phone and took off at a brisk pace back to his cruiser.

MINUTES LATER, MARCUS pulled into the secure back lot at Western Division. It was a flurry of activity with the shift change. Cops pulled in to the lot at the same time as Marcus and the next shift of officers ran around selecting cruisers and SUVs to hit the streets.

A rookie pulled in thirty seconds after Marcus, bottoming out and scraping his cruiser's undercarriage on the turn-in that had been patched over a dozen times with blacktop filler. Marcus glanced back in his side mirror. That rookie would learn, just as Marcus had, how to turn the wheel just right to avoid the same mistake in the future.

Marcus flung his door open and worked feverishly to disconnect his computer. He patted his pockets to make sure he had his wallet, phone and personal car keys, whipping his head side to side before getting out. The creaky door slammed shut with a thrust of his hip and he headed into the station, computer under his arm.

Access to the station from the parking area led cops strangely through the outdated kitchen and dining room. Rows of eight-foot folding tables more suited for a large family holiday get-together butted up end to end and were spaced in four rows tightly enough that cops had to twist their torsos and sidestep down the aisles when they wanted to eat at them.

A narrow path ran from the back door, past the tables on the left and candy and soda machines on the right, into the kitchen and out into the main hallway of the station.

Various offices dotted the hallway, including a computer room for filing reports and the offices of the division's leaders.

"Way to go, bro!" a younger Latino officer said, as they passed each other going in opposite directions.

The congratulatory greeting no doubt referenced his stolen car recovery so long ago that morning. But Marcus didn't catch his intent at first, and looked back over his shoulder after getting brushed by another cop. He started to thank him, but the cop was out the back door already by then.

Marcus hung a left in the hallway, buried his head and stomped toward the computer room. An email from the Latent Fingerprint Lab was waiting, or so he hoped. It was all he'd thought about on the drive to the station: had they been able to come up with a fingerprint match and, if so, would it be his guy?

Cutting off his train of thought, a booming "Kemp!" chased him down the corridor—the unmistakable voice of his lieutenant.

Marcus grimaced and stopped cold. His face flushed and he stopped breathing. He turned around slowly and stepped into his superior's four-walled closet of an office.

"Yes, sir?" Honestly, it perplexed everyone how the lieutenant even got behind his desk every day.

"Come see me after you're wrapped up," Lt. Berry said without looking at him. He put no inflection on any of the eight syllables.

Marcus took another half step into the office, held on to the door frame with his right hand, while securing his computer under his left arm. A bead of sweat ran down his spine and he felt the path it took in every uncomfortable centimeter until it stopped at the crack of his ass.

"I have the time now," Marcus said.

Lieutenant Berry, a fellow black officer, had responded to Marcus' suspected homicide that morning. Though he carried himself with a commanding presence, he was still one of the most approachable authority figures Marcus had encountered.

"No," he said gruffly, without breaking from his work. "Finish up. Then come see me."

Marcus gulped and his orifices constricted. He retreated out of the office with a "Yes, sir."

Continuing down the hallway, he needed to put up his patrol computer before going to the report room. Black-streaked scuffs lined the baseboards from where officers kicked the walls either in a rush to get out on their beats or out of frustration with a bad day on their return.

Marcus dropped off the computer in the tech room and skipped across the hall into a room with a double row of computers set back-to-back. Like all station's rooms, it was a tight squeeze, especially if you wanted to get to the back row on the side of the room facing the door as Marcus was intent on. There, he could check his email and prevent anyone from looking at what he was doing.

He only had one report to fill out: The meth couple. But when logging on to the computer, his focus was entirely on checking his email. His pulse quickened. There, in the inbox, was the email from the fingerprint lab. The subject line, "Fingerprint Analysis: 1 Positive Match Found," sent a wave of excitement through his chest. Marcus popped his head above the monitors to make sure no one was at the door or watching him in some other way.

Blowing out a long breath, he shook his hands like he was flinging off mud. When he opened the email, his eyes skipped from sentence to sentence, absorbing the general gist but focused on finding the payoff. There, two paragraphs down, his eyes glued to the name of his man.

Caleb Brighton.

Attached to the email was a file containing his records.

Marcus blew out another deep breath and looked up to scan the dark report room once more. He was still the only cop in the room, but not for long with the shift change in progress.

He opened the attachment and hit print. The laser printer, propped on a short, rusted filing cabinet in the corner of the room to his left, whirred to life.

He deleted the email from the lab, deleted it again from his email's trash can in a fit of paranoia, closed out his email and jumped up to retrieve the print outs.

"Come on. Come oooooonnn," he begged the printer, standing over it with clenched teeth, his fingers positioned ready to snatch the job from the tray.

By that point, he had forgotten all about the arrest report he was required to file. Once the three pages printed out, he grabbed them, folded them sloppily in half together and took off out of the room.

"Whoa, man!" McKenzie hollered. Marcus nearly drove his buried head into his friend's chin, the two meeting at the door.

"Sorry," Marcus said. He stuffed the folded pages into his back pocket. McKenzie said something else but Marcus didn't catch it, as he was already down the hall and headed for the lockers by then.

"Caleb Brighton," he said to himself, closing his locker after pulling out his gym bag, stuffing the report in and throwing the bag back inside the locker.

The name echoed in his head while he showered in a rush, wanting to believe he had his man. He just wanted to get back to his locker to confirm it. But his conscience berated him to slow down, to quit while he was ahead. Yet another part of him pressed to keep going. See it through. Why run the prints if you're going to give up now?

Then, paranoia chimed in. What if his lieutenant was on to him? But how? He must know something if he wants to talk to him. Boss was looking for him as he was breaking a dozen different policies, after all.

He washed briskly. Water flew off his half-soaped body and sprayed the checkered-tile walls of the open shower stall.

Wearing a ratty, once-blue towel tied around his waist, Marcus sat on the wooden-slatted bench in front of his open locker and held Caleb's reports. Wet spots spread on the pages. Realizing he hadn't dried himself off yet, he dropped the papers into his lap and wiped his wet hands and forearms on the towel around his legs.

Lockers began to rattle as more cops entered the room. Marcus jumped with the noise. He whipped his head from side to side like a seagull quick to a handout to make sure he wasn't being watched.

Marcus caught a whiff of locker room mildew, felt the drops falling off his body and recoiled. The locker and shower area smelled the same as it always had, but the sour odor took on a familiar offense, as if the molecules had been weaponized and fired directly into his nasal passages.

"God." He groaned, pinched his nose closed after snorting, hoping to expel the smell and the memories it seemed to carry.

Marcus looked down at the pages again and the feeling faded the more he focused. Flipping through the report, he scanned it more thoroughly than his previous rushed glance. A white, twenty-eight-year-old former Army veteran, Caleb had been honorably discharged four years earlier. Marcus' pulse quickened. Right age. Check. The photo of Caleb was a headshot from his service days. He was wearing fatigues and a matching green camouflage hat that flattened the top of his floppy ears at a 45-degree angle.

Instead of water from the shower, beads of sweat now trickled down Marcus' temples and along the side of his face, which he wiped away with a brush of his shoulders.

Garland. The city might as well have been bolded, underlined and highlighted with the most neon yellow ever. Garland was Caleb's last known address, and it was current, the report stated.

Though not Plano, where Bill worked and Marcus grew up, it was a neighboring city.

"Fuck yes!" Marcus growled, muffling the word by shouting it into his chest. He pumped his left fist. The energy built and the fist flew out stiffly in front of him as if suddenly possessed, and punched the flimsy turquoise door of his locker shut.

He had his man and his imagination threw him forward in time to meeting and thanking him. When, was still a question, but it would have to be soon. He wasn't completely confident Caleb could get away with Bill's murder yet, even with his intervention thus far. Marcus had no idea how Homicide was faring in their investigation, so he needed to get to Caleb before they did and help him get away.

But first, his lieutenant was waiting for him.

AFTER CHANGING AND gathering his things, Marcus stood in the door frame of his superior's office, a black gym bag slung over one shoulder. Dressed in thick, heather gray sweatpants and a navy blue, Nike dri-fit T-shirt, Marcus felt small as he waited for a response.

"Sit down. Close the door," the lieutenant said. His voice was smooth, carried in a deep register. Marcus followed instruction, sitting in one of two fabric-padded chairs across from his boss, the one closest to the door.

"Why did you want to see me—"

"Let me get right to the point, Kemp," he said. "I pulled your GPS when you didn't answer me earlier. And you were way over in Downtown. You care to explain that?"

The words stunned Marcus. He just sat there for a few seconds not reacting, the look on his face pained, as if a brick had just landed square on his face from four stories above.

"HR. I went to HR," he said.

"Look. I like you, Marcus. You know that," the lieutenant began. "But you went AWOL from your beat today for over an hour and—"

"And it won't happen again, sir, I…"

Marcus couldn't look the lieutenant in the eyes. He looked past him instead. He knew anything he added in his defense would be another lie—a strategic move—but dishonest still the same. His look glazed over, on to a framed poster of an Ansel Adams photograph of Yosemite behind his lieutenant's head. Marcus imagined he had inherited it with the office, but maybe he had an affinity for such things as black and white nature photography.

"Normally, I would let you off with a warning. But you know there's a mandate to stop this beat covering shit," Berry said. "We're going to have to look into it, open an investigation. If you were at HR, then it will be dropped."

Marcus looked at him, felt defiance growing inside of him. While he should have stayed calm, sat there and let it play out, his pride pushed an excuse to his lips he thought sounded plausible and reasonable.

"But, this is the first time I've ever gone AWOL and it just slipped my mind to tell you I needed to go by HR."

"Yes, well." Lieutenant Berry looked down at his desk and the wrinkles in the corners of his eyes thickened. "I also heard the call this morning might have shaken you and with what your mother just went through... Maybe it's a good thing you have the next two days off. You can get your mind straight and we can clear all this up."

"Who told you I got shook?" Marcus shouted. "McKenzie?"

"That's not important right now." Berry held up his palms to Marcus. After glaring at him with a raised eyebrow for a couple of seconds, the lieutenant straightened in his seat.

A simmering defiance danced under Marcus' skin. But he had no right to be defensive. With his two off days, Marcus had the time to follow-up on Caleb and put a bow on the day's twists and turns. This wasn't lost on him in the moment, but his bruised pride continued to egg him on.

"I don't get this, SIR," he said.

"Watch it!" the lieutenant shot back.

The phrase hit Marcus square in the jaw and it curled his lip. The warning rang in his ears as a threat, so similar to something his father would have said to him when he was a child.

Watch it.

The words Terry used to taunt his mother right before he would beat her.

"I'm just looking out for you here," the lieutenant added.

"Fuck you are!" Marcus instantly cringed at the sound of the words after they jettisoned his lips. He wanted to dive to catch them by the ankles and wrestle the three syllables back into his mouth. But it was done, and they served a purpose.

"Get out of my office!"

Marcus sank in the seat and then a room-shaking, "Get out!" from Lt. Berry made him jolt, jump up and run out of the station. Marcus stormed out of the back door, the metal-framed glass door shaking like Jell-O when he slammed it closed.

Feeling angry and disappointed with himself, he flung his gym bag to the ground and pulled out his phone, standing in the now-quiet parking lot.

He scrolled through his contacts and called an old friend, who answered after two rings.

"Marcus?"

"Hey, Brian. My man." Marcus tried to sound upbeat.

"What's up? I'm about to take off so…"

"Yeah, that's why I'm calling," Marcus said. "I need to catch a ride, to Dallas. Was hoping you could hook me up?"

There was a pause, then Brian said, "Uh, sure. Are you ok?"

"Yeah, why?" Marcus asked.

"You just sound, I don't know. Your voice is shaky."

"Can you fly me today?" Marcus asked, ignoring his friend's concern.

"Man. Today might be tough. But, I mean, if you're in a bind, I could fly you there overnight." His voice sounded sincere.

"That would be perfect," Marcus said. "I can pay you for the fuel."

Brian laughed. "You'll have to."

"No doubt. I, uh, hey. Can you hang on a second, Brian? I'm getting another call."

Marcus looked at his phone and the caller ID said, "Estrella Estates," his mother's assisted living facility.

"I gotta go anyway, Marcus. Just be at Montgomery at midnight."

"Cool man. I owe you!" Marcus said.

Switching lines, he answered the incoming call.

"This is Marcus. Ok. Wait. When? Shit. Ok, I'll be right there."

Marcus hung up the phone, grabbed up his gym bag by one strap and sprinted to his car parked at the far south end of the fenced lot.

His mother had just been admitted into hospice care.

12
STACEY KEMP

MARCUS STOOD IN the hallway outside the hospice care room where Stacey Kemp now slept. His attention shifted between looking in at her through the long sliver of glass inset in the white door and the conversation the hospice doctor attempted to have with him.

The doctor placed a hand on his shoulder in an attempt to corral his focus.

"Do you understand, Mr. Kemp?" she asked. Her brown eyes flickered.

Two female nurses in taupe scrubs sat with their heads cocked to the side behind her at the nurses' station, trying not let their eavesdropping look obvious. Their heads poking around the sides of their computer monitors.

Marcus blinked and looked at the doctor. She looked like a nice person. Her kind face calmed him. Of Indian descent, she had a thick head of hair which flowed over her ears. She kept it out of her eyes with bobby pins and silver metal, comb-wired barrettes, but she still brushed strangling strands aside every few seconds it seemed.

"Uh, yes," he fibbed.

His mother looked surprisingly comfortable in the bed. Resting on her back with her hands folded on her chest over the sheets, and a pleasant smile on her face. Not at all the way he slept: arms flailed, tongue hanging out and drool.

Marcus assumed the doctor had just informed him that his mother's body was shutting down, more or less, and her immune system hadn't responded like her PCP and oncologist had hoped it might. The only course now was to keep her pain to a minimum.

His throat was parched and felt like one side was sticking to the other. His words struggled to shimmy their way out and warbled doing so.

"How, how long does she have?"

The doctor took her hand off Marcus and her face dropped. She clutched the tablet she was carrying against her body.

"I can't answer that with any level of certitude," she said.

"I'm not going to hold it against you," Marcus mumbled, turning his head to his sleeping mother and then back at the doctor. "But we—I—need to know."

The doctor stared with glassy eyes past him down the hall. It took so long for her to respond that Marcus opened his mouth to repeat what he had just said in case she didn't hear him. He swallowed a gulp of air instead when she spoke up.

"A week, maybe three or four?" she said, her eyes now sharp and looking into his. "It all depends on Stacey. She's not eating right now, and we don't want to force her to, but if she does start eating again, she could make it a few more months." Her words trailed off and there was another long pause before she said, "But she *is* going to pass."

Marcus sighed and dropped his head. "Yeah, I know." He focused on the taut, brown Berber carpet of the hallway's floor.

"I don't want to leave you with an impression that's contrary to the truth," she added and again put her hand on his arm.

"Thank you," he said and motioned toward his mother's room, taking hold of the door handle.

QUIETLY LETTING HIMSELF into the room, Marcus sat in a chair at the side of the bed. It creaked under his weight. He grasped the bare wood armrests and squeezed, hoping to muffle any additional noise settling into place would make. The chair, it seemed, looked like it belonged in an old downtown library with dark, paneled walls and equally squeaky wooden floors.

Leaning back, he tucked his chin. The private room was quiet. His eyes drifted.

The bathroom was off the entrance to the room; a flat-screen television hung on the wall next to it, above a long, mahogany dresser with brass pull knobs. Set on top of the dresser was a live white orchid in a white ceramic vase with holes from which dried moss squeezed out.

A bank of windows ran the length of the far wall, covered with a heavy shade. When pulled open, the second-floor view looked west along the treetops of the surrounding central San Diego neighborhood. Too bad the Jacaranda trees were finished blooming, he thought. She would have appreciated the show of purple.

Traditional nightstands matching the dresser flanked the bed. A framed photo of a grassy meadow scene hung on the hay-colored wall above the bed. The room had a cozy feel, he summed up, approving.

Marcus looked at his mother again. They'd anticipated this eventuality. They had planned for it, in fact. None of this would be a surprise to her when she woke up. After her initial diagnosis, Stacey outlined an advanced care directive with her doctor. She and Marcus toured and selected an assisted living facility to move her into during treatments because she was adamant about not wanting her son to care for her. She didn't want him to see her at her worst: the vomiting, the frequent bathroom trips, and god help her, she would never make him bathe her.

Stacey wanted Marcus to remain her son, not become her caregiver and, though he was willing to do it all, he respected his mother's wishes. But Marcus felt a pressure building in his chest all the same. Guilt gurgling up like heartburn. Why hadn't he called her that morning? He squeezed the armrests tighter. The one day he hadn't in weeks. No, in two months! And it's the day she's admitted to hospice.

He knew she'd had an appointment for her doctor to visit that day to go over her latest test results and he had let it slip his mind. Bill's dead body had distracted him and thrown him off-kilter, sure, but that wasn't the reason. No, of course not. Marcus had blocked the appointment from his mind to avoid pain. As a way to distance himself from the likely negative news she would receive.

Moaning a pathetic sigh, he rolled his eyes. Regret pressed on him hard. He interlocked his fingers in his lap, squeezed as hard as he could and tilted his head to the ceiling. He tried to distract himself by forming images out of the texture of the popcorn. Instead, the ceiling blurred with the tears that puddled in his eyes. The salty tears stung, but he allowed the discomfort until they streamed from his eyes.

Marcus began to bargain with the universe. If God, Buddha, the Scientology wizard, Satan, or any other deity appeared and offered to save his mother's life right then, he would do anything to make it happen. He didn't believe in a higher power, but if doing so was a prerequisite to a life-saving intervention, he would have summoned the faith of a hundred radicals to heal his mother.

Marcus was sure the thought wasn't original, but his sadness didn't afford him the luxury of logical thought in the moment. The tears continued to pour down his face. He ground his teeth.

Hell, if it meant his mother would live, he would give up on this stupid undertaking. Even though he was a day, maybe two, away from being able to bury all his freshly-realized—

The thought stopped cold. His mind wouldn't complete the trade scenario. A rush of panic made him wonder why not. But he knew.

Trying to keep from making anymore sound, he bit his lip.

But Stacey stirred anyway, blinked awake and started to sit up.

The rustling of the sheets caught Marcus by surprise and he looked away sharply. He wiped his tears with his shirt before attempting to look at her.

"What's the matter, baby?" she said.

With a gulp, he looked up at her and gave her a failed smile. "There she is," he said.

Stacey sat up completely and pursed her lips.

"Well, how is Megan?" she asked.

Marcus shrugged. They had already discussed the status of the most recent break-up a few days earlier.

"Have you even called her, Marcus?"

"Called?" he said, smirking.

"You kids," she said, waving her hands. "A woman still wants to be called, not sent a text."

Marcus sighed. "Yeah."

"You know," she said. "I've been thinking—"

"Oh, boy," Marcus said. He straightened up in his chair and rubbed the side of his face.

Stacey ignored the interruption and continued. "I think your issue with women is a lack of trust. Not a fear of commitment."

Marcus sneered. "What's the difference?"

"And I think—no—I'm sure I'm to blame," she added.

Marcus rolled his eyes and glared at her. She stared past him; her own eyes unfocused.

"Back when I was preparing to move us out here and leave your father," she said, pausing to bite down on her lower lip. "The signs were there. You were in pain. I see that now."

"What... are you talking about?" Marcus said, his words slow and hesitant.

"You were so closed off. It's like you shut down. You didn't hang out with your friends, your schoolwork suffered..."

Marcus squeezed the armrests and he winced.

"I should have known," she said, trailing off.

A blood vessel under his left eye began to pulse. He leaned his left elbow on the armrest to cover the nerve with a finger. Marcus avoided eye-contact with Stacey whose face was still glazed over as though meditating.

"You must have lost ten pounds between the start of school and November."

The nerve would not stop pulsing. It throbbed and thickened and no amount of pressure he put on it helped. He pulled up on the corner of his eye and got the same result.

His ears were suddenly burning as well, yet his hands were clammy and cold. Stars appeared in his eyes when he shut them, whole galaxies hurling their planets through his swirling, black field of vision. His brain might explode if she spoke the shame of his past aloud.

Stacey took a breath and blurted out, "I ripped you away from your father and his family and you must have sensed it the whole time."

Her lower lip quivered. Her face flushed and her eyes were now the ones dodging contact with his.

"How could you be expected to trust anyone after that?"

She dropped her head and cried.

Marcus sat stunned. Maybe she was right. Not about him sensing the move, but the trust thing. The premise rang true.

He wanted to cry, 'No! You have it all wrong. It wasn't you! If I don't trust people it's because the father figure I respected more than my biological one betrayed my trust and molested me. Repeatedly. That's why I was a moody little shit for three months. I stopped hanging out with my friends because they would know I wasn't the same. They had already sensed it over the summer. And I didn't say anything because you didn't need any more pain in your life.'

The truth he just discovered poured from his heart but didn't escape his lips.

"You were so quiet on our drive to California, too," she said, through sniffs.

He knew he needed to say something to put a stop to this so she would stop blaming herself. He felt stabs to his chest, watching her dab her eyes with a tissue.

"Mom, listen to me."

She whimpered and looked at him with big cartoon-like sad eyes.

He arched one eyebrow and looked her in the eye.

"You did not ruin my sense of trust. You had to do what you had to do and I'm grateful every day that you took us out of that situation."

After a long pause, she looked up and said, "Really?"

"Yes." Marcus cleared his throat.

"You know I heard—" Marcus paused, not sure if he should complete the thought, but did. "Uh. I heard, every time he hit you..."

Stacey's head dropped again and her eyes fell to her lap.

He leaned forward and rubbed her upper back the way she used to do for him when he was young. Marcus cleared his throat again.

"Let's talk about happier things. Okay?"

"Okay," she answered.

Her eyes blinked and her face brightened.

"Remember the day we were walking on the beach, and—"

"There's been a lot of those," Marcus joked.

"Let me finish," she said, and swatted at the air.

He snickered and held his hands up as if at gunpoint and said, "Sorry, sorry!"

"It was the first time we saw *Valella valella* on La Jolla Shores," she said. "Remember?"

Marcus smiled.

The electric blue, jellyfish-like creatures were fascinating, like real-life aliens. Their deep royal and navy gelatin bodies glowed like sapphire jewels on that sunny day. Marcus was twelve and he and every other kid on the beach, and several adults as well, poked and prodded the odd visitors for signs of life.

Some of the more daring of the group—which included Marcus—picked the squishy *Valella valella* up. Giggles and shrieks pierced through the methodic waves. Smiling from ear to ear, Marcus cradled a perfect jiggling specimen in his open palm, and then, like serving fancy hors d'oeuvres at a cocktail party, twisted his lanky arm and held it up to his mother. She beamed back at him.

Lying in the hospice bed, Stacey looked much the same to Marcus as she had on *Valella valella* day. Her still-vibrant appearance complicated his acceptance with her diagnosis. Sure, streaks of gray now ran through her hair and the subsequent years were scripted in the prominent wrinkles around her eyes. But the symptoms made her disease known almost two years prior, she had been as active to that point as she had ever been;

much more than he remembered when they lived in Texas. Thinking through how to tell his mother he was going to Texas, her relatively healthy look was making it easier for him to rationalize the decision to himself.

Tears welled in Stacey's eyes again.

"I just remember watching you run around picking those funny things up, thinking how much I dreamed of sharing exactly that kind of experience with you back when I was trapped in our old apartment," she said.

Marcus offered his hand and she grasped it between hers.

"I got everything I ever dreamed," she whispered between sniffs. She leaned into his face.

"I know, Mom," Marcus whispered back through trembling lips.

They stared at each other for a few seconds and then Marcus cradled her head. He rested it against his where they remained until a knock at the door interrupted the moment. A nurse walked in.

"Are you all right in here," asked a middle-aged Filipino woman in brown scrubs.

"Yes, thank you," Stacey answered and then yawned.

"Ok. I need to check your vitals," the nurse replied to Stacey but stared at Marcus. She then nodded with a motion toward the door.

Marcus fidgeted but didn't budge.

"Oh, he's fine," Stacey said and waved to the nurse.

"No, it's ok," Marcus said, relenting. "I need to stretch my legs anyway."

He gave Stacey a peck on the forehead and walked out of the room. Once in the hallway, he rubbed his eyes and stretched before burying his hands into the pockets of his sweatpants and trudging down the hall.

A young nurse came toward him from around the corner, and with the two closing the distance between them to within a few feet, the brunette gave Marcus a big smile. Distracted, he didn't react quickly enough to return the smile. He didn't realize she had just flirted with him until he heard the chunk of a door latching opening. He looked back to catch a glimpse of her ample backside disappearing into a patient's room. A light fragrance of cinnamon wafted down the hall and into his nose then.

Marcus smiled, dropped his head and rounded the corner.

The three floors of the hospice care facility were configured on a square footprint with patient rooms along the perimeter and offices and nurses' stations in the middle. It's track-like layout made for a perfect alternative to pacing. It also made it so every patient received natural light in their room and administrative work stayed hidden.

Murmurs from a patient room caught Marcus' attention. He took note of a pine cone wreath hanging on the door, adorned with seashells, pieces of driftwood and white, plaster seahorses. The touch of warmth made him feel good about the place. He turned his gaze back to the hallway and stared down at the tightly-woven carpet.

His attention followed the yellow fibers running vertically in the carpet along the borders, about a foot out from the walls.

"How do I do this?" Marcus heard his mother's voice telling him stop mumbling.

The lines in the carpet tripled, his vision crossed on them. He stopped and shook his head and looked up. The hall felt desolate now.

On the next patient door, a string of homemade, fringed purple garland bordered the frame, making it look as if you were about to enter a birthday party.

Searching his pocket for his phone, Marcus realized he must have left it in his mother's room. He wondered if Megan had responded to his last text, even though he didn't expect she would. Had she even checked it? The thought occurred to him that he might receive a "Who is this?" text in response if she decided to delete his contact from her phone. His ears burned with the thought.

The anger didn't last long, though. Instead, guilt still lingered about missing his mother's doctor's appointment. That same guilt was now working him over about wanting to leave town, and go back to Texas of all places. He would have to tell her, simple as that. There was no way around it. Hopefully, he would be back well in advance of her, of her— Marcus couldn't, didn't want to go there.

It had been a while since he had moped; maybe he was a teenager the last time? He couldn't be sure. With each step, Marcus kicked his feet out in front of himself in an exaggerated fashion and sighed.

After making three laps of the floor, he approached his mother's room. Walking past it for the third time, he peeked through the glass to see the nurse sat on the bed next to Stacey. What was that about?

He decided he would do another slow lap and then if she was still in the room, he would investigate. The nerve under his eye still pulsed; slower than before but still as annoying as a persistent case of hiccups. He was sure it would keep up for hours.

"Ow!" a soft voice cried out.

He had bulldozed right into the brunette nurse leaving the patient room he'd watch her go into earlier.

"Oh, ow. Sorry!" Marcus covered his mouth with one hand and held his forehead with his other.

His head had knocked into her right shoulder.

"Really, I'm so sorry," Marcus said, too impatient for a response to his first apology.

"It's… it's ok," she said. The nurse rubbed her shoulder. She then looked up at him and her face brightened.

Her smile hit something in him and a chill went through his body. She reached up and rubbed Marcus' forehead, pushing his hand aside, which only intensified the tingle.

"How did you hit your head on my shoulder from all the way up there," she asked, giggling.

"I obviously wasn't paying attention."

She crossed her arms, faking like she was mad and said, "Watch yourself next time," and smirked. She brushed past him and winked. Walked into the admin offices.

Marcus stood there with a sheepish grin and imagined the nurse instead taking him with her to a small break room around the corner for coffee.

There, in a standing room only-sized space with a refrigerator butted up to a metal sink set. He stood behind the nurse, tracing the curves of her body with his eyes while she took down two ceramic mugs from the cabinet. Her hair bounced right above her low back. The cramped break room squeezed in on the pair and Marcus felt his body being slowly pulled toward hers. He moaned when she sat back snug against his lap.

"Should I forget about the coffee?" She couldn't have been more suggestive. Confident, she looked at him over her shoulder. The amber flecks in her irises fired at him like a muzzle blast.

Marcus licked his lower lip, locked into the fantasy.

He hugged her waist with his right arm. Pulled her tight to his body. She looked up at his face and the smell of cinnamon sent a chill down his spine. A tingle danced over his skin.

He caressed the side of her neck and she cooed. Their eyes closed simultaneously and they kissed. And kept kissing until the nurse pulled away only to gasp for air. After she cupped the front of his sweatpants, Marcus looked back at the closed solid door to the break room. The nurse grabbed his chin and turned his face to hers and kissed him.

Marcus squeezed her ass with both hands and pulled her in and then spun her around. She leaned over and held on to the countertop.

"I want you," she said, panting heavily.

The nurse's breathing deepened with each of their movements. He felt his heart beating almost as fast as it had when he discovered Bill's body. He sneered and recoiled at the comparison and refocused on the nurse. She moaned and bit her lip to quiet herself. Marcus pressed his chest on her back and rested his face on her shoulder. Her spicy fragrance rolled his eyes to the back of his head and he snapped out of the daydream.

What the fuck? Hadn't he done enough dumb shit for one day? Entertaining the fantasy shook him. Did his sudden thirst for self-destruction know no bounds?

WHEN HE RETURNED to his mother's room, he was relieved to find Stacey had already fallen asleep. Marcus soon followed.

He woke up an hour later, his head humming with regret. It also throbbed. A crick had formed in his neck from sleeping with his head flopped over the top of the chair's hard back support. He wiped away a crust of dried saliva from one corner of his mouth and tried to focus his eyes.

"I've been thinking about what you should say to Megan." The soft, yet alert voice of his mother.

Marcus groaned.

"Not this again."

"I'm sorry," she said.

"What?" he asked.

"You should say you're sorry," Stacey said.

Marcus rubbed his eyes and blurted out, "You don't think I've said tried that?"

Stacey sat still and didn't acknowledge him.

"Geez. I mean, enough!"

With this comment, his mother gave him a look that said, "Excuse me?" and he slunk.

"I really like her, Marcus."

Marcus stood up and pushed the chair away from himself with the back of his legs.

"Mom. Can we talk about this later? I have to tell you something that's a little more important right now. Okay?"

Stacey straightened up but didn't appear offended, seeing the pained urgency on her son's face.

"What is it?" she asked.

Clenching his eyes shut, he said, "I made plans to go to Texas for, for, um, for a thing." He rubbed the side of his face, his day-old stubble scratching with each stroke.

"Are you going to see your father?" Stacey asked, with a look on her face like a child opening a gift at Christmas.

"What? Nooo," he answered. Her question made him open his eyes and look at her and stop rubbing his face.

"Mom. I need to… I need to look into something."

She blinked at him.

"I can't say what it is."

Stacey smiled, but still said nothing.

"What?" he asked, confused.

"You don't need my permission, Marcus," she said, still smiling.

"Uh, yeah, I kinda do," he said, motioning with both his hands along her bed, displaying what he thought was obvious.

"Where in Texas are you going and for how long?" Stacey asked.

Marcus huffed. "Plano."

"Mmm. And for how long?"

"I'm hoping just for a couple of days." He dropped his head.

The silence lasted an agonizing eternity. Marcus kept his eyes fixed on his shoes. When he looked up, and to his surprise, his mother's eyes waited, gleaming with approval.

"I just…" The thought stuck in the back of his throat.

"Honey," Stacey said. "I'll still be here when you get back."

Marcus winced and looked away toward the bathroom.

Raising his head to look back up at her, he said, "I know you don't have an appetite, but try to eat something while I'm gone."

Her soft eyes stared into his sunken eyes and said, "Ok, but go see your father while you're there. Deal?"

13
NIGHT FLIGHT TO TEXAS

MARCUS SANK INTO the spongy leather seat, its cream hide cradling his posterior and core in luxury. The smell of rawhide, recycled air and the slight hint of fruit hung in the air; hisses and pops came from outside.

Five of the six executive seats in the Cessna Citation CJ4 private jet were vacant. Marcus would be the only passenger on this flight. With his back to the cockpit, he stared ahead at the opulent cabin trimmed in high gloss cherry wood and gold plating before him, nicer than he'd ever seen in any car, let alone an airplane.

Marcus squirmed. Each leather seat was adorned with a vibrant blue throw pillow and matching tasseled fleece throw— both in the brand color of the plane owner's technology company—with accompanying white Bose noise-canceling headphones resting on the armrests. He looked over at the polished wood console to his right and cocked his head, unsure what to make of the multiple inset metal rings. "Ah," he said, figuring they must be to secure champagne flutes mid-flight.

Textured fabric covered the non-wood portions of the consoles and looked as high in quality as any Persian rug he could imagine. Each Lazy Boy-like chair had ample legroom and was spaced so far apart in comparison to a commercial plane, it seemed it would take only a passenger of Marcus' size to touch a neighbor.

From outside came the sounds of metal buckles or latches being secured and he figured it was a mechanic, doing final checks in preparation of their departure. His friend, Brian

Wiggins, would pilot the flight and he had sent Marcus inside while he "zipped this baby up," as he put it.

Turning his attention to the black gym bag on his lap, Marcus unzipped it. "Ok," he said under his breath. He'd finished packing it a few hours earlier and knew everything he'd placed inside, but checked it again anyway.

He packed several sets of athletic sweatpants and Dri-Fit t-shirts first and then thought better, remembering how hot it might already be in Texas. A check of a weather app confirmed his hunch: no day below eighty-eight degrees on the seven-day forecast. Out went the sweatpants. In their place, he threw in a couple of pairs of Volcom shorts. Next, he added socks, an extra pair of shoes—black low-top Converse—boxers and a Dopp kit containing lotion, deodorant and other toiletries. A packing minimalist regardless of the destination, Marcus stood over the bag on his bed humming with his hands on his hips, contemplating what else he might need. He snapped his fingers.

Shuffling to the kitchen, he returned with three pop-top cans of tuna, a huge bag of peppered elk jerky he bought at a recent Ocean Beach street fair and a jar of unsweetened almond butter and tossed them all in the bag.

Then, he pulled down a slim, powder-coated, steel case from a closet shelf and dropped it on the bed next to the gym bag. The case had weight. It bounced on the mattress. A green square illuminated around his pressed thumb and the lid to the biometric gun safe sprang open after a click and a chunk.

Marcus pulled out one of the two spooning handguns inside, a Sig Sauer P229 Select Compact, checked the magazine and grabbed another loaded one. He walked to his nightstand and took out a holster for the gun from the top drawer, pushed the weapon into the leather and dropped it on top of the clothes in the bag. After stuffing a headlamp, batteries, a multitool and the first aid kit he used for hiking trips into the bag, he zipped it up.

On the plane, Marcus stared down at the 9mm handgun and reassured himself for bringing it, even if his intention for the trip was all talk, no action. He zipped up the bag and dropped it between his feet.

"Ready to go?" a voice behind him asked.

Jumping to his feet, Marcus spun around and saw his friend standing inside at the door of the jet. Brian motioned to someone outside and the hydraulic stairs folded up on itself and the plane's door was sealed closed with a chunk from outside.

"Man. Thank you again," Marcus said, extending his fist. Brian knuckled it.

"No problem, man. Missed you and Megan last week at the party." Brian referred to the unicorn-themed birthday bash at Fiesta Island he and his wife threw for their youngest daughter, Emma, who turned five-years-old.

"Ah, shit. You know I would have been there, but I had OT," Marcus said.

Brian took a second to respond, appearing to judge the excuse.

"We missed you all the same. The girls love you, but you know that."

"Yessir," Marcus said as one syllable in a slurry drawl, playing up his Texas heritage.

On one of the first days he hung out with his new California friends after school, Marcus referred to the preteens as "ya'll" and they couldn't believe their cool biracial friend was actually from the dirt-kicking, horse-riding, cowboy hat-wearing, great state of Texas. Then—starting with Brian— they all tried their best attempts at twangy Texas accents to poke fun at Marcus. All these years later, the friends who kept in touch from those days liked to remind him of his roots.

Brian shouted, "Ha! Damn straight!" He kicked out a heel and swung an arm in his best Cotton Eyed Joe dance step.

"You sure it's cool?" Marcus asked.

"It's all good, man," Brian said, putting a hand on Marcus's shoulder. "Not like I have anywhere to be for the next six or seven hours."

"Well, you were the one who suggested midnight," Marcus said.

Brian took off his white pilot cap and ran his hand through his floppy, dirty blonde hair.

"Got me there!" he shouted and then laughed.

Marcus didn't have to ask how Brian was able to accommodate his last-minute request. After flying F-16 fighter jets on three tours in Afghanistan, Brian was heavily recruited upon his discharge from the Air Force. He had offers from every legacy airline and multiple Fortune 500-type companies across the United States. One allowance of the generous benefits package provided by the company he'd selected allowed him to fly any of the company's three jets wherever, whenever with whoever. As long as it didn't conflict with the needs of the executives. Keeping his family in San Diego was the clincher in going with the company he did, but Brian took advantage of the perk. In the year-and-a-half with the tech giant, Brian had taken his small family on quick trips to the Bay Area, Seattle and Vancouver, and vacations to Mexico and Alaska.

Placing his hand back on Marcus, Brian's face got serious.

"Is everything all right?" he asked.

"Yeah," Marcus started, thinking about making something up to cover his tracks before realizing the truth would more than suffice. "It's, it's my mom. She doesn't have long."

Brian's face fell. "Oh, Marcus. So the surgery wasn't successful?"

Marcus shook his head.

After pausing for a few seconds, he went on but felt the need to bend the truth now to his good friend.

"I promised her I would get back to Dallas and track down my father so he would know."

"Yeah," Brian said, his arms now on his hips. "Man. That's, that's a tough thing. Poor Misses Kemp."

Marcus didn't say anything but noticed the nerve under his eye flinched for the first time since being back at the hospice facility.

"When you get back, I want to go by and see her. You have my word, man."

"She would love that," Marcus said.

Brian pulled Marcus in by the shoulder and gave him a bear hug that lasted a few seconds. Hard back slaps broke up the affection.

"What do you say we get this baby airborne?" Brian announced, giving Marcus an elbow jab.

"Yeah, man. Hey, you need me up there, or?" Marcus said, shifting his eyes and pointing at the cockpit.

"No, no, no!" Brian bellowed. "You ride here in comfort and class." He shot his face to the ceiling and extended an arm. "Enjoy the luxury only afforded to the one percent!"

Marcus covered his mouth to stifle laughter.

"Seriously," Brian said. "I have Jack Daniels to keep me company—kidding! Really, settle in and enjoy, my friend. Or get some sleep. You look like you need it."

"Thanks, man," Marcus said and chuckled.

Hell of a friend, that Brian. Marcus watched him step into the cockpit. Brian didn't know the full extent of his generosity, of course, but that in no way minimized the appreciation Marcus felt for him in the pit of his stomach.

Sleep. Brian mentioned sleep and that sounded good to Marcus. His body ached now that the adrenaline he'd mainlined for much of the day had worn off. But his mind was still on overdrive.

His thoughts were not with his mother or Megan, however. And they should have been on Caleb. Instead, his mind was fixed on his fucking father. Marcus plopped back down into the leather executive chair.

Latching the cross-body seat belt forcibly he began to seethe, reminded of his mother's last words to him, which had partly scripted the untruthful part of his story to Brian.

Go see your father, meaning, of course, to reconcile with your father. What if those were her last, *last* words?

Truth was, they weren't her last words to Marcus, since he stayed with her for another hour after he ran to her assisted living facility and brought back some of her personal things. But the words stuck out as her last to him anyway.

"Goddamn it." He felt upset with her and pissed at himself because of it.

The engines revved and seconds later the jet rolled forward. Marcus heard chatter he didn't understand from the cockpit. They took a right turn and came to a stop. Marcus looked around the cabin, expecting the lights to dim while they sat waiting to take off, but they remained at the same level. Then, the jet lurched forward and picked up speed, fast.

Startled, Marcus jerked and squeezed on to the armrests, knocking the Bose headphones off the armrest and into his lap. Within less than ten seconds, the Cessna was airborne. Instead of experiencing his stomach drop as it always did on commercial flights, the ascent was surprisingly gentle. After banking, he looked out the window to his right and saw sporadic white and amber lights dotting an outline of the neighborhoods between Montgomery-Gibbs Executive Airport and the black ocean, only visible from moonlight. He looked across the aisle through the window to his left and saw neighborhood lights that ran into a wall of darkness; the shadowed, jagged outline of the mountain summits in the east.

"May I have your attention?" Brian's voice came over the PA system as clear as if he was still in the cabin.

Marcus twisted into the aisle to look to the cockpit at his friend in the captain's chair.

"Thank you for flying with us this evening," Brian deadpanned, continuing in an exaggerated pilot impersonation with spot-on pacing and inflection. "This fifty-three-foot, four-inch Cessna Citation CJ4 is the largest, fastest and furthest flying Citation jet in the single-pilot class. As we pilots like to say: "In thrust we trust.""

Marcus smiled and sat back in his seat, leaned his head against the headrest to savor the rest of the monologue.

"Powered by two Williams International turbofan engines, each putting out over 3,000 pounds of thrust, we'll reach a top speed of 450 knots this evening. Or for civilian types, that's 517 miles per. So, sit back and enjoy this quick flight."

Then, changing to a raspy, Texas twang, Brian added, "Yer gonna be in Dallas in less than three hours, partner! Yeeeeee-haw!"

Marcus laughed and clapped his hands above his head.

"A-thank ya," Brian replied over the PA.

Thankful for the moment of levity, Marcus' smile soon faded. He snapped back to memories of his father. He had no intention of honoring his mother's request. Was that shitty? Sure.

There wasn't much he liked about his decision-making this day. It had been one questionable line crossed after another. And though he felt hollower after each indiscretion, as if he was scooping out his insides one shovel full at a time, he also found himself increasingly numb to the feeling.

At any rate, he was not going to look-up his father. That was for damn sure. He was going to Plano for only one reason. He didn't owe his father shit. Besides, Terry had attempted a reunion not too long ago. Right before his mother got sick, actually. And Marcus had told him he didn't want anything to do with him then. Stacey knew about it. Marcus had told her and she seemed accepting of his stance at the time. But why the change? Did she just need to know her son and his father were reconciled before she could leave this world? If that was the case, Marcus could simply just tell her all was right between them and she would never know the difference.

Marcus grimaced at the thought. This seemed a line a bit too perverse to cross, even for this day.

Terry had boldly shown up at the Western Division police station one day, two years ago and attempted conversation with Marcus that had felt more like an ambush.

"How the fuck did you find where I work?" Marcus demanded. His face red, he used his size advantage to pressure his father backwards and out of the lobby.

Once outside, Terry said with upturned palms and a lost child's look on his face, "I need to talk to ya—"

"So, you just flew out here to talk to me after all these years?"

Terry dropped his head and stroked his goatee. It was still full and well-trimmed as it had been in Marcus' youth, but was now mostly gray.

"I just, I just..." Terry fumbled to find the words and Marcus was not intent on waiting around for him to grasp them.

"The only thing I want from you, the only thing I've ever wanted from you, is for you to leave me the hell alone," Marcus said, his voice a snarl.

"But Marcus, I need ta tell you—"

"I have nothing to say to you."

"But I want-ta say—"

Hovering over his father with the body language of a schoolyard bully, Marcus chided Terry.

"Say what? Spit it out then."

Terry sighed. "I'm sorry."

"For what?" Marcus stepped back and crossed his arms.

Terry looked up at his son with eyes turned down at the corners and sighed again.

"Can we talk later?"

"No," Marcus said.

And they didn't. As far as Marcus was concerned, Terry flew back to Dallas and it was the last time he heard from him.

Recalling the memory had the opposite effect on him than it did when it had happened. Instead of getting riled up and the nervous energy keeping him up through the night, the memory affirmed his feelings and wiped him out. His eyes felt brick heavy.

Before he passed out, he decided to give the noise-canceling headphones a try. As soon as he put them on his eyes widened, realizing how loud the cabin actually was in comparison. What had been a smooth flight humming along, he was now transported to the quietest place on earth. He snapped his fingers in front of his face. Nothing. He pulled the round covers from both his ears and static whooshed again. Letting the headphones snap back on to his ears, absolute silence returned. He mouthed, "Crazy" and yawned.

MINUTES LATER, MARCUS told himself he must be asleep because he was floating on a surfboard on the clearest blue ocean he had ever seen. A pier materialized in the far distance to his left, stretching further than he could see. A tangerine sun hung just above the horizon line of saltwater and sky in front of him.

Megan was also there, suddenly appearing just to his left, also sitting on a surfboard. Rays of orange sunlight beamed behind her head and made the blonde highlights in her hair glow. She smiled at him. His chest warmed.

The water bobbed them gently up and down. The waves were picking up, yet were still too small to bother with catching one to surf.

"Whoa! Did you see that?" Marcus shouted and pointed at the horizon.

Megan shook her head.

What he had seen appeared again: A humpback whale breaching the water, rising several stories in the air, but not leaving the ocean entirely. Like a slow-motion train wreck, it crashed back down on its side. Saltwater sprayed in the air and droplets fell like a gentle spring rain on Marcus and Megan, even though the majestic, great beast was miles away from them.

They smiled wide-eyed at each other, taking in the phenomenon. The droplets continued to fall. Marcus and Megan both smiled, their faces pitched to the sky.

Then, another humpback's tail emerged from the quickly darkening water. The white underbelly of its fluke rose and rose and rose from the now solid, black ocean. With the base still at the water's surface, the humpback's fluke took up the entirety of the horizon; each end of the tail stretched to opposite points, the tips not visible. The fluke swelled in size and smothered the sun. The sky went gray.

The fluke remained suspended for minutes on end, and Marcus looked over at Megan with his jaw dropped, but the girl on the surfboard wasn't Megan. Instead, the hospice nurse stared back with an equally-shocked expression.

Confused, Marcus shook his head and turned back to the whale. The sky started to brighten slightly with bits of sunlight escaping from behind the whale. A loud crack broke through the sky, but it wasn't lightning. Marcus realized the whale's fluke was careening toward the surface of the ocean.

"Hold on!" Marcus screamed, reaching out his hand to the nurse, who took it.

The water shook as if they were on land during an earthquake. Their boards wobbled back and forth and even the sky shook somehow. The tail screamed down and Marcus saw its face staring back at him.

It wasn't a whale's face at all.

There was no upside-down whale smile or baleen showing.

It was Bill's face and he was laughing maniacally.

The fluke slammed the now icy waters with a violent impact, sending cascading rows of waves seven stories high toward Marcus and the nurse. Except now, the nurse was gone.

Marcus spun around, dove belly-down on to the surfboard and started paddling his arms with all his might. He felt the waves' energy bearing down on him. Surging under him and raising him up and up and instead of crashing down on him and burying him under the water, it hurtled him into the sandy cliffs stretching over the beach.

When the wave died out, the water returned to a calm lake and cleared to a transparent blue. Marcus woke up on the beach, convinced it had all been a dream. And of course, it had been, but he wasn't awake yet.

His eyes blinked open and Megan, the nurse, Caleb, his mother and Bill all stood around him in a circle, each shaking their heads in disappointment. Then, they disappeared in a puff of vapor, one after the other.

Marcus groaned awake and clumsily pulled the Bose headphones off his ears, dragging them over his face and bumping his nose.

He moaned and blinked his groggy eyes open.

Leaning forward, he rubbed his scratchy face.

"Shiiiiiit."

Marcus wouldn't have been able to tell you the last time he had a dream—or rather, nightmare—with Bill in it. He remembered when they started, certainly, beginning the very night he was first assaulted.

Waking up so many times in a cold sweat is what he remembered more than the substance of the nightmares.

Over the months of the abuse and after, Bill found his way into every possible scenario—good and bad, rational and ridiculous alike—in his dreams. It made it so Marcus never got a break from his abuser, even after the assaults had stopped.

There were several nights, during the time he was being molested, when he would wake up in a panic as if the world was crashing down, the guilt strangling the life from him. On these occasions, he would leap out of bed, his heart racing, and make his way to the hallway to outside his parents' room.

There, he would stand at the closed door for minutes—sometimes hours—working up the courage to take hold of the doorknob, turn it and enter to wake his mom and dad and tell them what Bill was doing to him.

Only once did he even get so far as to wrap his hand around the round, gold knob though. He stood, frozen, too afraid to turn the squeaky thing, knowing if he woke his parents, he would indeed have to spill his secret.

Countless times, he collapsed in the hallway from indecision. Balling, holding his hands over his mouth to stifle the noise. Tears streaming down his face and hands. Snot snorting out of his nose.

After dreaming an especially accurate retelling of Bill's sexual abuse one night, Marcus woke up hot and nauseated. He started down the hallway toward his parents' room but had to veer suddenly to the only bathroom of the small apartment where he purged his guts into the toilet and passed out next to it. Stacey found him a few hours later when she got up to go to the bathroom and put him back in his bed.

The dreams persisted in frequency and intensity. He wouldn't run to his parents—with the desire to at least—every night. But when he did, the fear of what it would mean if his secret was exposed outweighed the certainty of the nightmares continuing.

And so, he paced back and forth from his bed to their bedroom door on those nights and his nerve would ultimately fail him, beaten back by his tormentor's weak threats rooted in his immature mind.

On the plane, Marcus unlatched his belt, stood up and stretched. If he thought hard enough, he could probably have told you when the nightmares of Bill stopped and when he was able to go a full night torture-free. It wasn't too long after they moved to San Diego. After the dreams ceased, the memories began to fade.

The memories of Bill got even fuzzier with each passing year, or more specifically he was realizing, Marcus shoved them down deeper. Obviously, they never disappeared. The memories had just laid dormant, like a ticking time bomb ready to blow.

Swiping the last bit of grogginess from his face with his left hand, Marcus let out a moan. The dream he just had was fresh and although he didn't completely understand its meaning—if it had one—he awoke more defiant and resolute than he had felt all day. It was technically the next day, but all the same.

"Hey, buddy," Brian sang out when he saw Marcus step into the cockpit and sit in the co-pilot's seat.

"Hey, man. Thought you could use some company."

"I won't turn it down."

Marcus looked out ahead to see them ripping through thick billows of clouds that looked like the kind children draw. Even with jumping ahead an hour in time and bearing down on another time zone, the sun was a couple of hours from making an appearance. The sky was a grayish slate color.

"About an hour away," Brian said.

"Cool."

Then Brian asked, "Can I tell you something?"

"Yeah, man."

"I've been up here thinking about your mom."

"Oh yeah?"

"Yeah, I mean. What a lady."

Marcus nodded and looked at his friend.

"I remember this time she picked us up at the Gliderport," Brian started. Marcus closed one eye and the eyebrow over the other raised. "We were throwing all our junk into the back of the car and getting sand everywhere. I mean, it was a real snowstorm. At least that's how I remember it. Anyway, I remember getting nervous about what she would say, because, ya know, my old man killed us for tracking sand in his cars, and that really stuck with me, ya know?"

"For sure," Marcus said.

"So, I think she saw my face, or knew, or… I don't know. But she's smiling when I look up after getting everything inside and she just says, 'Did you have fun?' and I was like, 'Yeah, it was awesome!' or I think that's what I said."

Brian stopped talking but the look on his face showed he had more to say.

"I guess. I guess her kindness stuck with me, you know? I want to be the kind of parent she was. Is. Sorry."

Marcus exhaled in a big huff.

"Man," he said, and patted Brian on the shoulder.

"She was so cool, too," Brian said. "She took us everywhere. I never knew as a kid how much work that was, but damn!"

"Yeah," Marcus agreed. "She was amazing."

The two sat in silence for a minute, and then Marcus spoke up.

"You want to hear something funny she just told me?"

Brian spun his head to Marcus. "Yessir!"

"Ok. So, when we lived in Texas, my mom was a big church person."

"Really?" Brian said. "I always took her for the hippie type."

"Just wait."

Brian laughed. "Ok."

Marcus continued. "Yeah, so she went to church every Sunday, but my father and I stayed home. Fast-forward to when she and I are living in San Diego and I don't think she went to church once."

"Nice," Brian said.

"I mean, at the time, I didn't even give it a second thought. But when I was sitting with her at the hospital one day, thinking about her life, I realized how strange it was she never had to work on a Sunday and we always went to the beach instead. I asked her how she always had Sunday off from Gelson's—"

"The grocery store, right?" Brian asked.

"Yeah," Marcus said. "Get this: She told her manager when she got the job that she couldn't work on Sundays due to religious reasons."

"But… you two went to the beach every Sunday, not church, right?"

Marcus laughed. "Exactly!"

Brian slapped his leg and laughed, and Marcus broke out laughing as well.

"That's… that's hilarious!"

"I know, right?"

"Ok, she's a legend," Brian said, laughing.

"Totally," Marcus said with a big smile.

A FEW HOURS later, Marcus caught his first glimpse of Bill's killer at his last known address. Turned out to be a converted storage unit along a sketchy stretch of Garland Road in Garland, Texas, about fifteen minutes from Marcus' childhood home. By converted, the modules of the former self-storage facility were basically units for—as far as he could figure—manual workers.

Caleb was smoking a cigarette; it dangled from his lips while he rushed around inside his unit.

From his vantage point in the parking lot, Marcus couldn't make out yet what Caleb's business was. He rolled down the window of his rental car, a silver Mitsubishi Mirage, for a better look and the morning's sticky humidity smacked him in the face. A blinding sun pierced the cloudless sky and burned hot. Even though the temperature had not yet reached eighty degrees, it easily felt like ninety-five.

In a unit neighboring Caleb's, a crew of Mexicans were pulling out lawnmowers, edgers and weed trimmers and loading them on to a high-side trailer hitched to nothing. It seemed like the crew was getting a late start for a day of mowing and blowing in the sweltering heat, but Marcus figured they were just doing what they were told. Their jefe had probably dropped them and the trailer off at the unit to load up right before Marcus had shown up.

One of the crew was grinding something inside. A stream of sparks sprayed out of the open door to the unit like the end of a bundle of Roman Candles. After several minutes of this, the worker walked to the trailer with sharpened mower blades in hand.

The three-man crew loaded a few more odds and ends in the trailer, closed and secured the gate and then stood around.

In a large unit, two doors down from Caleb's, toward the entrance to the facility, an overweight white guy in overalls and no shirt raised a mid-nineties Chevrolet Cavalier on a lift. The mechanic had a serious Ron Jeremy vibe, right down to a greasy, black mustache and an equally grimy, thinning head of hair he kept tied back in a ponytail.

The whirring of an automatic tool kicked on an air compressor in the makeshift car shop. The drumming sound of the compressor dulled the sound of heavy traffic behind Marcus but appeared to take the Mexicans by surprise. One pulled a red bandana from his back pocket and waved it toward the mechanic's direction. All of them were yelling and bitching, but Marcus couldn't hear their words over the compressor.

Marcus watched all of this through the bars of the rolling gate to the fenced facility. It was the one point of entry, accessible by a code punched into a keypad. It must have been some years since the place had operated as an actual storage facility. The mud brown and dark orange sheet metal units had definitely seen better days. The same could be said for the surrounding area.

Sweat licked the back of his knees and nearly every other crease and fold of skin. Tapping his right foot mindlessly, Marcus wiped the sweat away and on to the back of his shorts as he worked up the courage to approach Caleb. But how?

He didn't want to go in guns-blazing, so to speak, and vomit all over the guy. And it appeared Caleb would not be hanging around for much longer anyway, as he was now pulling the door to his unit down by a length of yellow rope.

The mechanic's compressor had stopped pumping by this time and a screech cried out from the wheels of the sheet metal door. It *rat-a-tat-tat-tatted* along the track until the door thudded to the concrete ground. Caleb stomped a boot down on the door and crushed a padlock closed on the unit and started toward the gate.

Marcus perked up his head when he saw him approaching and just as quickly slumped in his seat, deciding he was not ready for Caleb to spot him or even to do what he had come to Texas to do.

Once he reached the black iron gate, Caleb bent over and tapped the side of a silver mechanical box that fed a thick chain connected to the gate. The gate kicked to life, jumped on the track and rolled open. It too made a squeaky, shrill sound as it lazily acquiesced and allowed Caleb to exit to the parking lot.

Dressed in dark jeans, work boots and a plain black, long-sleeved v-neck shirt, Caleb was even larger in person than Marcus had observed on the surveillance video back in San Diego. It had been difficult to judge his size standing next to the squatty Bill, but in person in was clear: Caleb was a Hoss, as the Texan in Marcus might have said. Much wider than himself.

Caleb stopped at the back of a Garnet Red 1969 Chevrolet Nova SS and pulled out a soft pack of cigarettes and a lighter from his back pocket. When he brought the flame to the cigarette in his lips, Marcus realized he wasn't wearing a long-sleeved shirt at all, but a short-sleeved v-neck. Caleb's arms were sleeved all right—with tattoos.

Solid black ink covered the entirety of his forearms, from wrists to the crook of his elbows. The color reminded Marcus of a shop rag sopped with used motor oil that had been left in an engine a couple extra thousand miles. What he could see of Caleb's arms above the penetrating black and below his shirt sleeves were intricate tattoos woven together, they too prevented any naked skin from spying through.

Marcus winced, visualizing the pain associated with such commitment. The hours of delicate torture Caleb must have endured while an artist monotonously colored in every inch of epidermis made his brain hurt.

After lighting the smoke and taking a few drags, Caleb smashed the cigarette out against the sole of his boot and flicked the stub into the bushes in front of his car.

Marcus didn't flinch, satisfied to watch Bill's killer fire up the classic muscle car, rev it a few times and gun it on to Garland Road, disappearing in short order.

Looking down at his shaking hands, Marcus felt exhilaration. Though he didn't know what his exact words would be or how he would explain who he was and why he was there, he felt confident Caleb would appreciate his effort.

For now, Marcus was content to go check in to a motel, call his mother to let her know he had arrived safely. Then he'd get some rest. Tomorrow would be a big day and he needed to work through all the unknowns before approaching Caleb.

14
INTRODUCING HIMSELF TO THE
NEWSPAPER MAN'S KILLER

Another chartreuse horse apple exploded against the kidney bean-red brick of the two-story office building that had once been home to *The Plano Register*. The brain-textured, softball-sized fruit splintered and splattered in every direction with Marcus reloading for his next assault. His face red-hot, tears of anger in his eyes.

"Fuck you!" he yelled in a teeth-clenching growl after rifling a third orb. It met the face of the building with devastating velocity, obliterating into chunks and leaving a pulpy smudge on the brick and grout.

Marcus wiped the sweat from his forehead. Whipped his head side-to-side to make sure no one was witnessing his bizarre behavior. He was still alone. The most recent economic downturn had treated the other businesses that once leased space in the business complex as harshly as the now digital-only newspaper. The property was a completely vacant building, save for a CPA office tucked in the far corner on the second level.

Marcus collapsed in a heap under the dappled shade of the Bois d'arc tree and sat on one of the fallen horse apples making him yell, "Goddamn it!" He leaned to one side and pulled the fruit out from under his butt. Leaning back against the tree's sturdy trunk, he half-heartily tossed it aside. Marcus fought the humidity, sucking deep to catch his breath, kicking away the other horse apples scattered around him.

A Molotov cocktail or a sledgehammer could have inflicted more damage to the building and would have been more satisfying, but the fruit had served its purpose.

He glared at the back of a five-foot wide, wooden board on wooden posts: a commercial lease sign staked in the grass a few feet in front of him. The empty newspaper office had been on the market for a while, evidenced by the degree of fade to the colored print on the front of the sign.

Marcus first noticed the newspaper's sign had been taken down when he drove by. But thanks to the non-sun damaged brick underneath, the stenciled imprint of *"The Plano Register"* was still visible.

He tore into the parking lot, brought the car to a screeching stop and jumped out with the engine running. He ran up to the front and shook the glass doors in violent disbelief, before staggering back to the car. As he leaned in to shut off the engine and pull out the keys, he'd looked up and saw the stately Bois d'arc just beyond the lease sign, and felt inspired.

With his panting decreased enough for him to close his mouth, Marcus fanned his neck using the collar of his shirt. Even sitting in the shade, the afternoon heat was suffocating.

An hour earlier, Marcus had woken from a long nap and drove back to Caleb's, but didn't find him there. Disappointed, he meandered back to Plano with no real purpose, driving aimlessly, and found himself at the site of his weekly assaults. The area looked much different than when he last saw it as an eleven-year-old.

The long-since completed overpass was showing its more than two decades of age. The Texas state-shaped flag emblems stamped on the top of each concrete support beam were faded from years of direct sun. The perpendicular, deep royal blue sections of the flags were now a pale baby blue and what should have been blood-red horizontal areas were instead muted and almost pink.

The lanes of the toll road above had been widened twice to accommodate the growing population over the years. Yet when Marcus last saw the site it was a skeletal mess of twisted rebar. Now, vehicles roared down the turnpike named for the first President George Bush.

And the field Bill used to park in was now a street leading to the on-ramp for eastbound traffic. Marcus was unsure at first if he was in the right place, but when he pulled over to the half shoulder and looked up at the overpass, something clicked.

Part of him was relieved to see the area had been paved over. The moment of satisfaction had been fleeting, however. A grim thought also mocked him of how people unknowingly drove over his past unaffected on a daily basis—every minute, in fact—and only he and a dead guy knew what had truly happened there.

The thought made him feel more isolated than ever. He wondered how many other boys, now men, could say the same for this place. Did Caleb feel the same? Was he glad it was paved over? Had Bill taken him to this spot after Marcus fled to California? Where did he take his prey after construction was complete and the location became heavily trafficked?

Transfixed by the questions and being back in the area, Marcus sat paralyzed on the side of a street he hadn't visited for decades. The area was barely recognizable, but flashbacks tormented him just the same. Bill's hands were all over him again. He saw his younger self thrashing. Frozen. Then weeping.

Newspaper print suffocated his nostrils.

Marcus tugged at his shorts, remembering the feeling of trying to make less of his legs show when he was in the car with Bill. He chided his younger self for not switching to wearing jeans on Fridays. Sure, it was too hot to wear jeans in the summer, but all these years later it seemed like a much better alternative. That made him think about the air conditioning. So, he turned down the air in the rental car from high to the lowest setting, getting a chill at the memory of Bill's mildew AC blasting him in the face.

Sweat beaded on his cheekbones and he could feel his ears start to burn. Surely his eye, or both, would start twitching any time now.

Marcus choked back tears. He looked across the street, his vision glazing on to a trio of young, leafed-out crepe myrtles not yet in bloom. Staring at peeling, papery blonde bark, Marcus tried to keep the memories from barraging his mind, but to no avail. Then, like when you're intently focused on finding a missing set of keys, searching the entire house with no luck, yet come across something else you lost a week before instead, a realization broke through.

Power. Bill had taken it from him. And though he was keenly aware of this fact intellectually, Marcus hadn't realized until this moment how it had affected him. How the need to regain power for himself had manifested itself over the course of his life. His career choice, for one. Becoming a cop to gain power.

His need to stick to a routine was another glaring example. Right down to how he packed his gym bag in the exact same order every night for the next day. Or how he took the same travel coffee mug and water bottle every morning and placed them in assigned cup holders in his car and corresponding cup holders in his police cruiser. How his world crumbled if he had a plan in place and it was upset or altered.

Some might call it type-A behavior, but he recognized his actions were born from a more deeply-rooted, traumatized place. From the need to control what he could in his life.

He balled his hands into fists and shook them. Pounded the top of the steering wheel and then squeezed it.

Get up. Workout. Shower. Work. Shower. Eat dinner, surf/go for a walk, go to bed. Rinse and repeat. Keeping to a routine allowed him to maintain power and control over himself and it was not only a comforting feeling but a necessary one. He wondered, had it really been so simple?

"Of course," he whispered.

A giggle broke loose from his chest. Then another and then Marcus couldn't hold back a torrent of body-jerking laughs leading into a rolling fit. His eyes watered, but this time not from sadness or fear, he realized. He wiped them away with his thumbs and looked at himself in the rear-view mirror, continuing to laugh uncontrollably.

New tears replaced the ones he wiped away, his face red and of the same disturbed nature he saw on many of those with mental issues on his beat back in Ocean Beach. Yep, he was losing it, he thought. Something was definitely broken. He sat, confused, unsure of what had caused the laughing fit, as nothing about any of this struck him as funny. Marcus may have laughed himself into insanity on the shoulder of the road atop his molestation graveyard. Instead, he was startled out of it by three raps of a knuckle on the driver's side window just then.

"Sir, you can't stay here. It isn't safe," said a Plano police officer, after Marcus wiped his eyes and rolled down the window.

"Is, is everything ok, sir?" the officer added when he saw his face.

Marcus looked up at the cop and blinked, hesitating to answer what should have been a simple question.

"Um. Yeah. I mean, yes. Thank you, officer."

The cop, a younger guy with an ironic Fu Manchu mustache—ironic or else Marcus hoped he had lost a bet—looked down at him with a suspicious glare. Marcus would have given the same look if he approached a guy crying and laughing hysterically in a rental car on the side of the road. And he would have known it was a rental because of how it didn't fit the driver. His knees were nearly even with his chest and the seat was pushed as far back as it could from the steering wheel.

Yes, he would have had some questions, and so it seemed this officer did as well. Yet, somehow, Marcus was able to pull himself together quickly enough, so he was let off with an, "Ok, then. On your way," without being required to show an I.D.

Marcus watched through the rear-view mirror and saw the cop get back in his cruiser and drive off. He breathed out a sigh of relief.

He didn't hang around long, whipping a U-turn and then driving with purpose to *The Plano Register*.

Sitting against the Bois d'arc tree, Marcus was still feeling the effects of the hot, early-summer Texas afternoon. His coastal San Diego skin sizzled, the shock to his system the equivalent of someone living at 0' elevation—which Marcus also did—and then hiking to the 14,505-foot peak of Mount Whitney in Sequoia National Park on a whim, without any preparation or training.

Marcus gathered himself and drove back to the self-storage facility turned rent-a-workshop for the second time that day. When he arrived, he had the urge to keep the car running so he could also keep the air conditioning blowing, but knew it could arouse interest. And he was still not ready to approach Caleb, who was there this time.

Sitting in the sweltering heat wasn't a much better option, but he had discovered an alternative when he'd been there earlier in the day.

Directly across from Caleb's unit was a low, four-foot-tall block wall encircling the property. Connected to the top of the block wall was an additional six-foot-high chain-link fence topped with rolling razor wire.

On the other side of the wall was the parking lot for a four-business, bricked strip center. All of the businesses—from what Marcus could gather—were Korean-owned retail shops: a tropical fish store, small grocer, Korean barbeque restaurant and a coin-operated laundry. These shops and the parking lot were obscured from the work units, however, as the property owner had long ago planted a hedge of red-tip photinia bushes along the expanse of the barrier. The plants had engulfed the chain link, and created a thick, organic screen.

Marcus parked in the lot, fortuitously shaded in the afternoon by the mammoth photinia. The hedge did have weak spots in spite of its coverage. Several sections had succumbed to disease or pest invasion over the years and looked like bare patches where someone had tossed a bucket of acid through. What few leaves were hanging on in these spots were brown and crispy. One such area was four feet from the ground, at the spot where the block wall and the chain-link met and was offset ten feet to the right of Caleb's unit. And through it, Marcus had a perfect covert porthole from which to view him.

Caleb appeared to be hard at work doing—it was difficult to tell for sure. Marcus was trying to figure it out when the car mechanic next door walked over and held out a power tool and told Caleb the wrench was running slow.

"It's probably the ball bearing," Caleb told him in a flat, benign accent. He wiped his hands with a red shop rag and took the tool. Turned it over, inspecting it.

"Well, shit," the mechanic said. His accent was tell-tale Texan—obvious from the way he pronounced shit as sheet.

"I'll flush it first, see if it's gunked up. But you're probably looking at a motor replacement."

Marcus kept his eyes on Caleb after the mechanic handed him the wrench and went back to his shop.

About an hour later, Caleb carried a flat, black Rogue workout bench outside, placed it just a few feet from the entrance to the unit and sat down facing the wall/fence/hedge. With the sun falling in the sky, shadows lengthened, creating shade where there hadn't been any before. A slight breeze picked up as well.

Caleb tinkered with a part, his hands covered in black grease which he wiped on a shop rag laid over his right thigh.

Marcus was again drawn to Caleb's sleeve tattoos and they reminded him of Megan's mermaid tattoo. He thought hers was the perfect representation of her personality. Unique and sexy. He shook his head to refocus his attention.

Why exactly he was staking out Caleb instead of approaching him, he wasn't even sure. Perhaps because he still hadn't come up with the right words. After all, what would he say when Caleb asked him why he didn't report Bill so he would have been spared?

What could he say?

It seemed so obvious and simple as an adult looking back on it. He should have told his parents or called the police. But as a child, both options were as intimidating as the abuse itself.

Then, Marcus wondered something else. Clearly, Caleb didn't report Bill or else the newspaper man would have been arrested, right? Marcus couldn't know for sure. He hadn't looked through court records or anything but, to the best of his knowledge, Bill had a clean slate.

The question made Marcus want to rush around the wall and confront Caleb right then and ask, "Why didn't *you* report Bill?

Huh?" But he didn't. Marcus was confused and grew more so sitting there thinking, trying to sort through everything.

He rubbed his head and then stroked his scratchy face, which made him huff and roll his eyes, annoyed he hadn't been able to shave for the last two days because he left his electric razor at home.

Rubbing his face with both hands once more as one might after getting off a long day of work, Marcus decided to put off his introduction. He would pick up a razor on the way back to the motel and come back the next morning fresh, rested and focused.

He leaned forward to start the car and stopped before firing the ignition. He looked through the hole in the hedge once more. Caleb was still working away, sitting on the bench, seemingly unaffected from killing a man just three days earlier.

Marcus daydreamed of how he would carry himself had he murdered Bill. It made a grin pop on his face. Yes, he would have liked the opportunity. Relished it, if he was being honest with himself. The thought of taking a life—that life—didn't make him flinch either.

Maybe that's what this had all been about. He wished he had been the one to stuff Bill in that trunk. Except, he would have strangled the life from the son of a bitch, forcing him to look him straight in the eyes as he did so. He daydreamed of Bill on his knees, looking up with shocked eyes, tears streaming down his round cheeks, begging Marcus not to go through with it.

"Don't be a baby," Marcus would have told Bill right before tightening his grip and squeezing. His grin turned to a sinister smile at the thought.

He wondered again why Caleb had chosen to bash Bill over the back of the head. At first, it made sense from a logical standpoint of throwing off the police, but it didn't make sense now. Not after envisioning a hit of the sweet juice of revenge and retribution. He didn't think he would have been able to keep a level, pragmatic head as Caleb had, and it made Marcus revere him even more than he already did.

Pulling out of the parking lot, Marcus felt his mind riding a wave of optimistic anticipation, again excited to meet Caleb the next day.

In his focused state during his stakeout, Marcus had neglected to notice someone had been staking him out as well. Parked across the street, in an old white van with dark, tinted windows, was a team made up of San Diego Homicide detectives and Garland police.

"Would you lookie there," Barnes said under his breath when he saw Marcus pull up hours earlier. And when he departed, Barnes turned to his partner Castillo and said, "We got him. We got them both."

AFTER PICKING UP a razor and shaving cream from a CVS, Marcus pulled into his motel and grimaced when he saw a burgundy 1996 Chevrolet Caprice low-rider parked in front of his ground-level room.

Sitting on the rear bumper was a thin, older, black male. He wore pale, blue-colored jean shorts and a red T-shirt, obnoxiously too long for even his tall torso.

"The fuck's he want?" Marcus said.

A purple Los Angeles Lakers hat rested on Terry Kemp's head, propped back with the bill facing skyward.

As Marcus inched the Mirage slowly closer, Terry stood up. Flicked his chin at Marcus.

The loose gravel of the poorly-maintained lot crackled like popcorn under the tires. Marcus pulled into a space next to Terry's Caprice. He hit the brake too hard and jerked himself to a stop. Still gripping the steering wheel with both hands, Marcus squeezed and thought for a split second about putting the car in reverse and leaving. But he turned off the car and got out instead. Reached back in and across the driver's seat to swipe up the white plastic CVS bag.

He didn't move with any urgency and saw Terry fidgeting at the back of their cars, anxious, but hesitant to approach.

The day's light was fading fast. The sun sat at the horizon line but was obscured by retail shopping centers, corporate buildings and nicer hotels than the one Marcus had booked. Orange and gold bands streaked across a stone-gray sky. Certainly, the sun's visual make-good for its hot temper that day.

"What do you want?" Marcus asked flatly. He walked to the front of his car without looking at Terry.

Skipping between the cars, Terry caught up to his son and stood a step down in the parking lot. He looked up at Marcus, who was now on the sidewalk in front of his room.

Terry's body language was already pleading before he spoke a word.

"And how did you find me?" Marcus added.

Terry hesitated, like he didn't expect the question. Instead of answering, he attempted to break the tension with a joke.

"Ain't you a little big for that Smurfmobile?" He let out a nervous laugh, pointing over to the Mirage.

Marcus ignored the question and instead repeated his.

"How did you find me?"

Terry sighed. "Uh, your mother. She let me know."

Marcus made a face, opening his mouth wider than necessary and shooting up his head Marcus. "Ah! Should have guessed."

"I need to talk ta ya, Marcus."

"Isn't that what you're doing?"

Marcus crossed his arms, the CVS bag swooshing and crinkling under one and his rental car key rattling against the hard-plastic keychain under the other.

Terry motioned his head to the room.

"Can we be inside?"

"Do you mean *go* inside?" Marcus said, his voice stern. "No, *we* can't go inside."

Terry nervously adjusted his hat and placed it back in its original, vertical position. Propped one foot up on the sidewalk.

He looked slight to Marcus—old, in fact. His goatee was still trimmed and neat as ever. But the skin around his cheekbones and eyes sagged now, and his arms were frail, almost skeletal.

Marcus wasn't close enough to him to tell for sure—keeping him at least an arm's length away—but he didn't pick up the pungent smell of stale cigarette smoke his father so notably wreaked of when he was a child.

"Look, I just want a coupla minutes ta make things right, is all," Terry said. His words now matched the urgent, pathetic body language he displayed when Marcus first pulled up.

Marcus didn't respond and instead glared past his father, letting his eyes drift onto the comically protruding, thin-walled tires of the Caprice. The gold-spoked rims glistened, despite the rapidly declining daylight. Above the tires, a couple of buffed and bonded spots around wheel wells appeared to be sloppy attempts at rust repair; flaws that took away from an otherwise well-maintained classic.

Terry flinched his body, threw out his palms for a reaction or response from Marcus.

"Look, can we do this some other time?" Marcus said.

"I really need-ta tell you some stuff and, I mean, when am I gonna see you again?"

Marcus uncrossed his arms, dropped them to his side and motioned forcibly with both hands, shaking the bag and the keys.

"I don't have anything to say to you—"

"But I do," Terry insisted.

Neither said anything for three or four seconds and then Terry spoke up.

"What are you doing in town, Marcus?"

Marcus cringed every time his father used his name. He loved his name but always imagined Stacey had chosen it for him. When Terry said it, however, he wished he had a different first name.

"That's my business," Marcus said.

When he saw Terry didn't react, seemingly not accepting his response, Marcus added with a shrug, "Seeing some old friends. What's it to you anyway?"

Terry sighed, dropped his head and removed his hat.

"Ok, man," Marcus said, stretching out the last word while pulling out his wallet from his back pocket.

Terry took a step forward on to the sidewalk and spoke up with confidence.

"Your mother told me she told you to get with me."

"HA!" Marcus turned his back to his father, inserted his room card into the door's keypad. The keypad buzzed and a green light illuminated.

"Boy, I—"

Marcus spun around and yelled, "Don't call me that!" He stuck a finger in Terry's face. "I'm not your boy. You lost that right when you beat my mother!"

Terry slunk back a couple of steps, lips pouted. He raised both hands like he was under arrest. After he'd stepped down into the parking lot, he dropped his arms, a look of defeat on his face.

"Cool, we're cool," he said, and looked side-to-side.

"Whatever," Marcus said, waving at him.

"Stacey knows how to get me if you change your mind." Terry now stood at the driver's door of the Caprice.

"I wouldn't count on it," Marcus said. He stepped into his room and shut the door.

15
CALEB'S DOTS DON'T ADD UP

THE NEXT MORNING, Marcus reluctantly opened his eyes. It wasn't the hundred ball-ping hammers smashing his skull, but nagging doubt giving him the most discomfort. The splotchy ceiling of the smoked-in, non-smoking room came into view when he raised his head. The cadence of the hammers behind his eyes doubled in speed. He rolled on to his side and the block of pain rolled with him, moving under his skin to his forehead like an air bubble trapped under a frozen pond.

"God… damn," Marcus moaned. He smeared a hand down his face, knowing he earned his state from the foolish attempt at self-medication the night before.

After his father left, anxiety squeezed his throat with an iron grip. Just sitting in the motel room wasn't helping matters. Needing to get something to eat anyway, he headed out and walked to a Tex-Mex place a few blocks from the motel where he finished off a plate of chicken enchiladas, refried beans and a heap of Spanish rice.

Before the waitress brought his meal, he downed a frozen strawberry margarita served in an oversized, classic margarita glass as an appetizer. He sat alone at a table large enough for a family of six. After the meal, he washed everything down with another margarita. The strong buzz took the edge off as intended, tucking the interaction with Terry into the background. He leaned hard into the feeling and wanted more. So, on his way back to the motel, he picked up two bottles of craft beer from a gas station. Back at the motel, in between clumsy swigs, he stared at the colorful artistic labels glassy-eyed, sitting on the end of the bed. After finishing most of the thick beers, he passed out in bed.

Now, propping himself against the bed's flimsy wooden headboard, he appreciated how the booze had washed away his father. But he lamented the fact it had not prevented Bill from making an appearance in his dreams again. The third time in as many sleeps.

An appearance? Hell, he shined in his leading role. Though Marcus couldn't recall the specifics, the dreams left a skittering, anxious imprint all the same. A feeling he had not experienced in years. Not since his regular nightmares of Bill.

As he scooted to the edge of the bed, head in hands, the pulsating pain relented enough for his mind to focus on that nagging doubt. Marcus walked over to the unframed mirror taking up the entire four-foot wall above the bathroom vanity. To his left was the room's open closet consisting of one bar with two permanent hangers, and to the right was the toilet and shower behind a wispy door made of particle board with large gashes of its faux-walnut veneer missing. Leaning over the sink and staring at the mirror, he ran his palm back and forth over his mouth and chin, judging whether he should shave again after having just done so the previous night.

"Nope," he said and recoiled at his own breath.

Leaning into the doorway to his right, he turned on the water to the shower. It was a tight fit, so much so the door wouldn't close when he sat on the toilet. While he let the water warm up, he picked up his phone from the nightstand and checked for a text from Megan. As expected, there wasn't one. There were, however, a stream of unchecked messages going back two days from McKenzie he had been ignoring.

The first was sent an hour after their shifts ended. When Marcus was with his mother.

"Wtf"

"What happened homie?"

"You there?"

Marcus slammed the phone back down on the nightstand and growled.

Steam escaped the door to the shower and fogged the mirror.

"Shit," he shouted, but not because of the shower. He picked up the phone and dialed the hospice care facility, remembering to check in on his mother.

"Uh, yes. Hi. Could you transfer me to Stacey Kemp's room? Sure."

After waiting on hold a few seconds longer than he expected, Marcus shuffled over to the shower and turned off the water, getting his arm wet right when a voice came back on the line.

"Oh, really? No, no, don't wake her. I'll call back later, thanks."

Stacey was asleep apparently. With his conscience clear for the time being, he turned the shower back on and got in. His mind returned to the nagging thought bothering him that morning.

Caleb's dots weren't adding up.

"Connecting," he said, correcting the incorrect turn of phrase he had been chewing on since awaking.

The dots weren't connecting all of the sudden. But why? Why did he wake up with such doubt? Marcus definitely knew Caleb was Bill's killer. He had video and a fingerprint as proof. But now he was wrestling with his motive where the answer had seemed obvious before.

After his shower, Marcus plopped on the end of the bed with a towel wrapped around his lower body. He dragged over his gym bag from in front of a long dresser. Retrieving Caleb's report from the bottom of the bag, he combed over the information in an attempt to cross-reference it with the Caleb he had seen with his own eyes the last two days.

"Military... Twenty-eight... White," Marcus read in a mumble.

"Muscular physique... smokes," he recalled from memory.

Marcus swatted the bed next to him with the report and stretched his neck from side to side, his eyes closed. Opening them, he stared ahead. A look of dumb confusion spread across his face, the look of someone with a hangover attempting long-from algebra in their head. His eyes connected with his reflection in the mirror over the dresser and it knocked him out of the trance.

"Military," he said, looking at the report. Then, his eyes found something he had seen a half-dozen times before and hadn't thought much of until then.

Under a heading that read, "Hometown," the city Longview appeared. Longview was a small town in far east Texas, 138 miles from Plano. Caleb's last known address was in Garland—his work unit—the only thing tying him to the greater Dallas area.

"He didn't grow up in Plano?" Marcus asked himself, slowly sitting up. His sloshy head was grasping to put a definitive pin in the meaning.

Growing more frustrated by the second, Marcus got dressed in a pair of shorts and a gray T-shirt. He rolled up Caleb's report and stuck it in his back pocket. Did a quick scan of the dingy motel room still smelling of stale barley and hops mixed with shower fungus. Even though he had paid for three nights, his look around the room was one of making sure not to forget anything before checking out. He spotted the keys to the rental car, swiped them off the dresser and ran out of the room.

Right after the door closed and locked behind him, Marcus snapped his fingers.

Once back in the room, he grabbed the gun from his bag and secured the holster to the waist of his shorts. He hesitated to flap his shirt down over it, debating for a second if he would rather hide the gun behind his back. Figuring he would play it by ear when he got to Caleb's, he tossed the end of his shirt over the weapon. Before leaving the room for the second time, he pulled Caleb's report out of his pocket and tossed it on the dresser.

It was a little after 10 a.m. when Marcus headed to Garland. He made a point to take a different route than he had the day before, as to not drive past the shuttered newspaper offices or the former construction site. Was he still dreaming of Bill because he had exposed himself to those signposts of his trauma? In any case, he didn't have the need to see either site ever again, so why chance it? The alternative course only added five minutes to the drive. No big deal.

The rental car's air conditioning was taking longer to cool down the interior than expected for a newer vehicle. The lag encouraged Marcus to crack the windows to force a breeze, but it was a stifling one. The temperature was well over ninety degrees already and the white sun looked like it was prepping a wallop for the day.

Marcus rocked in a gentle cadence to silence. Squinted his eyes and scanned the shopping centers, fast food restaurants and commercial buildings on both sides of the highway. Billboards for beer, strip clubs and the Texas Lottery whizzed past him. He looked beyond all this and for miles in every direction, all he saw was an expanse of sky.

It had never occurred to him until then how flat Dallas was. Driving around San Diego, he was used to seeing rolling mountain ranges, canyons and ocean. He realized how calm his home terrain made him feel. The views grounded him, settled his nerves, let him know—if nothing else—wild was never farther away than a glance in any direction.

The Garland Road exit was two miles ahead. The script Marcus had composed, edited and rewritten several times in his head over the last few days was now all marked up with red ink. Only one bullet point remained. It contained one, three-letter word in 72-point font.

Why?

The only question he needed answered right then.

Sure, he would need to ease into things so he didn't come off like he was interrogating Caleb. He was a cop after all and came across as one, he knew. But the question would be pressing against his vocal cords, ready to blurt out all the same. He would have to play it as cool as possible.

The south end of Garland Road looked like a flipped, mirrored version of the northern end. Fast food joints took up every quadrant of each intersection: Taco Bell, McDonald's, Popeye's and Jack in the Box at one, and Burger King, Arby's, Wendy's and KFC at the next, and so on.

There was a humongous warehouse building on his right taking up what seemed like three city blocks. A Costco or Wal-

Mart at one time perhaps. The Sit or Sleep furniture store now using the space was advertising an out-of-season "Black Friday" sale on outdoor patio items. Employees marched around yellow and blue printed "SALE up to 50% OFF" signs and a pink inflatable humanoid flapped and twerked on the corner of the intersection.

A panhandler on the left walked up and down the skinny median with a sign reading, "Need $ for beer. #truthbomb."

The light turned green. Marcus was two blocks from Caleb's. He cleared his throat and sat up straight. Interlocking his hands and resting them on top of the steering wheel, he cracked every finger of one hand simultaneously and then the other.

Marcus pulled into a shopping center neighboring the north side of the former self-storage facility. The heat of the day hit his face like opening an oven set on broil when he got out of the car. He cupped a hand to his forehead to shield his eyes and took the sidewalk over to the facility's parking lot.

With a vantage point opposite of what he had the day before, Marcus looked at his surroundings. His eyes were drawn across Garland Road, but nothing caught his attention.

The gate was closed when he approached, but he remembered how to gain access without a code to punch into the keypad, having watched Caleb use the method the day before. The gate lurched open and Marcus jerked his hand back through the bars after tapping a button on the side of the mechanical box.

The mechanic's compressor was hammering; the sound echoed off the concrete and drowned out all other sounds, including the squeaks and grinding from the metal-on-metal of the gate opening.

The grease monkey gave him a go-to-hell look when he walked by. Marcus nodded and it mellowed the mechanic, who dropped his head back under the hood of a white Nissan Frontier.

Caleb's door was open and Marcus could tell he was home from the sound of a ratchet cranking a bolt coming from inside. The craaaaank-click-click-click-craaaaaank-click-click-click ceased abruptly when Marcus stopped in front. Caleb looked up and their eyes met.

Neither said anything at first. Caleb walked from the homemade, wooden workbench lining the back wall of the unit over to the far wall to the left. Set against that wall was a five-foot-tall, heavy-duty steel tool chest on wheels.

With no sense of urgency, Caleb popped the socket off the ratchet and set both into one of the cherry-red drawers. The chrome socket clinked and the ratchet made a deeper thud. He pushed the drawer closed and it sounded like the track was lined with sand.

This was the first, unobstructed view Marcus got of the inside of the unit. It was more spacious than he imagined but overwhelmingly cluttered. He wondered what the exact dimensions were, but could easily tell it was an oversized unit. Not fully the width of the mechanic's space, but twice as deep, maybe going back thirty or forty feet.

Four, blue, 55-gallon steel drums were grouped together on the right side of the unit and another rolling tool cabinet, this one black, set behind them. Two industrial fans oscillating at full blast hung from opposite corners of the far wall and let off a hypnotic, zippering hum. The space was illuminated by two, four-foot-long, low-watt fluorescent strip lights hanging from the ceiling, suspended by linked chain.

Pulling a red rag from his back jeans pocket, Caleb gave it a snap at his side and stepped toward Marcus. Each of the men kept their eyes locked on the other.

Caleb stopped a few feet from Marcus, rolled his shoulders back and wiped his hands and arms with the rag. Wearing a sleeveless, black crewneck T-shirt, the intricacy of his tattoos was on full display.

Marcus stuck out a hand and said, "I'm Marcus."

Caleb continued wiping his hands with the rag, despite no more grease being present, leaving Marcus to remain in place like a mime. Then, he stuffed the rag in his back pocket and squinted, deep lines framing his face.

"I know who you are," he finally said.

Marcus dropped his hand.

"Okay." Marcus stuffed his hands into his pockets and felt his gun bump his right forearm. A bolt of panic rushed through his chest, not wanting Caleb to think he posed a risk. Trying to ignore it, Marcus cleared his throat and added, "I'm—"

"Look, I know who you are," Caleb said. "I also know you're a cop. So how about you get the fuck out of here."

Marcus scrunched his face. This wasn't going how he'd envisioned.

"Uh, ok. He cleared his throat again. Then held out his palms in front of his chest and said, "Listen, I'm here as a friend."

One eyebrow arched on Caleb's forehead and Marcus added, "Honest."

Caleb crossed his arms.

"No thanks."

"You don't want to know why I'm here?" Marcus asked.

"Nope."

"Ok, but I have questions for you."

"I figured. So, now that you've told me why you're here… peace," Caleb said. And with that, he turned around.

Frustrated, Marcus reached out and grabbed Caleb's left shoulder, attempting to turn him back around. The shoulder filled his palm the way a Thanksgiving ham would and Caleb didn't budge. When he did turn around of his own will, he appeared to grow two feet taller.

"Man, I did my job. Now get the fuck out!" Caleb growled. His eyes burned black and the stubble on his head bristled from his wrinkling brow.

Right when Marcus yelled, "What?" Caleb shoved Marcus in the chest and slung down the door to the unit with a thrust.

The aluminum door slammed against the concrete, missing Marcus' toes by a whisker. Marcus hollered, "Hey!" and banged on the door once with an open palm.

With a snort and a, "Goddamn it!" Marcus stumbled back a few steps. He kept cussing, staring at the gray wall in front of him.

"Fuck off!" came the muffled voice of Caleb.

Marcus slumped his shoulders and retreated.

"Shit, shit, shit. What the fuck?" He kept mumbling under his breath, walking back to the car.

Caleb's words repeated in his head.

"*I did my job.*"

The four words sent a shiver through Marcus, confirming the doubt he had awoken with. Caleb wasn't a victim of Bill's at all. There was no plot of revenge for a childhood—no matter the duration—robbed by molestation and abuse. Was there? Caleb hadn't plotted, bided his time and schemed a way to murder Bill and get away with it after all.

No, Marcus told himself. No. Rather, it seemed more likely Caleb was an assassin. His behavior said so. His personality said so.

Marcus pulled the driver's door closed once inside the rental car with violent frustration. Where did this leave him? Sweat poured down his temples but he kept the windows up and didn't turn the car on, his focus completely on weighing his options.

Bill was dead. That glorious truth persisted. And Caleb had murdered Bill. But it sounded like he had been hired. And if so, by whom? Perhaps another victim like Marcus, one who wasn't able to sneak off to California and instead had to let the horrific memories of the past eat away at his soul and mind? Or? Or what if Caleb simply meant he did his job, as in he did his part, and this was some sort of coordinated operation to rid the world of a very sick piece of shit?

"Fuck!" Marcus punched the steering wheel.

He was no closer to satisfying whatever itch had been tickled when he found Bill's corpse. Without answers to these unresolved questions, he couldn't go home.

The thought of how unsatisfying meeting Caleb had been made Marcus strike the steering wheel again. The enormity of everything he had done since pulling the business card out of his abuser's shorts was weighing down its hardest right then. He felt it pressing on his chest, churning in his stomach.

He punched the steering wheel three more times, but missed on the final fourth blow, his fist flying straight through and striking the instrument panel. The knob for the trip reset got him between the second and third knuckles, scraping away skin and immediately drawing blood. The miss sent him into a rage. He roared, grabbed the wheel with both hands and shook it with all his strength, the vibrations of his body sending sprays of sweat in every direction.

Then, calm. Marcus sat dazed, staring ahead at nothing in particular.

A second later, he opened the door and got out. Walking back to the gate, he hoped Caleb had opened the door to the unit already, given the facility wasn't air-conditioned and the discomfort would be too great, even with those big fans blowing.

He was right. The door was up and Caleb's attention was back on his workbench, where he stood working away.

"Hey!" Marcus shouted, his voice echoing. He stepped into the unit several feet so he couldn't be so quickly removed this time.

"Man, what the fuck did I tell you?" Caleb sneered, turning around.

As he did, the whites in his eyes mushroomed three sizes and he dove to his right, behind a motorcycle and the red tool cabinet.

Marcus swung his head around and saw the reflection of rolling lights of police cars approaching. Without hesitating, Marcus dove behind the quad of blue drums on the other side of the unit. A thought went through his head of how stupid the effort was. They were trapped rats with nowhere to go.

Two police cars came to a screeching stop in front of the unit. Then sounds of doors creaking open and crunching closed. Boots and shoes hitting pavement.

Almost simultaneously, a cocking sound of a pistol being chambered went off, coming from Caleb's direction.

"Caleb Brighton? Come out with your hands up!" said a voice from outside the unit.

The pale reflection of blue and red lights circled the perimeter of the inside of the unit, about five feet up the walls. From on his stomach, Marcus looked through a small gap between the left side of the barrels and some other junk and could see the boots of three uniformed cops, a pair of brown dress shoes and a pair of black casual shoes.

"This is Detective Barnes from the San Diego Police Department, Mr. Brighton. We are not coming in. We want to resolve this peacefully. So please, come out with your hands up."

Caleb didn't respond. Marcus twisted his body around on the ground to position his head so he could see Caleb, who was now positioned squarely behind the large, red tool cabinet.

Watching Caleb's body language, a nervous energy came over Marcus. A realization looking at Caleb's strained face. He's going to shoot his way out.

It didn't appear Barnes and the arresting party knew Marcus was there. At least, they hadn't called for him. How was that possible? He began to think through the ways, but cut himself off and told himself to focus on how he was going to get out of this or explain himself when caught.

"Caleb," said a different voice. "We need to take you in for questioning. Please come out."

Marcus caught Caleb's attention, their eyes meeting but then Caleb looked away.

A wheel of the cabinet squeaked when Caleb pressed against the steel case.

He then fired a shot over the top without looking.

The sudden bang made Marcus jump, and then the bullet hit some part of the aluminum unit with a ringing ping.

Shoes scraped frantically against concrete and bodies thudded against vehicles.

After the commotion settled, Barnes yelled, "Not cool, Caleb!"

"What the fuck are you doing?" Marcus whispered at Caleb.

Caleb just scowled back. His look said, "Thanks for bringing this shit to my door." And in fact, Marcus had done exactly that. And worse for Caleb, he had also found the only piece of evidence linking him to Bill's murder. And although neither of them knew it then, Marcus had allowed the detectives to intercept it.

Caleb waved his gun at Marcus, who still had his holstered.

"What?" Marcus whispered with a scrunched face.

Now lying on the floor behind the tool cabinet, Caleb pointed again, this time with his left hand, which was pinned under his body.

"Get out," Caleb said in a hushed voice.

Looking over his shoulder, Marcus saw what Caleb was pointing at: a door on the back wall, in the corner, obscured from the outside by the mountain of clutter on that side of the unit.

"Why? Marcus asked.

"Brighton!" another cop yelled out. "Throw out your gun and come out with your hands up!"

"What?" Caleb whispered back to Marcus.

"Why did you kill him?"

"Fuck off." Caleb then added with his eyes, *I'm going for that door so stay out of my fucking way.*

But Caleb didn't make an immediate move for the door. Instead, he rose up into a crouched position behind the cabinet with his back facing the tool bench behind him, and fired two shots above his head, knocking out both florescent light strips. Thin glass rained down and several copes shouted "Whoa!" in unison. The two shots also startled Marcus, making him jump again.

Caleb dropped his right arm on to the top of the cabinet and began walking it to his left, toward Marcus. In one fluid motion, he started firing in methodic succession at the police cars. Caleb kept his head hidden behind the taller middle portion of the steel tool cabinet, using his shooting arm as leverage against it to push the shield at the same time.

A bullet hit and shattered a side mirror on a police cruiser, a window and then another; air hissed and whined when another bullet pierced a tire. The arresting party immediately returned fire. Bullets sprayed into the unit and tinged and clanked off the numerous metal surfaces, the majority striking Caleb's rolling shield.

Marcus covered his head with both arms and pressed his body to the floor, trying to flatten himself as much as possible. Two seconds later, he caught a ricocheted bullet in the back, just below his shoulder blade. He wailed from the sudden, excruciating pain. He clapped a hand over his mouth.

Marcus rolled on to his left side, keeping his face—now dripping with sweat and tears—pressed to the concrete. He hesitated and then lifted his head to see Caleb and the cabinet rolling steadily along. Caleb was more than halfway across the unit when a series of clicks snapped off on both sides and the chaotic meteor shower of bullets ended.

Marcus didn't waste any time and started to inch toward the door. It was only a few feet to his right, behind an eight-foot mountain of long, Rubbermaid storage containers stacked three wide and the black tool cabinet.

This was the perfect time to escape. Marcus grimaced. The police were reloading and their full attention was on Caleb, who he just saw drop the empty magazine from his gun and click in another.

The deep, penetrating smell of gun powder hung in the air unlike Marcus had ever experienced. Even at the firing range and at police academy, the smell had never been as concentrated as now, burning his nostrils with its sourness.

He reached up for the doorknob, putting his feet under him and working himself into a low squat. When he looked back, Caleb was in a crouched position.

Then, Marcus saw something blink to life on his face. The whites of his eyes now full and bright. His attention snapped to a single focus. The look of enlightenment. Marcus craned his neck to look back over the top of the blue barrels and saw Barnes, skulking ill-advised into the unit. He was a few steps in, gun pointed stiffly in front of him, but Marcus wasn't sure he could see Caleb with the lights shot out and experiencing what he assumed was a harsh transition from the intense, broad daylight to the dark storage unit.

But what he knew for certain: Caleb saw Barnes in sharp detail, like a cheetah patiently waiting in the camouflaged cover of dried grass for the moment to attack a weak, unassuming gazelle.

Caleb slowly rose from his crouch, gripping his pistol between two hands in front of his body. A snarl plastered on his face. Barnes blindly inched forward, steadily closing the fifteen-foot gap between the two.

Marcus could sit and watch this scene of survival of the fittest play out and know Caleb would be right behind him through that door to potential freedom. The chance of getting the answers he sought still alive and well, or... Or he needed to snap back to reality and protect Barnes from being gunned down. And he needed to make the decision immediately.

16
PINNED DOWN

A BONY FINGER pressed to the gray lips of the sideways-turned woman. Sweeping green pine trees obscured her face from the eyes up and the slightest upturn at the corner of her mouth hinted at a grin. *Shhh*, she instructed in breathy seduction.

Marcus shot at the inked woman on Caleb's left bicep, his bullet striking her in the cheek. Caleb yelped from the sudden hit, like a wounded wolf caught in a snare. He twisted and jerked his body violently from the shot, the motion drawing him out from behind his rolling tool cabinet shield and leaving him unprotected. This allowed Barnes to see his target for the first time, his eyes catching Caleb's movement the way a motion-detecting security light captures a passing figure at night.

Marcus streaked through the back door a split second after he squeezed the trigger and one or two seconds before hearing the *POP POP POP* of Barnes firing into Caleb's center mass. A roar of anguish cried out and the thud of his body hitting the floor came a second or two before the rush of feet scuffled and pounded into the unit.

Off and running, Marcus sprinted down a long, skinny corridor illuminated by one solitary light that blinked on when he burst through the door. The dim light was maybe forty yards from him. Far enough he needed to hold out a hand in front of his body as he ran, as he could only make out the first few feet at a time. Running past door after door on both sides of the hallway, he took the passage for a fire escape route of sorts.

His heart pounded against his chest. What had he done? He'd allowed Barnes to kill the only person who could answer his questions. *Not now.* There'd be plenty of time to wallow in regret and self-pity later.

Marcus stiff-armed the metal push bar on the door that emerged without warning using the heels of his palms, just like his days as a college tight end evading a tackle in the flat.

Outside, he slammed to a stop to keep from running into the perimeter wall and fence. Darting his eyes left to right, he saw no one in pursuit. He planted his foot onto the ledge of the gray block wall, grabbed the chain-link fence and scaled to the top in a few quick motions. He paused, once there, to survey the barbed wire coiled along the top in a fat, spiraling roll. Marcus thrust himself up and landed his chest on the sharp barrier. He cursed, rolling his body over the wire, the barbs digging into the flesh of his arms, chest and back. In one last effort to contain him, the barbed wire snagged his shirt but it tore easily in a slow, ripping sound and he tumbled to the ground on the other side of the wall.

Dazed yet frantic, Marcus looked up and saw the piece of shirt. He kicked up off the top of the block wall, reached up and snatched it between two fingers and took off running to his rental car as soon as he landed.

The drive back to the motel was a panicked blur. He pushed the car to 80 mph on the on-ramp to the highway. Whipped his head back and forth while he merged. Caught a glimpse of his face in the rear-view mirror. Dust coated his temples and cheeks; his eyes were wide and wet, and a trickle of blood leaked from his left nostril. Bullet fire still rang in his ears.

Drivers honked with his erratic lane changing.

If Barnes and Castillo and the rest of the arresting party didn't know Marcus was in Caleb's unit when they rolled up, they definitely did after he shot Caleb. They knew *someone* was in there at least.

"Fuck!" Marcus punched the steering wheel.

When he felt his right nipple suddenly get hard, he looked down at the hole in his shirt from the run-in with the barbed wire and realized he had cranked the air conditioning on high. His tattered, blood-dotted shirt flapped in the artificial breeze.

How had they found Caleb? There was no way he'd left fingerprints on the car or on Bill, right? Marcus had been as surprised as Caleb was by police suddenly showing up.

Fear and worry had his mind spinning and adrenaline stoked his panicked state. His thoughts glazed his eyesight over and he nearly rear-ended a mini-van, stomping the brakes and changing lanes to avoid a collision at the last second.

It wasn't until he was a few miles from his exit that he noticed he was still holding his gun. It was shaking, dangling in his hand with his fingers loosely wrapped around it. His right palm resting on the steering wheel.

Out of nowhere, an aching pain throbbed from his back. He grimaced, the lines at the corners of his eyes deepening as the pain intensified, his body awakening to reality.

Marcus set the gun on the passenger's seat, leaned forward and twisted his arm behind his back to feel for the source of the pain. He strained and grimaced more. His cheeks reddened when he held his breath.

The wound was just out of his reach, like an itch you need someone else to scratch for you. Marcus huffed, letting out his held breath and dropping his hand. But then as quickly tried to reach for the wound again. This time he felt the surrounding skin and it was hot to the touch, burning. He visualized it as a field engulfed in flames, encircling the deep, festering spot where the bullet entered his body.

When he looked at his hand, wet blood stained his fingers but didn't drip off them. So, there was that bit of positive news. The sight still made him remain leaned forward to keep his back from touching the seat for fear of blood soaking through his shirt to the cloth seat of the rental car.

Just before pulling into the hotel, Marcus returned his gun to the holster clipped to his shorts. Once parked, he got out, rushed into the room and immediately pulled off his shirt in one motion, yanking it by the back of the collar over his head.

Breathing heavy, shallow gulps of air through his mouth, Marcus darted to the mirror and turned his back toward it. He twisted and contorted his body, but when he wasn't able to find a good angle, he popped his butt up on the vanity and strained again to find the wound.

The area around it was as red as it imagined and blood smeared the majority of that side of his back. Then, he spotted the site of the wound, just below his right shoulder blade. It was a mess of red and purple blood and was too enflamed to see the actual hole from this angle.

And he still couldn't reach or touch it to inspect it either. He tried several times, each time giving up with a huff and a choice curse word.

"Fuck, fuck, fuck." And with that, he gave up. He paced in front of the mirror, wiped up the blood he could reach with a white hand towel.

Just then, his phone buzzed in his pocket and kept buzzing. His lieutenant calling.

"Shit." He heard his own pathetic voice. He stared at his phone and it continued to vibrate for what seemed like an eternity before finally going to voicemail. His skin tingled and he felt his insides flush from head to toe, starting at his chest and working in opposite directions. He pulled off his holster and tossed it and the gun on top of his gym bag.

The phone chimed. Shaking by this point, Marcus opened the phone and deleted the voicemail without checking it.

"What the hell am I going to do?" He now sat on the edge of the bed, head in hands.

Digging his knuckles into his temples in a twisting motion, he ground his teeth and tears fell to the worn carpet.

Several minutes later, Marcus was still pressing his fists into the side of his head and was now rocking when his phone vibrated again beside his leg.

"Where are you man?" A text from McKenzie.

Another popped up after it on the locked screen.

"We are all worried about you Marcus. Call—"

Marcus cursed and stood up, looking around the room before walking to the bathroom sink. There, he cupped handfuls of water to his mouth from the faucet.

With each greedy slurp, he looked at his disheveled appearance in the mirror and then away, unable to look at his own face for more than a second at a time.

"Look at you, Marcus." He shook his head. "It's time to turn yourself in."

After a dozen handfuls of water, his mind began to argue with itself.

Slurp. What have you really done wrong?

Slurp. Bill deserved what he got. And Caleb killed him, not you. *Slurp.*

The back and forth knotted his stomach. Seven years on the Ocean Beach beat and four in El Centro before had taught him humans were capable of going to great lengths to fool themselves. It's always easier to blame anyone and everyone before yourself.

He picked up the phone and dialed, wondering if he was doing the same. After waiting impatiently on hold—slapping his thigh and yelling, "Come on!" several times—he was connected with his mother.

"Hi, Mom."

"Marcus? What's wrong?"

"Nothing."

"I can hear it in your voice, son." Her voice was weak, yet firm.

"I'm just," he started and paused. "I'm, just tired, is all. Ready to come home."

She bought the excuse long enough for Marcus to change the subject. Taking a gulp and squeezing his eyes shut, he asked, "Could you give me Terry's phone number?"

The request surprised Stacey, distracted her of all her concerns. She carefully recited the number to her son.

"Thanks, Mom. Be home soon."

"Love you, Marcus. I'm so proud of you."

The words made Marcus cringe and he didn't think that was a good sign.

IT TOOK TERRY roughly ten minutes to get to the motel room. Marcus crept to the door and let him in when he heard the *knock-knock-knock... knock... knock* cadence he told him to use.

"What you got into?" Terry asked in a high-pitched voice, taking a step inside the door. A look of shock grew on his face and he glided to the side to let Marcus close the door.

"Just get inside," Marcus replied.

"I'm in, I'm in. Didn't tell me you was beat to hell."

"Yeah."

Terry stared at his son, not wide-eyed as such, but startled and a bit confused all the same. Marcus avoided his father's eyes, not for reasons of shame, but more out of hesitancy with his decision to ask Terry for help.

"Get in the shower. Clean off your face and, and that blood and shit," Terry said, pointing and waving his finger at Marcus' back. "Got to see what we're workin' with."

Marcus hadn't thought of cleaning up until Terry mentioned it, and so he followed the instructions. He returned a few minutes later wearing the same soiled shorts he had on before the shower; the back of the waistline stained with his blood.

"I can feel it," Marcus said in a panicked voice. He rushed up to Terry, who was sitting on the edge of the bed facing the bathroom. "I need you to get the bullet out!"

"Shit, you got shot?" Terry said.

"Yeah. I'm pretty sure."

Terry whipped off his Dallas Cowboys hat and fanned his face with it.

"Well sit down." He put the hat back on his head loosely and then swatted the mattress next to him.

Marcus sat down facing away from Terry, who put his left hand on Marcus' left shoulder as a way of balancing himself as he began his inspection. His hand felt along his son's back gently until he reached the wound, touching it with two fingers.

"Ow!" Marcus yelped and jumped.

"Sorry," Terry said softly. "I need a light, hang on."

After fishing his cell phone from his jean shorts, he raised the flashlight back to the wound and said, "I can't tell if there's anything in there."

"Did you look?" Marcus asked.

Dropping his arms, his left with the phone in it bouncing on the mattress, Terry said, "The hell you think I'm doing?"

Waiting a second for his point to land, he added, "'Sides, it's not bleeding much."

"That doesn't mean anything," Marcus said. "Ok, hang on."

Marcus pulled his gym bag on to the bed, took out a first aid kit and handed it to Terry over his shoulder.

"There's all you'll need. You have to spread the wound and see. Use the tweezers, then go from there."

When Terry didn't respond and Marcus didn't hear the first aid kit open, he turned around to see his father staring down at it in his hand.

"What's wrong?" Marcus asked.

"Nothin'. It's just." Terry looked up at Marcus. "I'm glad you called me is all."

After a couple of seconds of silence, Marcus said, "I had no choice."

Terry unsnapped the kit open and Marcus turned his head forward.

"Bend over," Terry said. "You a fucking giant, kid."

Marcus complied, resting his forearms on his thighs, keeping his back straight enough to set dinnerware for two on and serve a meal.

"Relax, relax," Terry said, patting him on the middle of his back gently with an open palm.

Terry held up his cell phone, using it to light his work. He moved the tweezers into position. Three of fingers came off the phone and their tips pressed on Marcus for leverage.

"Hold still now," he said.

Marcus grimaced and put his head in his hands when Terry pulled at the wound. He sucked through his clenched teeth when he felt the cold tweezers spread his flesh apart.

"What do you see?" he said. The words vibrated out as though he were shivering coatless in a snowstorm.

"Hang on," Terry sang.

Marcus could feel what he guessed was the corner of the phone pressing on the hot skin just above where he was pulling and then a release.

Terry sat up, held both arms out, and declared, "I don't see no bullet. I think you're good."

"You sure?" Marcus asked.

"Yep. Lemme clean it up and put a bandage on it."

"OK," Marcus said.

Terry got up and came back with a warm, soapy hand towel and began cleaning the area, using slow, gentle strokes. Marcus flinched when it first touched his back but the feeling of instant soothing calm collapsed his chest. He blew out a big breath.

"So, how you get shot?" Terry asked bluntly. He tossed the hand towel on to the sink counter.

"It's complicated," Marcus said.

"Kinda like why I'm doin' this and not a nurse?"

Marcus groaned. "Something like that."

Thoughts of the shootout and the situation he had put himself in hadn't been far from top of mind since he escaped. But he had been able to temporarily shove everything aside to focus on fixing his wound. With Terry's question, however, panic came rushing back again. He tried to hide it, burying his head in his hands. What had seemed justifiable only a few days earlier, now felt cheap and useless. Adding to the feeling, the realization that he would never get the answers he still needed with Caleb dead.

"Still hurt that bad?" Terry asked, hearing Marcus moan when applying the Neosporin.

Marcus coughed. "Yeah."

The confines of the tiny motel room seemed to shrink in on him with every second. Same as back at the scene of the stolen car with Bill's body in the trunk and evidence in his pocket. His forehead beaded with sweat and the perspiration dripped to the floor. Not sure if he was going to cry or scream, Marcus instead punched his thigh, once then another two times.

"Whoa!" Terry said, jumping off the bed. When he got around to the front of Marcus, he set a hand on his shoulder.

"I fucked up. I don't know what to do," Marcus said, looking up at him.

"Naw," Terry said. "What happened?"

Marcus shook his head.

"Ain't nothin' we can't handle," Terry said.

Feeling a suffocating pressure on his chest, his breaths turned to gulps and pretty soon Marcus couldn't catch his breath.

"Boy. Boy. Calm down," Terry said in a soothing voice.

Marcus stood up and placed his hands on his hips and sucked deep pulls of air through his nose until his lungs couldn't hold anymore. Then exhaled through puckered lips. He moved one hand up to his side and pinched his fingers around his oblique to feel his core inflate and deflate with each series of deep breaths.

After six or seven rounds of this, Marcus caught his breath. He opened his eyes to see Terry staring at him with a pained expression on his face.

"I, I," Marcus stuttered and Terry jumped in.

"You can tell me. I ain't no snitch."

Marcus sat back down on the bed. After one last big breath in and out, he reluctantly shared with Terry what happened in Caleb's work unit, but didn't mention Bill.

"I don't get it," Terry said. "Why would you be in trouble? Sounds like you saved your buddy's life."

"He's not my buddy," Marcus said, referring to Barnes.

"'Cause you tried to arrest the guy yourself? Is that it?"

"No, I wasn't trying to arrest Caleb. I, I was trying to make sure he wasn't arrested for this murder I found in San Diego. I told you it's complicated."

Terry looked at Marcus out of the corner of his eye, pressed his lips together and scoffed.

"I think you're a hero and think the cops will think so, too."

"You don't get it," Marcus said and sighed. "I need to turn myself in."

"Fuck that!" Terry yelled.

"But I stole evidence. Twice! And I... I..." Marcus trailed off, dropped his head and plopped back on the bed.

There were several minutes of silence and Marcus felt done, defeated and resigned. And he likely was. Marcus told himself he was going to do the right thing.

"Listen," Terry said. "I'm going get us some food and we can talk some more 'bout this. Ok? You need some food in ya."

"Sure," Marcus said.

Terry nodded, turned for the door. When he reached the handle, he looked back. Marcus was flopped on to the bed spread eagle. Terry scooped up the room card and the keys to Marcus' rental car from off the dresser. Marcus didn't object.

Terry wasn't gone long. The crinkle of paper bags and the jingle of keys stirred Marcus. When Terry walked in, the smell of grease, hot bread, cheese and griddled beef grabbed his full attention.

Marcus moaned. "Oh, man." He sat up and saw Terry holding two orange and white Whataburger bags. He licked his lips and scooted to the end of the bed. He watched Terry pull the food out of the bags and set it on the dresser.

"Be back, got drinks in the car," Terry said and shuffled off.

Marcus partitioned one of the burgers and an order of fries to one side of the dresser and stood over them ready to pounce.

"They the same?" he asked when Terry returned to the room.

"Yeah, Monterey Melts." Terry rubbed his hands together and let out a snicker.

Marcus unwrapped the burger and greedily chomped into the two patties, melted Pepper Jack cheese and sautéed peppers and onion.

"Ohhh, man." He moaned with a full mouth when the fatty juices hit the back of his tongue.

The two stood next to the dresser and devoured the meal. At several points they locked eyes and smiled at each other.

"Thanks," Marcus said, when he finished. "I needed that." He wiped grease from the corners of his mouth with a napkin and moaned in satisfaction a bit more.

"Good, right?"

"Oh yeah," Marcus said. "I must have been ten or eleven last time I had Whataburger."

"Yeah," Terry crooned with a wide grin. "They don't have them out by you, huh?"

Marcus tossed the napkin in one of the bags, sighed and dropped his shoulders with contentment.

Both of the men stood in place for several minutes in food-coma silence.

After a while, Marcus got serious. "Can I ask you a question?"

Terry nodded.

"Shoot," he said and then realized his poorly-timed choice of words. "Shit, I didn't mean it like that!" He held up both hands with a wadded napkin trapped in the webbing of his thumb.

"It's cool," Marcus said, and chuckled. "No, I was gonna ask, why are you trying all of the sudden? Why are you helping me? I mean, you didn't give a shit about me all those years, but now?"

Terry dropped his head and did a nervous shuffle with his feet.

"Shit's getting real," he said, in a subdued voice.

"I'm sorry," Marcus started, but then scowled. Then corrected himself. "I mean, I'm not sorry, but—"

"I know, I know," Terry said. "I deserve it."

Marcus bent down to his gym bag and winced. He grabbing his side with pain radiating from his wound. He fished out a shirt and gingerly put it on. Then returned his eyes to Terry.

He raised his eyebrows to let Terry know he was waiting for a response.

Terry wiped the corner of his mouth with the wadded napkin and moved into a stance with his feet close together and his hands behind his back.

"I feel shitty for the way I treated you and your mom." He stared at the ground. "Talk 'bout fucking up."

As if he didn't hear the words or more likely had waited his entire life to hear them and they rang hollow, Marcus shook his head and huffed.

"I needed a dad!" he said.

Keeping his eyes trained to the floor, Terry sighed deeply and didn't respond.

"I'm not tryin' to say, 'boo-hoo, you ruined my life,' or anything," Marcus said, pantomiming by rolling his fists at the base of his eyes with a pouting face.

Terry looked up, cringed at Marcus' face.

"I let you down, I know," he said in a low, shaky voice.

Marcus looked away.

"I'm tryin' now," Terry said.

"What about then?" Marcus whipped his head back, his forehead wrinkled.

They stared at each other in silence for a few long moments. Terry tossed his napkin at the small, lined trash can next to the dresser but missed.

"I want to hear from you *why*," Marcus said.

"Why?"

"Yeah. Why. Why did you hit Mom and why were you never around?"

Terry took a step toward Marcus, then twisted his body and collapsed on the end of the bed, interlocking his hands on his lap. He stared ahead with a glazed look as if he was trying to put himself back in that time. After a few seconds, he dropped his head.

"Truth is, I don't know why, son."

Before Marcus could say anything—only a squeak getting out—Terry outstretched his right hand, looked up and added, "All's I know is that's not me now and I'm tryin'. I was a shit father and a even shittier husband. I know that!"

Shifting his weight to his left leg and crossing his arms, Marcus said, "But Mom's forgiven you, I guess?" His tone came out snotty, like the teenager his father had never met.

"Yeah, somehow," Terry said cautiously. "That make you mad?"

"Honestly? Yeah. Yeah, it does! I mean, what the fuck?"

Terry dropped his head again, this time so far it practically fell in his lap.

Marcus was hot. His temper jumped like a flame fed starter fluid. He seethed; saliva spraying out from his clenched teeth with his next words.

"Did you even fucking care when you came home and we were gone?" He held his fists tight, shaking at his side. "Did you?"

"I tried to make it up," Terry said, but the words were too quiet for Marcus to hear.

"Well?"

"Well, what?" Terry asked.

"Did you care that we left you? Or did us leaving actually give you the life you wanted?"

Terry turned his head to the left and said something inaudible.

"Speak up!" Marcus demanded.

Terry groaned something.

"Louder, old man!" Marcus was leaning into his words now, literally. His body lunged forward, balanced on the balls of his feet, keeping him from falling forward with each rebuke.

Terry turned his face to meet Marcus and, with tears resting in his saggy eyes, confessed in a meek voice, "No." A fat, round drop blinked from his left eye and fell to the ground.

The word knocked Marcus backwards, as if it took him by complete surprise and punched him in the chest.

"But I care now," Terry pleaded immediately. Tears fell from both eyes now.

He said something else but Marcus only heard buzzing.

"Wow," Marcus said. He began rubbing his forehead.

"I tried to make it up to you," Terry said.

Not hearing the words, Marcus said, "What?"

Now Terry started to hyperventilate. Tears trickled down his cheeks and soon he was gasping for air through body jerks. He turned away, hiding his face from Marcus, who still burned hot. He watched his father's bony shoulders bounce with each short, violent breath. Through the tears and shortness of breath, Marcus squinted and cocked his head, unable to understand what his old man was saying.

"Huh?"

"I fucked... your... life... again," Terry managed, hiccupping out every word.

"What do you mean?"

Looking at Marcus, his saggy cheeks wet, Terry couldn't talk for blubbering.

"Calm down, man," Marcus said, rolling his eyes.

Terry followed his instructions and mimicked the breathing technique Marcus had used just an hour earlier: One big draw of air in, hold on to his side, and let the breath out. After several rounds of this over a few minutes time, Terry had calmed down.

Marcus sighed, turned around and began to pace in three-step turns.

Calming down himself, Marcus thought how unexpected it was that he had opened up to his father. How he'd let out some of his built-up anger. He equally didn't expect his father to be so apologetic. Or cry. It momentarily distracted him from his bigger dilemma.

From behind him, Terry said, "You said I didn't ruin your life."

"And you didn't," Marcus said, not turning around to look at him.

"But I did," Terry insisted. "Twice. I thought I was fixing the first fuck up when I hired that boy. But turns out, I'm fucking up your life all over again."

Skittish, Terry rubbed his forehead and didn't look up.

Marcus perked up, but wasn't quite sure he understood what his father meant. He stopped pacing and turned around with his hands on his hips, his eyes wide.

Terry dropped his head into his hands and bent over into his lap, sniffing back the last of his tears. Though muffled, Marcus heard Terry's next words in booming clarity.

"I killed that newspaper man for you and I thought that would be that."

17

BY WAY OF RETRIBUTION

"WHAT DID YOU just say? What are you talking about?"

Marcus' eyes were wide, focused on his father with panicked confusion. Terry didn't answer and kept his head down and face hidden.

In two steps, Marcus rushed to stand in front of him. He bent down and grabbed both of Terry's shoulders and shook him.

"What did you just say?" Marcus repeated. Each subsequent word climbed an octave higher leaving his mouth. He shook his father again, this time harder than the first and it tossed the Cowboys hat from his head, sending it tumbling to the ground. Shaggy, gray-accented hair splayed out in the hat's absence.

Terry's bony shoulders dug into Marcus' palms as he squeezed them firm. Unaffected by the jolting but responding anyway, Terry raised his head.

"It's true," he whispered, when his face finally met his son's.

Marcus gasped and just stood there, squeezing his father's shoulders with his jaw dropped open. He tried to say something but nothing coherent came out.

Terry spoke up and said, "I found out about Bill, and… what… what he did to you." His eyes darted to the side. "I tried to fix it."

Marcus stumbled back a step and stood dazed, his arms dangling lifeless at his sides.

"You know?" Marcus whispered the words so quietly they could have been just to himself, but Terry heard him.

The older man bent over and picked up his hat from the floor and put it on. He sat up, rubbed his right arm with his left hand and said in a reluctant voice, without looking up, "Yeah."

Marcus tripped backward a step, doubled over and grabbed his knees, expecting his body to lurch and his senses buckle at the realization of a third person knowing he had been molested.

Memories of those awful nights he hovered outside his parents' closed bedroom door, trying to work up the nerve to divulge his deepest, darkest secret—the one secret tearing up his insides and twisting his thoughts—rushed back to him.

The motel's musty carpet swirled in front of his eyes, so he clenched them closed, hoping to stop the sensation. But the blackness swirled instead.

Marcus saw his pre-teen self, collapsed on the floor, rocking uncontrollably against the wall of the apartment. Knees tucked to his chest, hugging them so tight his ribs would be sore the next day. Taken to the point of sobbing most of those late nights, he would suck in each body-rocking gasp and hold it like a breath when trying to get rid of the hiccups, in the hopes it would have the same effect. He remembered the salty taste of tears streaming down his face and into his mouth. How he told himself he had to stop crying before he went into his parents' room because his father would tell him only babies cried.

Terry said something, but the words were garbled in Marcus' ears.

When he started to sway involuntarily, he felt a hand squeeze his shoulder and then his other. It was Terry turning him around, guiding him to sit on the bed.

"Here, take this," Terry said. Marcus didn't respond.

Terry pushed a Whataburger cup into one of his hands and squeezed his own around it, ensuring the drink wouldn't fall.

"Drink."

Marcus did so absent-mindedly and his eyes shot open when the carbonated sugar hit the back of his throat.

"There he is," Terry said in a tone Marcus had never heard from him before.

Looking up at his father, he pushed the Styrofoam cup back to him.

"I, I, I don't understand," he said, watching Terry set the drink down on the dresser.

His father relaxed on to the dresser in a half-sit with his feet planted on the ground at a 45-degree angle. Pressing his lips together, he breathed out an audible puff of air from his nose and said, "These the times I wish I still smoked."

"When?" Marcus asked.

"When what?" Terry asked.

"When did you find out? How?"

Terry rubbed the side of his face, scrunched his nose and closed one eye. Got lost in thought. Then, he spoke up.

"You know his newspaper was on my delivery route all those years," he said. "One day I saw that sick fuck looking all goofy at some young boy when I was in there. Got me thinkin'. Thinkin' how you was 'bout that same age when I sent you to work for him that one summer."

Marcus dropped his head. He remembered the goofy look— as Terry put it. It was really a glare of possession, and only intensified as the abuse went on.

Soon as Bill pulled out the chewed-up pencil from behind his ear, Marcus knew the look was coming and his heart sank every time. Bill's excited eyes fixed on him through round glass lenses, the tip of his tongue pinched between his front teeth and poking out of his thin lips. Sweat beaded on his lumpy forehead. With a tuck of his chin and a tilt of his eyes, he said, "You are mine, Marcus Kemp" without uttering a word.

Terry continued.

"Yeah, so, I gotta funny feeling and found a guy to follow him."

"What, like a private detective?" Marcus asked.

"Sort of. I mean, yeah. Just a guy that a guy at work put me on."

"Did a guy at work connect you with Caleb, too?"

"Naw, but that was after this," Terry said. He was still rubbing his cheek, now slower, and pulling at his skin and pinching his loose jowl with each downstroke.

"My guy didn't find nothin' but I knew Bill was a piece of shit—" Terry ended his sentence short, as if he had more to say but stopped himself. He paused from rubbing his face, looked to the side and shuttered.

Marcus breathed a heavy breath, the skin between his eyebrows folding in two rows. He wondered what new tricks Bill employed over the years to escape detection, because he sure as hell was molesting boys up until the day Marcus found him dead in the trunk in San Diego.

What he wouldn't have given for a private detective to be tailing them when Bill took him to the construction site all those Friday afternoons, all those years ago.

"Then I hired Caleb," Terry said.

"When was that?" Marcus asked.

"A few months ago."

Eyes widening, Marcus asked, "So you just found out about this?"

"Aw, naw," Terry said. Waved his hands. "I found out a couple years ago. Was trying to figure out what to do about it."

A look of confusion—complete with ridged forehead, squinted, fluttering eyes and an open mouth looking like someone trying to avoid smelling a stench—spread across Marcus' face. Terry saw he needed to illuminate more of the story for his son.

"The next time I saw that asshole at the paper, I charged him up!" Terry said. "I slammed him up against the wall in his office and yelled right in his fat face. He was all shaking and crying and shit."

Terry grinned momentarily, but then a look of anger returned to his face, and he put his fists up like he was reenacting pinning Bill to the wall.

"Did you touch my boy? That's what I kept yelling at him."

"Did he admit it?" Marcus hung on Terry's words.

"No." Terry slumped. Then, on a dime, excitement returned to his face.

"That motherfucker say he didn't know what I was talking 'bout. I wanted to punch him in his stupid glasses!"

Terry's chest heaved, making his body rock itself back and forth slightly. Marcus sat up straight, still glued to the story.

"Anyway, I couldn't get him to admit it," Terry said. "But I knew."

"How?"

Terry didn't think on this at all.

"Fuck. The way his eyes looked every time I said your name. Can't describe it. Was nasty. Like just saying it gave him a charge."

Cringing at his own description, Terry looked away.

Marcus didn't cringe, but instead, his body tensed in fury.

"Weren't you afraid he would be suspicious of you after that?" Marcus asked. His fists were clenched so tight his nails dug into his palms. "Is that why you waited two years to have him killed?"

Terry looked at Marcus in the eyes.

"Naw," he said, shaking his head. "It was one of my last days before I retired, just worked out that way."

Terry explained how Bill grew smugger by the minute and by the end of their interaction, he was jovial and even chuckled walking him to the front door.

"He knew you couldn't prove anything," Marcus said.

"Motherfucker," Terry said into his chest.

"Sorry, I'm just having a hard time wrapping my head around how you killed a guy on a hunch, even if it was correct," Marcus said.

Terry's head dropped.

Marcus added, "You didn't even need to know what he did to me back then?"

"I know enough," Terry replied, not looking up.

They both sat in silence for a minute.

"When I figured out he'd done something to you," Terry said. "That's when it hit me."

"What hit you?" Marcus was still fuming, visualizing the encounter and Bill's shit-eaten grin.

Terry gulped.

"The shit dad I was."

The words snapped Marcus from his daydream. He blew out a large breath. Terry did the same.

"Yeah," Terry said after a few seconds.

"Why? Why did that make you realize that?" Marcus asked. His focus was back entirely on Terry, and his words sounded as if he knew the answer but still wanted to hear it.

Terry shoved his hands in his pockets and looked at his sneakers.

"'Cause. I'm the one that punished you by making you go to that job."

Marcus rubbed the back of his neck and stared up at the ceiling. Like any son, Marcus longed for his father's approval as a child, even in spite of Terry's many flaws. It had been years— hell more like a couple of decades—since he could say he cared for his father or sought his favor. But now, after hearing Terry lay out his twisted path to redemption for all of his sins, Marcus felt conflicted.

He had trained himself over the years to remember his father as the uncaring, neglectful person he was. When memories of his father's detachment weren't enough to keep Marcus solely focused on hating him, all he needed was to recall the beatings Terry gave to his mother.

Then, a thought popped in his head.

Marcus blinked, bucked his head and looked at Terry.

"When you came see me in San Diego? Was that after your run-in with Bill?"

Terry's eyes widened. He nodded.

"Yeah!" Terry jumped to his feet. "I was trying to fix things. Like I said. I wanted to tell you what I found out. But—"

"But, what?" Marcus asked, looking up at him.

"I seen how much you still hated me. So, I wanted to do something to really fix it."

Marcus paused for a moment and blurted out, "Like murdering him?"

"Well, yeah," Terry said. "Took me a coupla years, but when it worked out, it worked out."

"What does that mean?" Marcus asked, still sitting on the bed with Terry now prancing in front of him.

Sunlight had stopped burning hot behind the room's drawn curtain, even though it was still a couple of hours from sunset. The air conditioning unit rattled under the window, having been working overtime just to keep the room cooled to seventy-five degrees.

"Caleb found out he was going to San Diego and I told him to do it there and leave Bill for you to find," Terry said. His words oozed with pride and he pushed out his chest like a victorious rooster at the end of a frenzied cockfight.

"*You?*" Marcus said, drawing the word out. "You left his body on my beat?"

"Yeah," Terry said. "I wanted to let you know I took care of it. That I fixed it."

Looking at Terry, Marcus recalled a memory of a cat that once dropped a dead rabbit between his feet when he was a child. He was sitting on the broken-down back porch at Terry's mother's house when the family had gone over for a visit one weekend. His father had the same look in his eyes as that cat had before it jumped in his lap. The look said he hoped bringing home a dead rabbit would mean he would receive some love and pets of approval for his cunning predator skills.

Marcus wrinkled his nose.

"What?" Terry asked.

"Nothing," Marcus said.

"I couldn't just call and tell you I was gonna kill him, uh, have him killed," Terry said, correcting himself as if there was a difference.

"How the fuck did Caleb know I would find the body?" Marcus asked, standing up. His nose flared.

"He watched you one day, I guess."

Marcus erupted.

"What? Are you fucking kidding me?"

"Calm down, man." Terry put his hands up and held them out in a defensive manner.

"God," Marcus whined, and turned his back to him. "That actually scared the shit out of me seeing him and—"

"But you wanted him dead, right? Least you were happy after the shock of it all." Terry smiled.

"Ha!" Marcus said loudly, with no laugh.

"I'm wrong? You just said you weren't trying to arrest Caleb today. So?"

Marcus didn't answer and looked away.

Of course, Terry had it correct, but Marcus had not admitted his motivations out loud to anyone, including himself.

With his father illuminating things, Marcus found himself quickly losing his admiration for Caleb. Not because he didn't appreciate what Caleb had done, but because he was beginning to see he was not the mastermind he believed him to be. Caleb was immaterial, really. He was only as useful in getting the job done. The blunt force object. The gun. The knife. Caleb was the murder weapon. Terry was the will behind the weapon.

"Who else knows about this?" Marcus asked.

"Which part?" Terry asked. But before Marcus could answer, he added, "Nobody. None of it. Just me, Caleb and now you."

Marcus stood up and started pacing along the side of the bed closest to the window and Terry sat back down against the dresser. For the next ten minutes, both men kept their heads down; Marcus pacing and Terry sitting. Huffs grunted intermittently from Marcus; long, dejected sighs escaped his father.

Marcus caught Terry looking at him a couple of times when he made the turn back toward the wall with the dresser. He noticed that proud look Terry had displayed while describing his plan to have Bill murdered had turned into a sagging face of regret. His eyes were no longer wide and excited as they had been, but deep and withdrawn. Each time their eyes met, Marcus turned his head away quickly and rubbed his left forearm.

"I don't even know why I punished you back then," Terry said.

Marcus kept pacing, keeping his hazy eyes on the worn carpet he knew from the smell of the room to be littered with generous traces of cigarette ash, piss and shit.

It was true, Terry didn't get involved with disciplining Marcus as a child and the one instance he did, when Marcus and his friends started the fire on the vacant patio in the apartment complex, was the outlier. There were several instances when Marcus acted up as kids will do, right in front of his father and it was as if Terry was oblivious.

His apathy didn't go unnoticed from Stacy, who would glare at her disinterested husband and later voice her displeasure of having to be the constant disciplinarian.

"For whatever reason, maybe I was tryin' ta prove I could be a dad. I don't know. Maybe I just…"

Terry trailed off and dropped his head. He kicked the toe of his left sneaker with the heel of his right, over and over and the sound of his breathing got louder.

After about a minute or two of this, he huffed and said, "I'm so sorry."

The words stopped Marcus cold and he flicked his eyes over to his father and a warm feeling flooded his body. A feeling he hadn't felt for his father in a couple of decades.

Walking the step or two over to the window, he pulled aside the heavy fabric curtain and poked his face close to the glass, nearly pressing his nose to the pane, and looked up.

"It's getting dark out there—cloudy."

"Yeah? "Probably rain, I'd guess," Terry said.

Still looking out the window, Marcus said, "When it gets cloudy like this in San Diego, it doesn't mean it's going to rain. Tripped me out the first couple of years. We just call it June Gloom."

Terry snorted. "Huh." He walked over to Marcus and stood next to him and put his hand on Marcus' left shoulder.

"I'm sorry," he repeated. "I thought I could fix things. I didn't know what else to do. I got so angry at Bill, but I know I was mostly mad at myself."

It was becoming clear to Marcus. By way of retribution, Terry believed he could atone for his past mistakes and wrongs and rid the world of the only human who hurt his son more than he had. Without turning around, Marcus said, "I'm not mad." He let go of the curtain, turned around and added, "I *am* going to turn myself in, though."

Terry smacked with one side of his own mouth and asked, "Why would you do that?"

"I'm a police officer, Dad. I broke the law."

Stepping backward, Terry plopped on the side of the bed.

"I'd try to stop you, but I know you won't listen."

"It's not that," Marcus said. "There's no way out of this. But either way, I got what I was after."

"What's that?"

"Answers," he said. "Closure."

Terry drew in a deep breath through his nose that raised his torso up. He blew out the air with a moaning sigh.

"I ain't gonna turn myself in but you do what you gotta do," Terry said.

Marcus understood he was talking about implicating him for the murder and Terry confirmed as much.

"If it helps you, I deserve it."

18

DECISIONS

WITH HIS BLACK bag at his side, Marcus climbed the cracked concrete steps of the two-story, pagoda-shaped headquarters of the Garland Police Department. Stopping a step below the top, he turned, closed his eyes and inhaled the faint smell of sweet fungi hanging in the heavy air of the early evening. A cool wind was blowing in and had already taken the heat off the day. Rain was coming, and soon. The earth had opened. The soil's pores impatiently awaited its arrival.

So, too, were the San Diego Homicide and Garland Police detectives waiting for Marcus. He'd called them, let them know he was coming in, before leaving his father at the motel room.

When he walked through one of the heavy glass and steel entry doors, Castillo reached out a hand for the gym bag. Marcus extended it to him.

"There's a gun on top," he said, relinquishing the straps.

Castillo nodded. "Thanks," he said.

A GROUP OF four uniformed officers stared intently at him from behind Castillo. At the lieutenant's side was one detective in a suit Marcus didn't recognize. The cops looked ready to pounce, but Castillo held out a palm at his side to keep them at bay.

The lobby hummed with activity—plain-clothed people Marcus guessed were residents, going in and out of the building, there for any number of reasons. Cops milled about, others leaving and coming in. The hushed surrender taking place just feet inside the entrance drew everyone's attention and Marcus felt their judging eyes.

Taking a step toward him, the suited Garland detective held out his hands and asked flatly, "Do you mind?"

Marcus shook his head and raised his arms like a scarecrow. "You've come a long way, Marcus," he thought to himself and rolled his eyes.

After the detective finished searching him, he held up Marcus' cell phone, wallet and rental car keys and nodded in satisfaction. With the affirmation, Castillo dismissed the uniformed cops and the two detectives escorted Marcus to the second level of the station.

The Garland detective opened the door to an interview room and held it open with an outstretched arm. He sucked in his body to let Marcus and Castillo by. Marcus heard him whisper something at Castillo as he entered, couldn't make it out.

Once all three were inside the room, they directed Marcus to take a seat on a flimsy aluminum chair behind a large oak table taking up a majority of the room. After he sat, they left the room.

Over the years, he had escorted plenty of suspects to dimly-lit rooms such as this for questioning and the irony of the shoe being on the other foot wasn't lost on him.

What did take him by surprise was how calm he felt, as if he was resigned to his fate already. Whatever it might be. With his hands outstretched and resting on the table, fingers laced, Marcus was practically at ease.

He hadn't worked out the details of what he would say when the detectives returned or even if he should say anything when questioned. Yet, somehow, he was fine. His pulse was steady, stomach quiet, his skin dry and no flush of panic.

On the drive to the police station, Marcus had thought through his limited options but hadn't settled on any of them as a definitive course of action. He could twist the story, make himself out to be some sort of vigilante hero figure. Maybe he wanted to be a detective and stole evidence from Bill's body to go on an adventure to prove he could identify and apprehend a killer on his own. But why would they believe that? What would motivate a beat cop to go rogue, to risk his job instead of taking the normal path to becoming a detective? Stupid.

Then, there was the issue of what to do about Terry and his involvement. If Marcus turned him in for hiring the hit on Bill, his secret would surely get out and the media would have a field day.

"Father avenges cop son by hiring killer to bludgeon his molester." Marcus smirked after seeing the headline flash in his mind like a Broadway marquee. But it faded quickly when he told himself there was no way he wanted his past getting out. But, as Terry had implied, turning him in might be the best way to lessen his own punishment.

The only other option, as he saw it, was to admit to everything: he stole and tampered with evidence and obstructed justice. Admit to everything. Except for his motive, that is. They would want a motive and what should he say? There, he was at a loss. Even still, as he waited for detectives to come back and question him with no definitive plan in place, he felt more at peace than he would have expected.

Twenty minutes passed and he still hadn't made a decision on which option to go with, so his mind drifted to his mother. He would make her his call. Marcus scrunched his face. Rubbed his cheeks, thinking about her in hospice and how he wasn't ready to lose her.

To his credit, Marcus had done his share supporting her, assisting Stacey throughout her health issues—from managing her wishes, making changes to her living arrangements and accompanying her to every doctor's appointment. Well, except for the last appointment. He still felt he could have done more.

Of course, if he ever expressed that regret or disappointment in himself, Stacey would outright dismiss his concerns. She regularly thanked him for his support, her eyes holding back tears as she did so. But her appreciation made him feel even more inadequate.

Perhaps the quality he cherished most in her was how she could be his biggest champion in the moments when he was hardest on himself. However, she didn't overlook his faults. No, not by a long shot. She was genuine enough to call him on his own bullshit when it was warranted, too.

The more he thought about what remained of his mother's future and all the things he wanted to tell her and ask her before she left him, the more his stomach tightened. He wanted to be with her.

MORE TIME PASSED.

The only thing hanging on any of the room's walls was an old clock, one from an elementary classroom in the '60s. Plain and ordinary in every way. The hands read six twenty-one.

A few minutes later, the door opened and the detective who'd frisked Marcus when he surrendered entered, holding a paper cup.

"Water?" he asked, and set it on the table within arm's length in front of Marcus.

The white, middle-aged man lingered for a couple of seconds, but Marcus didn't get the impression he was trying to get him to talk or would say anything further himself. He just hovered and scratched his mustache for a few seconds and then pressed his lips tight, sucking the rust-colored whiskers into his mouth.

Without ever making eye-contact, he said, "Welp," in a thick drawl and left the room. It was as if the detective just wanted to get a look at the San Diego cop who skirted his team's surveillance. Marcus swallowed the water in two gulps right after the door closed behind the detective.

Ten more minutes went by and Marcus found himself tracing the grain of the table with his left thumb. The lacquered surface was worn and rough in spots. When his thumb caught a groove, he would stop and go over the spot again. The table reminded him of the one he worked at when he was eleven in *The Plano Register* newsroom.

Another twenty minutes went by.

Marcus thought about Megan and her bright, beautiful face. How he missed her and what he would try to do to win her back if he got out of this mess. Or rather, when he got out of prison.

Stacey was right: he needed to apologize to Megan, and just not over the phone, but in person. He owed her that much. Memories of orange-glowing sunsets, crashing waves, walks on the OB Pier, dinners in his apartment and mornings waking up to her smooth, naked body all filled him with feelings of both encouragement and regret.

Just then, while recalling a hike they had taken one time— almost an hour after being led into the room—the door handle clicked. Marcus turned to watch the silver handle inch down, but the door didn't open. The handle sprang back to its resting position as if the one turning it had changed their mind. A couple of seconds later, the handle clicked again and the door flew open.

In walked Lt. Castillo. He made immediate eye-contact with Marcus, and dropped a yellow legal pad and pen on the table, along with a clipboard securing a thick stack of photos and papers. The aluminum chair across from Marcus clanked when Castillo dragged it out from the table.

"How's your partner?" Marcus asked.

Castillo settled uncomfortably in the chair. He stroked his goatee with his left hand, exhaustion all over his face.

"Barnes is good, man. Happy to be alive." Castillo's serious face didn't match his positive words. Then, pointing a finger at Marcus, he added, "And that's thanks to you."

Marcus couldn't tell if he was flattering him to lay the groundwork to get a confession out of him, or whether it was a genuine expression of gratitude.

There was no smile on his face, and in fact, it was morphing more into a look of confusion. His eyebrows furrowed down over squinted, heavy eyes and he tucked his round chin, the hair of his goatee curling over his bottom lip. Castillo had come into the room with a thought and Marcus had interrupted it. His face was indeed one of confusion, but also of strained focus.

"We'll get back to Barnes," he said. "Really though, thank you."

The unguarded appreciation caught Marcus by surprise. He blinked, straightened his shoulders and rocked back against the chair.

Castillo rested his elbows on the table and connected his knuckles together in front of his face.

"You gotta help me with something," he started.

Marcus had seen the lieutenant's tone and posture before from suspects who pleaded with him not to write them a ticket or arrest them. But Castillo wasn't the one in trouble here, so he had Marcus' full intrigue.

"Who was the dead guy?" Castillo said. "The one in the trunk in OB."

If Marcus had any bluff in him, it went right out the window with that question. His eyes went from calm to vacant; his body collapsed and he exhaled sharply.

San Diego Homicide still didn't have an ID on Bill. Even after killing his murderer. That was a surprise to Marcus.

Castillo took note of his reaction and said, "Do you know who he was?"

Now Marcus felt the familiar flush of panic he had been so accustomed to the last several days. To deny or confess? Both felt to him like flight responses. His chest began to vibrate and pinpricks danced under his skin.

Closing his eyes, he pitched his head to the ceiling and exhaled a breath that skipped four or five times on the way out, like a smooth pebble skimmed across a still lake.

"You ok?" Castillo asked. "Need some water or—"

"No," Marcus said, holding out one hand.

He opened his eyes, looked at Castillo. He exhaled another breath, but this one didn't hesitate.

"I don't know what I was thinking," Marcus began.

The look on Castillo's face softened and he sucked in air to ask a question but stopped short.

"I didn't think I would do this," Marcus said. He leaned forward mirroring Castillo's pose, setting his chin on top of his cupped hands. After blowing out a short, hard breath, he said, "His name was Bill Kaulbier. He was an editor at *The Plano Register.*"

Castillo shrugged.

"It's a local paper. Next city over," Marcus said.

"How do you know this, Marcus?"

"I should have told you at the scene, but something hit me when I opened that trunk and I saw who was inside."

"So, you knew him? Castillo asked, confused. "The deceased?"

"Yes," Marcus said. He let out a slow breath through his nostrils, and maintained eye contact with the lieutenant.

His eyes fell onto the table. Heavy breaths prefaced his next words.

"What I'm about to say," he said, looking back at Castillo, "I've never said out loud or told any other person. Before Monday, I never thought I'd see him again."

In his peripheral vision, Marcus saw his hands and arms were shaking. Castillo leaned back and took his elbows off the table, resting his hands in his lap.

Marcus had not intended to divulge his secret, but here he was, on the brink. It wasn't that he was swayed by Castillo's trusting ear or that he felt admitting it would absolve him. No, it really came down to the sudden realization of how every time his abuser was brought up in any way, he felt as powerless as he had in the front seat of the newspaper man's car so many years ago.

Not more than a couple of hours earlier he had told Terry he found closure and answers, and, at the time, he believed the former was because of the latter. But in this moment, he wondered if he could only grapple true closure by facing the horrors of his past and telling someone about his abuse.

Yes, he felt Bill's smothering presence: seeping into his thoughts, molesting his dreams, hijacking his emotions. Each time he was snapped back to the place of being the helpless eleven-year-old with no recourse other than to let what was going to happen, happen. Bill was dead, and for that, he was deeply appreciative. His actions over the past few days had proved as much. But Bill's mental control over Marcus hadn't died with him. Moving away and putting years between the abuse had worked at suppressing memories, but he was beyond that now. The only way now he could hope to move on, he surmised right then, was to come clean.

"When I was eleven and lived here in Plano, Bill molested me over the course of seven weeks. Every Friday. In his car at a construction site. When I found his body in the stolen vehicle, all those horrible memories came flooding back. I thought I had buried all of that—everything he did to me."

Marcus paused for a breath and then continued.

"I, I don't know what I was thinking. I wanted to find the person who killed him and, and…"

"And what?" Castillo urged.

"And help him get away with it," Marcus said, dropping his head and pressing his forehead against his fists, hiding his face.

Castillo didn't reply and Marcus stayed in the same position, where he stared at the grain of the wood table.

After a few seconds, Castillo sighed and said, "I'm sorry that happened to you, Marcus," and let out another sigh.

Marcus sat back, his arms collapsing on to the table. "Yeah."

There was silence for what likely felt to both much longer than the actual thirty seconds that elapsed.

Castillo asked, "So, the shootout. Tell me about that. You were there to… do what exactly?"

"I don't know," Marcus said. I guess I needed to find out why he killed Bill."

"Yeah, Castillo said. "I get that."

Over the next hour, the two of them went over the details of Marcus' rogue mission in detail. Marcus shouted "Huh!" and shook his head when Castillo told him how Barnes saw him dropping off the AirPod at SDPD headquarters and how practically every lead they'd had was from tracking him.

Castillo looked at Marcus in amazement when he told him about finding the AirPod underneath the utility box at the convention center.

They broke down the events at Caleb's scene by scene and again Castillo's tone was one of almost reverence when they got to the part when Marcus shot Caleb to protect Barnes.

The Garland detective came in once to give Marcus more water and another time to make sure Castillo didn't need his assistance. Marcus found it odd the detective, or maybe his supervisor, ceded authority to the out-of-town lieutenant. But they had obviously worked out an arrangement.

A little after 8 p.m., they seemed to be wrapping up and Castillo said he would return, but needed to visit the men's room.

A minute later, a disheveled Dt. Aaron Barnes burst through the door slurring, "Come here. Come here," and motioning to Marcus to stand up.

The light blue, long-sleeved dress shirt he wore was untucked and every other button or so was undone, revealing a generous amount of his hairless chest and stomach. One side of the shirt's collar was flipped up and flicked his ear when he turned his head that way. When it would brush him, he swatted at it in a slow-motioned, much delayed, innate response, not quite piecing together he just needed to flip the collar back down.

Barnes pulled in Marcus tight for a hug, squeezed him and blew hot, alcohol breath into his ear.

"Thank you, brah. Thank you."

"Yeah," Marcus said, wincing and trying to pull away a bit. But Barnes kept his hold and pulled him back in, touching his nose to Marcus' cheek.

"You saved my life, bro," Barnes said slowly, ensuring he got every word correct.

Marcus nodded and said, "Yes. Okay."

Barnes let go of him, but then grabbed him by both shoulders before he could escape.

"You don't understand!" he cried. The volume of his own voice made his eyes shoot open. Marcus didn't respond, and like a child who realizes they're using an outside voice during a church service, Barnes hiccupped and sheepishly whispered, "You saved my life."

His eyes then blinked and his head swirled in a tight circle, making his body sway just slightly. "Jesus, you *are* a big fucker," he said, looking up at Marcus. He didn't let go right away, continuing to squeeze his shoulders.

Marcus smirked and then laughed.

"Okay, okay," Castillo sang out, coming back into the room. He pulled Barnes off Marcus and drove his partner back toward the door. Barnes resisted a bit, shouting out something incoherent, but Castillo's size advantage was no match for his impaired state. Barnes hovered for a second and was then escorted out of the room by a Garland officer who was holding the door open.

"Sorry about him," Castillo said with failed-smile. He sat down and motioned for Marcus to do the same. "He's been blowing off some steam."

"Yeah, I can tell," Marcus said, still smirking.

Castillo settled into his chair with a shimmy and then braced what he was about to say by pumping his arms.

"Ok. I know I just left, but I need to leave you again. I will be back, but I just can't tell you when."

Marcus cocked his head slightly.

"Not an interrogation trick," Castillo said, holding up his right hand like when swearing on a bible in court. He huffed, dropped his hand and gathered the yellow legal pad he had filled with notes during their time together. Once he stood up, he grabbed the clipboard as well.

Standing at the mouth of the door, he turned and looked back with confused eyes but also a warm smile at Marcus.

"I need to make a call. A few calls, actually. Sit tight."

19

A BURIAL

WHEN MARCUS RETURNED from Texas, he was a free man. For the time being.

Castillo didn't put Marcus under arrest or read him his rights when he came back into the interrogation room. He only relayed a message from San Diego that the Police Chief and City Attorney were "involved in a dialogue" about his situation. And that Castillo and Barnes would fly him back to San Diego the next morning.

A day later, Marcus was summoned to SDPD headquarters.

When he walked into the building on Broadway in downtown San Diego—the same place he had violated so many policies just days earlier— his lieutenant greeted him at the entrance.

He led him to the office of the Chief of Police, pausing briefly at the closed door, pointing at it and nodded to the administrative assistant sitting behind a desk outside the office. After Lt. Berry knocked on the door with two quick raps of his knuckle, the two entered the office and the lieutenant closed the door behind them.

"Hello, Officer Kemp," the chief said, seated behind his desk. He motioned to both to sit in the chairs across from him.

"Chief," Marcus said, dropping his head.

After both sat down, the chief got right to the point.

"The City Attorney is declining to pursue charges against you at this time, Kemp."

The words were the exact opposite of what Marcus had prepared himself to hear and he sat stunned as a result.

Berry shifted in his seat and put his right hand on the back of Marcus' chair, stared at him.

Feeling his glare, Marcus fumbled over his words, saying, "I, uh, I. I don't know what to say. Thank you, but how?"

The chief cleared his throat and leaned forward. Rested his elbows on the desk and folded his hands together.

"She came to the same conclusion as we did," he said. "While you violated numerous department policies—"

"Which you will be held accountable for," Berry interjected.

The chief raised a palm to the lieutenant and continued.

"The end result was that Homicide identified and apprehended a suspect they were able to prove was the killer of the victim you discovered on your beat."

Marcus felt his heart racing while he stared the chief in the eyes, not blinking. He was gripping the armrests of his chair so tightly that his fingers began to tingle.

"I, I—"

"I'm not finished," the chief said. "This department owes you a debt of gratitude for saving the life of one of your colleagues. But under the—" The chief paused, cleared his throat before continuing.

"Because of the extraordinary circumstances, you will not be honored in any way for saving Detective Barnes' life. But it did factor into our decision process immensely."

"Yes, sir. Of course," Marcus said.

"Your lieutenant sees promise in you, Kemp, and so do I."

"Thank you, sir."

"However, we don't condone your actions and so you will serve a three-month, unpaid suspension before being allowed to return to duty."

"Is that it?" Marcus blurted out.

"Is that it?" the chief repeated, his head tilted to one side.

Flustered, Marcus waved his hands and said, "I mean... I feel like I deserve a much harsher punishment."

The chief let out a sigh and Lt. Berry growled. Waving his index finger back and forth between Berry and himself, the chief said, "WE put a lot of thought into this and WE believe this is the best result for all parties concerned. Do you understand, officer?"

"Yes, of course," Marcus said without hesitating and then dropped his head. "Sorry, sir. I appreciate all you've done for me—"

"Listen. You're only going to discover your... well. That's only going to happen once. So, we see this as an isolated incident you can learn from and move on," he said, then cleared his throat. "I want you to think how you can use your experience and your past, to benefit others. Will you use this time away from the force to do that, Kemp?"

"Yes, Chief," Marcus said.

The meeting concluded after another five minutes, at which point Marcus and Berry walked out of the building together, not saying anything. Marcus felt dumbfounded. His lieutenant played the role of a parent who was making sure the lesson sank in.

"Call me next week, Marcus," Berry said as the two started to part ways in the parking lot.

"Yes, sir. And, thank you again."

The lieutenant stopped and took one step back toward Marcus.

"Call me," he said.

THREE MONTHS LATER, Marcus gripped the metal railing on the starboard side of a sixty-two-foot Offshore yacht named, "Just the Beginning."

Peering down into the pale blue water, he watched the creamy sand floor sweep by. Saltwater frothed at the edges of the yacht's slight wake and dissipated almost as instantly as they methodically cut through the bay. The sun shone on Marcus' face when he looked back to watch the beach shrink from view.

The yacht puttered to a stop when it reached open ocean and turned; the vessel's port side now facing the vast Pacific and its starboard side toward the mainland.

"You ok?" a soft voice from behind him asked.

"Yeah," Marcus said.

He let go of the railing and Megan hugged her arms around his body. Marcus embraced her back and rested his chin on top of her braided head. He drew a deep breath.

"She would have loved this," she said.

Pulling away from her just enough so he could see her face, Marcus smiled.

"She should. It was her idea."

"But you planned it," Megan said.

"True."

"You're a great son, taking care of her—honoring her wishes."

Later, with the sun climbing in the sky, Marcus spread his mother's ashes in the cool ocean. As the saltwater began sweeping her away, she consumed his thoughts. He could still feel her hands squeezed around his wrist when he told her what Bill had done to him. It pained him to tell her, but he knew she should know.

On the way back into the harbor, his father came to mind. Terry was out there with a secret of his own to keep now. Where he'd go or what he would do with it wasn't for Marcus to worry about now.

He had the sun on his back and the woman he loved holding him tight. Tomorrow he would get his badge back and work a new beat, now as a detective in the Child Abuse unit. The work would be hard. It would be painful. But Marcus knew it was work he needed to do.

ACKNOWLEDGEMENTS

There are many people to thank for helping to make my debut novel a reality.

Thank you to my good friend, Chuck Cox, for inspiring me.

To my sisters, Alisha and Arielle, thank you for always cheering me on. To Eric, you're an awesome brother.

Thanks to Stephen Golds for being an incredibly supportive friend. Can't wait to share a drink with you, mate. To Bobby Mathews for the solid suggestions. My man. To the excellent authors who so graciously provided blurbs and support for this book. And to all of my friends in the writing community for their encouragement and support.

My thanks to Philip Ellsworth and Eric Hungarter of the San Diego Police Department for entertaining my many questions. Thank you, Eyal Wigdor, for talking private planes with me.

I'd also like to express my appreciation to everyone at Red Dog Press, obviously. Thank you, Sean, for finding value in my work and turning me into a published author. I'll be forever grateful to you for making my dream come true. Thank you to Meggy Roussel and the BARKeting team for sharing my work on your side of the pond and mine.

Special thanks to my wife, Sharon. She gave me the space to work and tolerated my mood swings and distant behavior, including staring off into space and randomly typing notes into my phone over dinner—and all of the time, honestly. I couldn't ask for a better partner.

Lastly, thank you, reader. I'm beyond grateful you spent your hard-earned money on my book. It means more to me than you'll know. If you enjoyed this book, I would be incredibly appreciative if you would leave me a positive review on Amazon or Goodreads. Thank you.

ABOUT THE AUTHOR

Curtis Ippolito lives in San Diego, California, with his wife Sharon.

He is a communications writer for a nonprofit biological research facility. He has previously been a writer in the health care industry, and is a former newspaper reporter.

Follow him on Twitter @curtis9980 or get in touch via Red Dog Press.

CPSIA information can be obtained
at www.ICGtesting.com
Printed in the USA
LVHW042110150922
728486LV00004B/315